The Cyberthief and the Samurai

IT'S MESMERIZING STORYTELLING.
IT'S EDGE-OF-THE-SEAT READING.
AND IT'S TRUE.

FIND OUT . . .

HOW A CELLULAR PHONE SCAM LED POLICE
TO KEVIN MITNICK'S DOOR . . . AND HOW
THEY LET HIM GET AWAY.

HOW MITNICK BREACHED TSUTOMU
SHIMOMURA'S PERSONAL COMPUTER
SYSTEM.

THE AMAZING PLACE WHERE MITNICK
STORED HIS STOLEN DATA—INCLUDING
20,000 CREDIT CARD NUMBERS—AND HOW IT
BECAME HIS FATAL MISTAKE.

HOW THE PROGRAM CALLED SATAN—THE
DEVILISHLY DANGEROUS SECURITY
CHECKING SOFTWARE THAT CAN
TRANSFORM A SIXTEEN-YEAR-OLD INTO
AN EXPERT CRACKER—FELL INTO
MITNICK'S HANDS.

WHY THE FBI CHASED MITNICK FOR TWO
YEARS . . . HOW THEY ARRESTED THE WRONG
MAN . . . AND HOW SHIMOMURA RAN CIRCLES
AROUND THEM TO FIND MITNICK
IN *SIX WEEKS*.

QUANTITY SALES

Most Dell books are available at special quantity discounts when purchased in bulk by corporations, organizations, or groups. Special imprints, messages, and excerpts can be produced to meet your needs. For more information, write to: Dell Publishing, 1540 Broadway, New York, NY 10036. Attention: Special Markets.

INDIVIDUAL SALES

Are there any Dell books you want but cannot find in your local stores? If so, you can order them directly from us. You can get any Dell book currently in print. For a complete up-to-date listing of our books and information on how to order, write to: Dell Readers Service, Box DR, 1540 Broadway, New York, NY 10036.

THE CYBERTHIEF AND THE SAMURAI

by Jeff Goodell

A Dell Book

Published by
Dell Publishing
a division of
Bantam Doubleday Dell Publishing Group, Inc.
1540 Broadway
New York, New York 10036

ISBN: 0-440-22205-2

Printed in the United States of America

Published simultaneously in Canada

March 1996

10 9 8 7 6 5 4 3 2

RAD

For Jerry

Contents

ACKNOWLEDGMENTS   xiii

INTRODUCTION   xv

I. FLIGHT   1

II. ORIGINAL SIN   29

III. THE CHASE   109

IV. ENTER THE SAMURAI   213

V. SNOW JOB   309

Even paranoids have real enemies.

—Delmore Schwartz

THE
CYBERTHIEF
AND THE
SAMURAI

ACKNOWLEDGMENTS

This is a work of journalism. There has been no fictionalization. In telling the story, I have made judgments and interpretations, but I have gone out of my way to be fair and factual in every detail.

My thanks to Steve Ross, my editor, for suggesting that I write this book, and for his patience and incisive editing. And to my agent, Flip Brophy, who never wavered. Bob Love, my editor at *Rolling Stone*, trusted me to go after this story the day it hit the news. My researchers—Ellen Kosuda, Racheline Maltese, and James Oberman—were heroic.

I would also like to express my gratitude to the many people I interviewed during the course of writing this book. Susan Headley, Lewis De Payne, Ron Austin, and Justin Petersen were all generous with their time. The technicians and engineers at Sprint Cellular, AT&T Wireless Services, and Colorado SuperNet answered more questions than I had any right to ask. I am also indebted to *Cyberpunk* by Katie Hafner and John Markoff, which I recommend to anyone who wants to learn more about Kevin's youthful adventures, and was the source for much of the material about Kevin's early hacking exploits. For details about Richard Feynman's life, I consulted James Gleick's *Genius: The Life and Science of Richard Feynman*.

Finally, I owe my biggest debt of gratitude to Jon Katz, whose support, friendship, and craziness helped me through some very tough times. And to Michele, who lovingly put up with her absentee husband, and to Lulu, who not-so-patiently put up with her absentee Frisbee-tosser.

INTRODUCTION

On February 16, 1995, cyberspace went Hollywood. That morning, on the front page of *The New York Times*, in a box in the top left corner—the spot traditionally reserved by the *Times'* editors for the second most important story of the day—was the headline: "A Most-Wanted Cyberthief Is Caught in His Own Web." Beside it was a photo of the cyberthief himself, Kevin Mitnick. He looked fat and bloated. Glasses. Dark hair. The picture of a nerd gone bad.

By contrast, the man who captured him, Tsutomu Shimomura, whose photo appeared inside the paper, looked impish and exotic. Long, dark hair flowing over his slender shoulders. Bright, slightly buggy eyes. Asian. The picture of a samurai warrior.

The dramatic opposition of these two characters played out in the story too. It was written by John Markoff, the *Times'* ace technology reporter, in classic *Times* style: cool, factual, authoritative. But the story had the shape and feel of a Hollywood western. It was a cyberduel between two archetypal characters, a tale of pursuit and cell phones, of mysterious computer break-ins and complex digital sleuthing.

It was more than just a great yarn. The story also tapped into rising fears about high-tech crime and computer espionage. Over the last decade or so, the engine that runs the American economy has gone digital: from Wall Street to Wal-Mart, businesses are relying more and more on computers and electronic networks to track and control daily transactions. Banks are rushing to set up shop on the Internet, medical records are forwarded over phone lines, corporate computers have become prized information vaults. As more and more valuable information goes on-line, the risk that it will be misused or stolen skyrockets. Fifteen years ago, a wayward hacker couldn't do much more than inconvenience a few university researchers. Today, he could conceivably shut down an entire country.

That's the fear, anyway. In fact, the days of the

digital desperado riding free and easy on the electronic frontier were about over. By the winter of 1995, cyberspace had become a fairly civilized place: there was digicash and cyberbabes, web stars and pet chat, electronic AIDS quilts and digital family trees. More and more, the electronic frontier was starting to look like real life. It was a stubbornly democratic world, to be sure. Computer networks took the power of the media out of the hands of the few and delivered it into the hands of the many. But it didn't show any signs of altering the human spirit. On-line, people had the same desires and emotions, the same social problems and cultural battles. And the same thirst for heroes and villains.

Kevin and Tsutomu fit the bill nicely. All you had to do was look at the pictures and you could see that Kevin was the bad guy. In the first paragraph of the *Times* story, he was identified as a "31-year-old computer expert accused of a long crime spree that includes the theft of thousands of data files and at least 20,000 credit card numbers from computer systems around the nation." (About ten paragraphs later, the *Times* pointed out that there was no evidence Kevin ever profited from those credit card numbers.) Besides having swiped thousands of megabytes of proprietary software, according to the *Times*, Kevin had broken into a North American Air Defense Command computer in 1982. There was no mention of how he got into this military computer, or what his intentions might have been—was he showing off to friends, or was he trying to launch a missile?—but still, the implication was there. He was a dangerous virus in the system, an evil genius who could roam the world via the global Internet. "He was arguably the most wanted computer hacker in the world," a United States Attorney in San Francisco was quoted as saying. "He allegedly had access to trade secrets worth millions of dollars. He was a very big threat."

And Tsutomu, well, he was straight out of central casting. At the San Diego Supercomputer Center, where Tsutomu worked as a computational physicist, the halls were abuzz with speculation about who would play him in the movie. "Maybe Keanu Reeves, if he grew his hair long? Or maybe Tsutomu will insist on an Asian actor," one administrator mused the day after the story appeared. Plopped there in the sleepy pages of the *Times*, Tsutomu reeked of hipness and heroism. He was a wizard's wizard, a mild-mannered scientist who had been living a mild-mannered life in his beach cottage near San Diego until someone was foolish enough to break into his home computers. Then Tsutomu was forced to defend his personal honor and the public good. Over a period of several weeks, with the help of a pocketful of gizmos and home-brewed hacker-tracking software, Tsutomu accomplished what law enforcement couldn't: he finally put Kevin Mitnick behind bars where he belonged.

It was a compelling story, one that played off our deepest fears and anxieties about the technological revolution that was unsettling our lives and changing the way we work and live.

But was it really all so simple?

I

FLIGHT

1

Something weird was going on. In late December 1992, Ed Loveless, a senior investigator for the Department of Motor Vehicles in Sacramento, was alerted that someone was using DMV access codes to get unauthorized information from DMV computers. They were asking for, in DMV lingo, a "soundex": a DMV document which contained, among other things, a person's photo, thumbprint, driver's license number, and address.

This was not, in itself, so weird. Loveless, a veteran with twenty-three years in law enforcement, including a stint as a police chief in a rough 'n' tumble cowboy town in northern California, had witnessed virtually every kind of fraud and cockamamie scheme known to mankind. DMV computers are a gold mine of personal information, and although they are carefully monitored against intruders, security breaches are not uncommon. Often it involves a disgruntled DMV employee who is selling personal information to bill collectors or angry ex-spouses.

As usual, the first thing Loveless did was check out the return phone number the intruder had left: it was disconnected. Then Loveless checked out the number to which the soundexs were being faxed—it turned out to be a Kinko's copy center on Ventura Boulevard in Studio City, near Los Angeles.

Now, *that* was weird. Loveless did a little checking on the IDs the intruder was asking for, and was surprised to find that they included those of a Federal Bureau of Investigations agent and a well-known computer hacker named Justin Petersen, who at the time was using the alias Eric Heinz. Loveless discussed it with the FBI, who knew all about Justin Petersen, and who suggested that it was probably not a DMV employee who was messing around with the DMV access codes—it was another hacker.

So on Christmas Eve, Loveless set a trap. When the intruder called to have another soundex faxed to him, Loveless called Shirley Lessiak, a DMV investigator in the Los Angeles area. The DMV has their own police force, which looks into everything from driver's license forgery to odometer rollbacks. Because this case involved the misuse of a DMV computer and access codes, it was being handled by the internal affairs division, to which Lessiak had been assigned for the last several months. Loveless explained the situation to her, and they devised a plan: Lessiak would stake out the Kinko's in Studio City. Loveless would fax a soundex to the shop, just as the intruder had requested— except it would be of a John Doe. When the intruder came in to pick up the documents, Lessiak would nab him.

Lessiak was not thrilled with the assignment. It was, after all, Christmas Eve, and she was hoping to get home early to her friends and family. But duty called. And while the stakeout shouldn't be a big deal, it would be foolhardy to go out there alone. So she checked around the office, but because of the holiday, there was no one around to accompany her. She finally reached an old friend of hers, another DMV investigator named Cary Shore, on the police radio. Years ago, Lessiak and Shore had been dispatchers together at the California Highway Patrol. He agreed to meet her at Kinko's at 11 A.M.

Lessiak and Shore made an odd pair: Lessiak was an attractive brunette, thirty-eight years old, trim and athletic, wearing a pair of slacks and low shoes and an air of cool professionalism. Shore was a big, beefy guy with a somewhat less disciplined demeanor. When they arrived at Kinko's, they were met by an FBI agent, who had stopped by to lend a hand.

They took the manager of Kinko's aside and told him about the dummy fax that was going to be sent from the DMV office in Sacramento, and about how they planned to question and probably arrest whoever picked it up. The manager had only one request: wait until the perp gets outside to make the arrest. Lessiak agreed—it was her first mistake of the afternoon, and one that she would regret for years to come. She arranged for the clerk at the fax desk to signal her when the person arrived to pick up the document from the DMV—"just glance over, catch my eye," Lessiak told him. He seemed nervous but willing.

With everything in place, Lessiak and Shore set up camp in the desktop-publishing area at Kinko's, which was just across from the fax center. That way, they could pretend to be fiddling around with the computers while they kept an eye on the clerk at the counter. After an hour or so, the FBI agent decided he'd had enough. He wasn't going to wreck his Christmas just to nab a hacker. At about noon, he nodded a polite good-bye and left.

Another hour passed. Lessiak and Shore talked and doodled and took turns going to the bathroom. They started giving each other looks that said, Nice Christmas Eve, huh? Oh, the glamorous, sexy life of a law enforcement officer. Sitting on your butt at Kinko's while the rest of the world is wrapping presents and decorating Christmas trees.

They were just about fed up with this whole operation when Lessiak noticed that the clerk at the fax center had been called away to help a customer at the other end of the store. Another clerk was filling in—one who knew nothing about the sting, or the signaling arrangement with Lessiak. There were several people at the counter, and Lessiak was getting worried, wondering if any of them were retrieving the DMV fax. That would be just her luck. But as she was about to walk up to the counter to see what was going on, she noticed a heavy, dark-haired, twenty-something man pulling a fax out of an envelope. His back was to her, she couldn't see his face, but she could see the faxes as he looked them over—they were the dummies from the DMV. This was her guy!

She noticed him stiffen as he looked through the faxes—he knew they were dummies, and now, presumably, he knew he was being set up. Lessiak watched him warily—she had no reason to think he was dangerous, but like any good cop, she assumed nothing. She hoped this whole thing could be done very quietly. Just follow him outside, ask him a few questions, take it one step at a time. Just keep cool.

Without looking around, the dark-haired man began to walk toward the back door. Lessiak and Shore followed, maybe ten feet behind. They were just waiting until he got outside . . . but then just as he was about to reach the back door, he spun around—he practically bumped into them—and started walking toward the front door.

Lessiak and Shore stepped quickly out of his way. Their eyes didn't meet, there was no suggestion in the man's face that said he'd seen them. At first, Lessiak thought he'd just forgotten where he'd parked his car. When he got a few feet away, they began to follow him toward the front door. When he was about to reach the threshold, he spun around again! It's an old countersurveillance trick, Lessiak realized. He apparently suspected someone was following him. He never looked Lessiak or Shore in the eye, never gestured to them . . . but he knew. Lessiak and Shore stepped aside and tried to look as if they were occupied with some papers on the counter. Once again, the man headed for the back door. And again, just as he reached the back door, he spun around and headed for the front door . . . and just as he reached it *he spun around again!* Clearly, he was playing a game with Lessiak and Shore. But he had still not looked them in the eye.

Finally, the man exited through the back door. Lessiak, and then Shore—who was a little slower on his feet—followed quickly behind. They watched as he took a turn in the parking lot, then walked about 20 feet to a pay phone. He picked up the receiver and pretended to make a call. Lessiak did not see him deposit any coins or dial a number. He just stood there, pinching the phone between his shoulder and his ear, waiting for them to approach.

Lessiak stepped up to him. Shore was a few yards behind her, still trying to catch up. With her right hand, Lessiak began reaching into her belt pack for her badge.

"What do you want from me?" the man said, turning toward her suddenly.

She flipped open her wallet to show him her badge. "I just want to ask you a few questions—"

He tossed the faxes at her and took off across the parking lot. Instead of immediately running after him, Lessiak made her second mistake—she grabbed for the papers instead of the perp. It was human reflex. But it gave the guy a few seconds' head start. By the time Lessiak wheeled around and went after him, he was already a hundred feet ahead of her. Cursing under her breath, she chased him across a parking lot crowded with Christmas shoppers lugging packages and trailing children. He ducked behind a couple of cars and then made a few quick turns and disappeared into the holiday hubbub.

When Lessiak returned to the office, she called Loveless and told him what had happened. He asked her to have the fax pages fumed for prints. Meanwhile, he faxed her a photo lineup. Could she pick out the guy's face? Lessiak looked over the lineup. Her eyes fell on a somber, chubby-looking man with short hair and glasses. Yep, there he was, that was her guy. Kevin Mitnick.

The name meant nothing to Lessiak. She didn't know about his troubled youth, his broken family, or his history of run-ins with the law dating back to the early 1980s. She didn't know that he had been convicted of computer fraud in 1988, or that he had recently served time in Lompoc Federal Prison Camp. Or even that, a little over a month earlier, a warrant had been issued for his arrest for probation violation. And, of course, she could never have guessed that over the next few years, this big, lumpy, unthreatening-looking guy would be considered a menace to society.

All she knew was that, for a man his size, this guy Kevin Mitnick could really run.

2

Twenty-seven days later, on January 20, 1993, the wired generation took control. Bill Clinton was inaugurated as the forty-second President of the United States. At his side on that chilly day behind the Capitol was Al Gore, his Vice President and dedicated technowank. The Clinton/Gore Presidential campaign had been a high-tech gabfest, with lots of talk about fiber optics, the information superhighway, and the power of technology to transform the economy.

When Clinton and Gore took office, you could

smell the silicon in the air in Washington. It was a generational shift. Bumped into the background were the aging establishmentarians who watched the MacNeil/Lehrer report every evening, worried about their kids spending too much time playing video games, and still thought having a secretary take dictation was the height of power. Young, cyber-hip Democrats uploaded into town. They brought their *own* video games. And who needs secretaries when you've got e-mail? Gone were ditto machines and rotary dial phones and Olivetti typewriters. In were laptops and modems and screen savers with flying toasters.

It wasn't just Democrats, of course. Close on their heels was Mr. Third Wave himself, Newt Gingrich. He had risen to power by exploiting new media venues like C-SPAN, and he, perhaps more than anyone, saw the political implications of this far-reaching communications revolution.

But there was a downside. As more and more information went on-line, so too did more and more anxiety. Everyone had heard about the mythical sixteen-year–old hacker who had a computer in his bedroom, a Doritos-fueled troublemaker who, with a modem and a laptop, can access credit reports, steal credit card numbers, and generally raise electronic hell. What happens when the real bad guys, the mobsters and the blackmailers and the kidnappers, start offering these kids all the Doritos they can eat in exchange for a few hours of their time?

Corporations were worried, the government didn't have a clue.

✢

In an effort to stay ahead of the curve, the U.S. House of Representative's Subcommittee of Telecommunications and Finance held a series of hearings. They were chaired by Representative Edward J. Markey of Massachusetts, whose district includes the Massachusetts Institute of Technology, and who was one of the most technologically savvy pols in Washington.

The first session was held in the old Rayburn Office Building on April 29, 1993. Besides the handful of congressmen on the committee, there were about two hundred people in attendance—mostly lobbyists with their Brooks Brothers suits and pocket phones. They welcomed the chance to see which way the wind was blowing on all this: there are big bucks at stake in telecommunications regulations.

Congressman Markey spoke briefly about the purpose of the hearing, then introduced John Gage, director of the science office at Sun Microsystems. Gage, professorial looking in his dark suit and glasses, had come up with the idea of putting on a little dog and pony show for the congressmen. Sun engineers had built a small electronic city in the hearing room, complete with a couple of high-powered Sun computers, telephone switches, a full connection to the Internet, and several large video screens. The staid old hearing room had been transformed into a digital command post from the twenty-first century.

Gage began his testimony. Roaming around the room like a brilliant but slightly daft impresario, he dropped little nuggets of wisdom intended to put the congressmen at ease amidst all this talk of computers and the Internet and cellular phones. He read aloud from an article in that morning's *New York Times*, which talked about "a new generation of telephones that have small display screens," "new hand-held computers," "personal digital assistants," and "interactive television services."

He grimaced.

"How do you know when something new is coming?" he asked aloud. "You know it when the language, like that language, is ugly. You can not tell what these things are. What is a personal digital assistant? What is a telephone that has a small display screen?"

He paused, turning to face the array of computers and display screens that made up the electric city. "These are all telephones with large display screens. We have built a city here for you. It is a city that shows you a fundamental shift in how all communication works."

Gage went on to explain how the whole world was going digital. Pictures, sound, voice, information, they're all the same. They can all be reduced to bits and bites and sent over a telephone line.

"There's no way to stop digital technology," Gage said. Even as he spoke, equipment was transmitting images and sound from the hearing room onto the net, and from there out to (potentially) millions of computers around the world.

About fifteen minutes into his talk, Gage moved to the topic of cellular phones—how vulnerable they are to electronic eavesdropping. He began with a basic question: "What is a cellular phone?"

A slight, long-haired Asian man stood up from within the middle of the electronic city, where he'd been sitting with a couple of other techies, quiet and out of sight. He was dressed in a T-shirt and sweatpants, and had the air of an eccentric grad student who had just been dragged in from a research lab. He held up a plastic bag labeled as having come from an AT&T phone store.

"This is Tsutomu Shimomura from the San Diego Supercomputer Center," Gage said. "He just went out and bought this. We will open it up, and take out this device that you all know."

Tsutomu opened the bag and took out a brand new cellular phone, still in the box. While Gage explained that cellular phones are really just cheap little computers with radio receivers in them, Tsutomu opened the box and slid out the phone. Then he went to work. He removed the back of the phone, fiddled around, punched a few buttons—there was a nervous, almost mechanical quickness to his movements.

"I think it's together," Tsutomu said. "Let's see."

He turned it on. Red lights flashed.

"It works," Gage said.

"So let's let this thing go and start scanning; we'll start at zero. Let's go up to channel three hundred."

Static filled the air in the hearing room. Then voices: a man talking to a woman. Men arguing. It was hard to tell exactly what anyone was saying. The cell phone had been programmed to stop briefly on each of the forty or so channels on the network, effectively eavesdropping on a good percentage of the cellular conversations going on in the capital area. They were channel-surfing the inner highways of Washington!

The lobbyists went pale. All this time, they thought cellular phone calls were safe. They were talking on the *phone*, for chrissakes. It's supposed to be *private*. And in two seconds, Tsutomu takes a regular phone and turns it into a listening post.

This was, of course, against the law. Altering cellular phones and eavesdropping on private conversations is a felony offense. For the sake of this demonstration, however, Tsutomu had been granted immunity. Still, an FBI agent was in the room, keeping a watchful eye on him.

Even Markey, savvy as he was, seemed taken aback. "So the point is, Mr. Gage, you can buy an off-the-shelf phone, go into a phone store, program it and turn it into a scanner that can pick up everyone's phone calls in the neighborhood or in the town in which you live?"

"Exactly," Gage said.

✣

If Washington lawmakers and lobbyists wanted to learn a little more about the gaping security holes in the electronic world, all they had to do was flip open the premiere issue of *Wired*, which hit the stands about the same time Tsutomu was making his dramatic demonstration. *Wired* spoke to the heart of this newly emerging digital culture: *"Wired* is about the most powerful people on the planet today—the Digital Generation," the editor/publisher, Louis Rossetto, wrote in the first issue. The purpose of the magazine, Rossetto noted, was to discuss "social changes so profound their only parallel is probably the discovery of fire." The magazine, printed in wild Day-Glo colors, lived up to the hype, and would go on to win a National Magazine Award in 1994. In that premiere issue, there were articles about libraries without walls and about how technology is changing the art of war, as well as one titled "The Incredibly Strange Mutant Creatures Who Rule the Universe of Alienated Japanese Zombie Computer Nerds."

But the story that would have caught a curious congressman's eye was called, "Cellular Phreaks & Code Dudes: Hacking Chips on Cellular Phones is the Latest Thing in the Digital Underground." It was written by John Markoff of *The New York Times*.

"Meet V.T. and N.M.," the article read, "the nation's most clever cellular phone phreaks. (Names here are obscured because, as with many hackers, V.T. and N.M.'s deeds inhabit a legal gray area.)" V.T. was described as "a young scientist at a prestigious government laboratory" with "long hair" and a choice of clothes that "frequently tends toward Patagonia." The article went on to celebrate V.T. and N.M.'s escapades on the edge of the law, painting them as brilliant rebels who have cracked the secrets of cellular phones. There was, for example, the tale of how V.T. manipulated technicians at OKI into revealing the special codes needed to access the cell phone software; of turning the phone into a scanner and eavesdropping on private conversations; of hooking the hacked cellular phone to his laptop and watching as it draws a map of each phone call being placed in the area. V.T. and N.M. speculated about using a hacked cell phone to track someone who is driving through traffic with a car phone, unaware that his or her phone sends out regular beeps that are easily monitored. And then there is, of course, the possibility of free phone calls—although V.T. and N.M. claimed not to be interested in anything as mundane as that. "If you're going to do something illegal," V.T. was quoted as saying, "you might as well do something interesting."

Every self-respecting phone phreaker in America knew that V.T. was the pseudonym of Tsutomu, and N.M. was his friend Mark Lottor, who was well-known in the computer underground for selling kits that transformed OKI cellular phones into surveillance devices. Lottor had once been the roommate of Kevin Poulsen, the first American hacker to be indicted for espionage (the charge—which many believed was unjustified—was eventually dropped in exchange for a guilty plea on other, unrelated hacking crimes). A few months before the *Wired* article was published, Lottor had been charged with several counts of computer and communications fraud stemming from a break-in at Pacific Bell in the late 1980s (the charges remain unresolved).

Not that anyone thought of Lottor as much of a criminal. While awaiting the resolution of his case, he had established a respected Internet consulting business, Network Wizards, and was well liked by many in the net community. Besides, if everyone obeyed the laws, the digital revolution might never have happened. Lawlessness, anarchy, and disrespect for Big Brother have been a fundamental part of the culture from the very beginning, fueling innovations right and left. In this world, it's never been easy to distinguish a genuis from a criminal, or a white hat from a black hat. "In that sense, it's still like the wild west," says John Perry Barlow, one of the founders of the Electronic Frontier Foundation, a watchdog group for civil liberties in cyberspace. "There's not a huge difference between the Wyatt Earps and the Billy the Kids."

3

"If you were going to go after a company," a security expert asked Kevin, "where would you look first?" The discussion was happening, as usual, on the telephone. For Kevin, the phone was his living room and his playground, his lifeline and his safecracking tool.

"I might look in their garbage," Kevin said. His voice sounded confident, assured, laced with pride, bending back a little here and there in a deliberate effort to be humble. "That would be a good start," he continued. "You might learn a little about the company, you might find an organization chart. In the late 1970s and early 1980s, I used to routinely go through phone company garbage. I'd find their manuals, a lot of employee lists. In 1981, I found passwords to one of their sensitive computers in the garbage. It was torn up, but someone with the time and patience to put it together—"

"One thing we do know about you is that you're very dedicated to your task, right?"

"It takes a lot of persistence and determination," Kevin said. And here the pride rose in his voice again. "It was a game, and unless you played the game well, you didn't get too far."

This exchange took place exactly one month prior to Kevin's near miss at Kinko's. A few weeks earlier, the FBI had put out a warrant for his arrest, claiming he had broken probation by messing around with Pacific Bell's computers and was performing unauthorized wiretaps on law enforcement officials. By this time, his reputation for being one of the most dangerous hackers in cyberspace was well-known. No one understood what motivated him. A quest for fame? Power? Money? A political agenda? He was regarded as unrepentant, amoral, nasty, fearless, and persistent.

None of this came through during this exchange on the phone. He sounded earnest and exceedingly polite. Ray Kaplan, one of his few friends in the security business, had offered him a few hundred bucks to participate in a teleconference on computer security. Also on the line were Jim Settle, then the head of the FBI Computer Crimes Squad, as well as other law enforcement officials, security experts, and *New York Times* writer John Markoff.

They had all gathered to hear Kevin hold forth, and to get a glimmer of understanding of how he operated. There was an odd kind of rapport among them. They were like warriors who had decided, for the moment, to lay down their arms and, if only for one night, sit around the campfire and share their tales of battle. Of course, no one knew where Kevin was—he was speaking with them from an undisclosed location.

As usual, nobody was too impressed with Kevin's technical knowledge. Kevin reveled in his under-standing of complex computer and telephone systems, and was particularly good at keeping up with the latest bugs in the software that ran Digital Equipment computers. But as he freely admitted in the conference, his technical skills took a back-seat to what hackers commonly refer to as "social engineering," that is, manipulating people to give you what you want. Kevin was expert at this. Why spend hours trying to guess the password for a corporate computer system when you can call up one of the system administrators and pose as his boss's boss and get him or her to tell you the password? Of course, to pull this kind of performance off, you've got to be good. Authoritative. Impatient. Knowledgeable. You have to know that boss's assistant's name. You have to know the lingo of the company. You have to know the procedures. You have to have the skills of a grifter, a con man.

In one case, for example, Kevin had tried to gain access to a Digital Equipment computer at a small company that had written a piece of software he wanted. "It was a two to three person operation run out of somebody's house," Kevin told the conference. "Social engineering was out of the question." Instead, Kevin and a friend inserted a Trojan horse—a piece of software that looks legitimate, but contains a secret code which would allow him "backdoor" access to the computer—into a routine software update program that was being distributed by Digital at the time. Then they carefully wrapped it up in a Digital box, enclosed an actual Digital packing slip in a sealed plastic wrapper, and delivered it to the company. "We didn't want to mail it, because that would be mail fraud, and that would be pretty serious," Kevin explained. So they decided that they would have someone dress up as a UPS courier, knock on the company's door, and deliver the package. "It was done very professionally," Kevin boasted. Ultimately, however, the ruse didn't work—"They were too lazy to install the software update."

Near the end of the conference, the moderator asked Kevin the $20,000 dollar question. While he was in Lompoc Federal Prison Camp in 1989, had professional criminals ever suggested that they might . . . um . . . go into "business" together someday?

"Every day," Kevin said, almost laughing. "A lot of people that were in Lompoc—and these people were not the dope dealers, and the murderers and stuff. They were the financial crime wizards of the community. They are the type whose wife and kids came up in a Mercedes Benz to visit them. They were pretty well off. And a lot of these guys wanted my telephone number, or wanted me to get in contact with them when we were both released so we can work together on the outside. They didn't tell me specifically what they wanted to do, but I'm sure it wasn't to get together for a root beer."

Before saying good-bye, and in effect vanishing underground for the next two years, he offered a final warning: "Some time they're gonna lock up somebody who really wants to use this technology for crime. I don't believe, in the past, I used it as a tool to commit crime. I believe I was an electronic joyrider having fun in cyberspace. But when somebody gets out there who really wants to do some damage, if the real bad guys get the technology, then you're going to have a big problem."

❖

Four weeks later, Kevin ditched Officer Lessiak at Kinko's. Now he was on the run. He never admitted it to any of his friends (or if he did, they won't admit it), but that close encounter must have scared the hell out of him. He knew if he got caught, he'd be doing time. How long, it was hard to say. It depended a lot on the judge. Maybe four months for breaking probation. Maybe six months. What else did they have on him? Kevin couldn't be sure. If he was listening in on the private conversations of FBI agents, in effect trying to track them while they tracked him, well, that was serious business.

The sanest thing for Kevin to do right then would probably have been to stop and turn himself in, take his licks, and get it over with. Susan Headley, another friend from his early hacking days, says she urged him to do it many times. "He would always say, 'I can't, I can't do it, I can't,'" Headley recalls. For one thing, he had no money. And without a good lawyer, he was afraid he'd never be able to defend himself successfully. Besides being paranoid by nature, he'd had plenty of bad experiences with law enforcement over the years. He was afraid he'd be blamed for every illegal computer intrusion that had happened in the state of California in the last ten years.

For Kevin, prison was a black hole where black things happened. He'd survived his time at Lompoc, but next time he might not end up in such a comfortable place. He had heard stories about what happens to young men in prison. He knew the jokes about picking up the soap in the shower. And it must have terrified him. It touched a dark place in his soul that he rarely talked about. It stirred memories better forgotten.

Besides, Kevin possessed a kind of righteousness. There were many, many holes in computer and network software—everyone knew that. It was a flawed universe. Why shouldn't he exploit it? If he didn't, someone else would. Someone who wasn't quite so evenhanded. In a sense, he was doing everyone a *favor*. He was pointing out flaws in the system before they could be exploited by someone who could really cause trouble. He was the virus that made the entire system healthier. People should be *grateful* to him.

So he chose a life on the run. He gave himself over to the adolescent romance of the fugitive, a life modeled after his favorite movie, *Three Days of the Condor*. It was a life on the fringes, getting shitty jobs under various aliases, moving from town to town, living like an electronic phantom. He kept in touch with old friends by phone, torn between his need for human contact and his fear of getting caught. He thought as long as he was smart, as long as he watched his back, he'd be fine. He knew there were only a handful of cops in the world who understood computers and computer crime well enough to track him down. And he knew they were probably too busy to bother.

Besides, he was not doing anything different from hundreds—maybe thousands—of dedicated hackers and crackers out there, guys like himself who probed the weaknesses in the communications system. It was not like he was selling stolen software for money. Lord knows he could, but he wasn't. And he wasn't raping women or kidnapping children. So if he wasn't physically hurting anybody, and he wasn't making any profit, well, what was the crime? He was just messing around—*an electronic joyrider.*

⚜

For Lessiak, this was not fun and games. A few weeks after her encounter with Kevin, she saw a man standing outside her office at the DMV. He looked like Kevin. Before she could be sure, he fled. She did not see him again. But sometimes her cold phone—a secure, unlisted phone she used at her office to make outgoing calls—would ring in the middle of the day. She'd pick up the receiver, and she would hear a computer dialing on the other end. Nothing like this had ever happened before. Weirder still, for the next five months, she was paged every night between midnight and 5 A.M. This number, too, was supposed to be unlisted, available to only a few people at the DMV. She would wake up and turn on the light and she would see error messages. Or it flashed a phone number in San Francisco. When she dialed, it was disconnected. The paging continued every night. Her sleep was destroyed. Was it Kevin? Was he getting his revenge? She never knew for sure. But then one day, the calls stopped. It was as if somebody had decided she'd suffered enough, and now the bill was paid.

II

ORIGINAL SIN

1

Panorama City, California, where Kevin grew up, is neither panoramic nor a city. It's a bleak, forgotten plot of real estate in a distant corner of the San Fernando Valley. To spend even a short amount of time in the area is to feel a particular kind of despair, one that comes from shabby strip malls and postwar apartment buildings that seem to sag in the heat. Apparently there was a brief spurt of prosperity here in the 1940s and 1950s, when the farmland was paved over and the majority of the houses built. But it's been downhill ever since. The palm trees look depressed. The bougainvilleas bloom reluctantly. Then there's smog. Traffic. Drugs. Strip malls. The urge to escape.

Kevin was born in Van Nuys on August 6, 1963. His father, Alan Mitnick, had grown up in the Detroit suburbs, one of four children in a lower middle class Jewish family. After graduating from high school, Alan joined the military and was transferred to California, where he met Rochelle (Shelly) Kramer. They were married in 1962. They were just kids: he was nineteen, she was eighteen. Just over a year later, Kevin was born, their first and only child. They moved into an apartment in the valley because it was inexpensive, but still within striking distance of Hollywood. Alan was interested in the music business—he would later have a brief career as an independent record promoter.

By the time Kevin was three years old, Alan and Shelly divorced. Shelly was left to raise her son on her own. She went to work as a waitress at Fromin's, a well-known deli in the valley. Shelly's mother, Reba, often looked after Kevin while Shelly went out and earned a living.

When Kevin was five years old, Shelly married again. Her second husband was a regrettable choice: a former military officer, he was fifteen years older than her, and according to police records, he sexually abused Kevin. It was not something that was talked about openly in the family, but others have confirmed the allegations. Kevin rarely spoke of it himself. It's easy to speculate that abuse by his stepfather—to whatever degree it occurred—might have had something to do with Kevin's anger and bitterness in later years, especially his desire to attack people in authority. That may be too simple an interpretation, however. About the only thing that can be said for sure is that early sexual trauma rarely leads to emotional well-being.

Not surprisingly, Shelly's marriage to the former military officer lasted only a year. The following year she moved on to her third husband, Howard Jaffee. That marriage also fell apart. This was dad number three for Kevin, and he was still only seven years old.

Kevin was a troubled kid. His only sibling was a half brother named Adam, born shortly after Kevin's birth father Alan remarried, and who quickly became the apple of Alan's eye. Kevin got shunted aside, raised by a mother who loved him dearly but who had a tough time with the complexities of single motherhood. There was no one taking Kevin to Little League games, no one taking him on camping trips to Lake Arrowhead, no one explaining this succession of father figures. His world was Panorama City. Studio City. Commerce City. Universal City. It was traffic lights and TV, telephones and divorce and frozen food. He and his mother and the man of the moment never had money. They never lived in a real house— just a series of flimsy apartments. Other kids might have been toughened by growing up in this hard-scrabble world; on Kevin, it had the opposite effect.

He was diagnosed as "hyperactive," and received medication—Ritalin and Dexedrine—until he was eleven years old. He suffered from chronic allergies, especially when outdoors. He complained about an irregular heartbeat, but doctors who examined him concluded that it was probably the result of stress and anxiety. He never drank or did drugs. But he did eat. According to his mother, "he could eat a Sara Lee cake in a single bite."

✛

As Kevin grew older, he turned inward. He became a shy, fat, lonely teenager with a seething anger inside. He dropped out of high school (he later returned to get his G.E.D.). The usual attractions of teenage life in LA had little appeal for Kevin. He sometimes went to the beach or movies with friends, but he was awkward around girls. He didn't drink. He didn't do drugs.

In 1978, Lewis De Payne, who would become Kevin's best friend and early mentor, met Kevin via ham radio, when De Payne overheared someone boasting about making illegal long distance calls with stolen MCI codes. De Payne, who was three years older than Kevin, was already an expert phone phreaker. Before long, the two of them got together and started swapping secrets. Kevin was only fourteen at the time, but his skills were already impressive.

What movies were to the destitute and unemployed during the Depression, the phone lines were to many kids of Kevin's generation. Hacking was an escape, a refuge, a fantasy life. Back in those days, the phone network was wide open. There were no computer switches yet, no security to speak of, no laws—it was a parallel universe just waiting to be explored. You could make free phone calls anywhere in the world, you could bounce from New York to Texas to Singapore to Cairo, you could leave messages for the Pope at the Vatican switchboard.

The Kit Carson of phone phreakers was a guy named John Draper, a.k.a. Captain Crunch, because he figured out that the whistle that came in the Captain Crunch cereal boxes worked at precisely the right frequency to allow him to manipulate AT&T's long distance phone system, which used a series of high-frequency tones to switch its calls. Then there were Steve Jobs and Steve Wozniak, the founders of Apple Computer, who made pizza money when they were teenagers by selling blue boxes—a box of whistles, basically—around the U.C. Berkeley campus.

In those early days, Kevin and Lewis would plot their adventures at a Shakey's pizza parlor in Hollywood, along with Susan Headley, a big blond ex-rock star groupie turned phone phreak and masterful social engineer, as well as Steve Rhoades, a quiet, mild-mannered kid who understood the hardware of the phone system as well as anyone.

They were bound together by their secret mastery of the phone system, and by the thrilling sense they shared of having found a trapdoor to another world.

Around 1980, phone companies started replacing mechanical phone switches with computers. When that happened, Kevin and his pals went digital, too. It required a quantum leap in skills, but it also quintupled the fun. Because by now they had discovered the Arpanet, the forerunner of today's Internet. It was originally designed for academic use, as a way for scientists and researchers to easily share information. And when ambitious young phone phreakers like Kevin discovered this, well, it was truly cool. The phone line became a kind of information spigot—it was connected to computers all over the country, and they were packed with interesting stuff. Suddenly, hackers were *inside*. They knew secrets. They had *power*.

An entire generation of kids were transformed. Patrick Kroupa, a former hacker in the New York area and cofounder of Mindvox, an early and influential computer bulletin board system, described what it was like to grow up at that heady moment. "Led by an oddball contingent of misfits, dropouts, acidheads, phreaks, hackers, hippies, scientists, and students, guys who could say, 'doOd [sic], got any new wares?' with a straight face and really mean it, the 1980s saw the rise of the first empires and kingdoms of cyberspace," Kroupa wrote in an essay that has been widely distributed on the net.

"When I first became an active participant in this electronic nervous system, I was a little over ten years old. My early understanding of this 'place' was shaped by a handful of people whose skills I admired and sought to emulate, yet whose lives I felt great pity and sadness for. They were building the cult of high tech in hope that it would somehow save them from whatever they thought had prevented them from attaining happiness anywhere else.

"Everything really was this big beautiful game, and here we were with an overview of the whole jigsaw puzzle, and the sudden power to do anything we wanted to do with it. For the first time in recent history you could reach out and change reality, you could do stuff that affected everything and everyone, and you were suddenly living this life that was like something out of a comic book or adventure story. . . .

"It was a very interesting time and place in which to grow up. Of course, the problem was that a lot of us didn't grow up.

"One day you wake up and come to realize that you're seventeen or eighteen going on ninety. You understand that everything in the whole world is comprised of bits and pieces of lies and half-truths, everyone is inherently corrupt, including you; a lot of kids who used to be your friends are now all grown up with no place to go and getting busted for such things as fraud and grand larceny; and you have utterly lost touch with anything even remotely 'real.'

"We had spent our entire childhoods jacked into this alternate electronic universe, locked into playing our overly developed personas, and almost no time figuring out who we were and what we wanted out of life beyond 'further, better, more.' "

2

In the late 1970s and early 1980s, hackers and phone phreaks were still just smudges on the cultural landscape—hardly anyone knew anything about them, nor did they care. The PC revolution was just taking hold—only a tiny percentage of Americans owned computers, and virtually no one beyond the scientists and academics who used the Arpanet were on-line yet. A Macintosh was still something you baked pies with. No one had heard of the "digerati," or of "cybersex," or of "cyber-punks"—William Gibson, the science fiction writer who was defining the imaginative borders of the electronic universe, did not coin the word "cyberspace" until 1982. Laws were vague. Security was nil. It was all still virgin territory, as wide open and beckoning as the western territories had once been.

For the most part, hackers and phone phreaks were portrayed in the media as ingenious pranksters. No one could imagine them causing serious trouble. In 1980, a story in the *LA Weekly* about Lewis De Payne was respectfully called, "The Phine Art of Phone Phreaking." In 1982, ABC's *20/ 20* ran a show about phreakers and hackers titled "The Electronic Delinquents." They were bizarre, strange kids, lost maybe, but no real danger to anyone.

Kevin, as usual, pushed the envelope. His troubles began in 1981, when he and De Payne and another pal decided to pull a pretty bold stunt and attempt to gain access to Pacific Bell's mainframe computer in downtown LA. Kevin and his pals had been dumpster-diving at Pac Bell plenty of times, but they had learned all they could from the old tech manuals and employee lists that turned up in the trash. Now they were after bigger game: they wanted the passwords that would allow them virtually free run of Pac Bell's computer system.

To gain entry into the Pac Bell office, it would never have occurred to Kevin in a million years to jimmy open a window or climb in through a ventilation duct. That was clearly *breaking the law*. Instead, he talked his way in. He wasn't committing a criminal act—he was just taking advantage of a weakness in the system. Right?

At 1:00 A.M. on a Sunday morning on Memorial Day weekend, Kevin, De Payne, and another friend strolled up to the Pac Bell building and started chatting with the security guard. Kevin, who was only seventeen at the time, demonstrated remarkable poise. He made up a story about how he was pissed off because he had a report due Monday and he had to come in over the holiday to work on it. Then he and his friends signed the logbook (two of them used fake names) and strolled right in. An hour or so later, they walked out with an armload of valuable manuals, as well as a list of codes to the digital door locks and other valuable info. They waved good-bye to the guard, and then went to Winchell's Donuts to celebrate.

They didn't have much time to play with their new goodies, however, because Susan Headley, under investigation for other charges, blew the whistle on them to police investigators. At the time, prosecutors were also after Kevin for an earlier incident in which he and his pals were suspected of breaking into the computer of a small company in the Bay Area and raising havoc—apparently deleting files and causing the printer to spew out adolescent witticisms like "FUCK YOU! FUCK YOU! FUCK YOU!"

So Kevin's lawyer cut a deal. After returning all

the stolen materials, Kevin pled guilty to one count of computer fraud and one count of burglary—both felonies. He was sentenced to one year probation.

✤

In the small, status-conscious circle of LA hackers, getting busted was a badge of honor. It seemed to give Kevin a new sense of identity and power. It also helped him make new friends. One was an awkward, pimply kid named Lenny DiCicco, who was two years younger than Kevin, and who, in those early days, looked up to him as a role model.

In 1982, they were busted together for strolling onto the campus at the University of Southern California and using their computers to get access to privileged accounts, read private e-mail (always irresistible for Kevin, who was, not surprisingly, obsessed with his own privacy), and use the USC computers as a base to explore the Arpanet. It was run of the mill stuff, no different from what hundreds of teenage hackers were doing around the same time. Except Kevin got caught.

This time, Kevin went to jail for six months. Although Kevin was nineteen years old at the time, and legally an adult, he was sent to a juvenile prison in Stockton, California. It drew the toughest kids in the state—murderers, shooters, druggies. While he was there, he underwent a diagnostic study administered by the California Youth Authority. According to court records, he was described as having an "unsocialized nonaggressive type personality." The study found no evidence of psychosis, but it did say that Kevin possessed minimal judgment, lacked insight, and was immature. In one evaluation, a psychologist described him as wanting to "vent his frustrations and anger [with computers], rather than use acceptable social methods to deal with his troubles."

By the time Kevin was released, the era of the electronic delinquent was about over. With a little help from Hollywood, hackers were being transformed into a national menace.

3

The premise of *Wargames* is simple enough. Matthew Broderick plays a hacker. He has a computer in his bedroom (something that Kevin was too poor to have until much later), an "attitude problem" at school, and a taste for junk food. When he's in danger of flunking biology, he hacks into the computer at school and changes his grade. One day he notices an ad in a magazine for a company that is producing new video games, so he decides to hack into their computer and have an advance look. He sets his modem to dial randomly, then hits on a number that he believes gives him access to the video game company's computer. In fact, he has stumbled into the computer that controls NORAD, the U.S. military's strategic defense system. He easily gets into the computer and begins playing a game called "Global Thermonuclear War." Although Broderick doesn't realize it, he has set the NORAD computers off on a countdown to nuclear war.

Of course, having triggered this global disaster, only Broderick can stop it. Unbeknownst to anyone at NORAD, their computer has run amuck, and thinking that it is still playing a game, it plans to launch an attack on its own. After being arrested by the FBI, Broderick pleads with them to let him help. He eventually escapes, slinks around in the NORAD operations center (causing one general to shout, in the movie's most memorable line, "Get that little bastard out of the War Room!"). He eventually tracks down the eccentric programmer who wrote the software that is controlling the computer. Broderick convinces him that the computer has gone nuts, that global thermonuclear war is minutes away. Finally Broderick, his girlfriend/ sidekick (played by a winsome Ally Sheedy), and the eccentric programmer rush back to NORAD and break in just as the missiles are about to be fired from their silos. Broderick saves the day by convincing the out-of-control computer to play tic-tac-toe with itself, thereby teaching it the futility of games, including the "game" of global thermonuclear war. Credits roll.

On one level, this is all unbearably silly. The handsome, noble hacker with the attractive girl-friend/sidekick (yeah, right), the NORAD computer run amuck (it even talks), the bumbling bureaucrats. But the movie skillfully exploits the anxieties of the atomic age—that we are just one computer keystroke away from annihilation—while at the same time, introducing a new gunslinger into the vocabulary of pop culture: the computer hacker.

The movie was responsible for a huge change in the public perception of hackers. Matthew Broderick played a good kid, decent, white, middle class, just out to have fun. There was nothing threatening about him. And yet he could do magic in his bedroom. He could turn on his computer and connect it to his telephone and dial a number and gain control of the world. It was, in its own un-threatening way, a terrifying notion.

The movie changed how hackers saw themselves, too. Until *Wargames,* hackers were toiling in the cultural darkness. Now there was a little swagger in their keystrokes—*don't mess with me, or I might get pissed off and launch some missiles.* Hackers played into this idea, exaggerating their conquests, spinning tales of drama and intrigue. It also inspired a whole new crop of kids to take a look at the fun that could be had in cyberspace. In a strange way, the movie became a touchstone for a generation.

And of course, some hackers claim to have poked

around in NORAD computers. One of the folktales of Kevin's teenage years was that he accessed NO-RAD in 1982. It was impossible to verify. But even in those days, when computer security was still an afterthought, getting into a NORAD computer was a different thing entirely than having the capability, the know-how, and the will to launch a missile. It was sheer paranoid fantasy. It made for great movies, but it wasn't a real-life risk.

Not surprisingly, given Kevin's Velcro-like quality of getting blamed for every crime in cyberspace, he often gets named as the inspiration for *Wargames*. "Not true," says screenwriter Larry Lasker. "I wrote *Wargames* in 1980—long before I'd ever heard of Kevin Mitnick." But like much about Kevin's hacking career, the line between fact and fantasy is a fine one.

4

Not long after he got out of jail in Stockton, Kevin bought a vanity plate for his black Nissan Pulsar that suggested he was beginning life anew. It read: "X HACKER."

If Kevin would have lived up to his proclamation, his life might have ended up no different than dozens of other successful people in the computer business. They mess around when they're kids, but then when they get out of high school, they run smack into the real world and they begin to realize how much is at stake with these stupid little hacker games.

For Kevin, the lesson didn't stick. Whatever the reason, not long after he was released from juvenile prison in Stockton, he got into trouble again.

He had taken a job at a small company owned by a friend of the family, where he worked at a computer doing clerical duties and other mundane tasks. But then he started doing a little electronic spelunking at the office, and before long, another arrest warrant was issued in his name. He was suspected of getting unauthorized access to TRW credit reports, as well as using fraudulent access codes to make free long distance calls.

This time, Kevin got wind of it and split. He was gone for almost a year. He spent at least some of that time in northern California, where he took classes at Butte Community College under an assumed name. Later, some reporters, eager to play up Kevin's status as a threat to national security, would account for this missing year by claiming he had visited Israel, implying that he was an agent for the Mossad or some such nonsense.

In September of 1985, Kevin enrolled in classes at the Computer Learning Center of Los Angeles. This was the first sober, mature move of his life. It was an indication that he wanted to put his past behind him, that he wanted to somehow channel his fascination with computers into a decent living. The Computer Learning Center was a respectable technical school, and their graduates usually went on to decent, if not glitzy, jobs in the computer industry.

Kevin was a serious student, but he got more out of the class than just technical skills. One evening when he was working in the computer lab, he happened to strike up an e-mail conversation with a short, somber, attractive brown-haired woman who was sitting across the room. After a little chitchat, he invited her out to dinner—a bold move for a guy who didn't have much experience with women—but she turned him down. She was engaged, she told him. He persisted. Maybe next week, she told him.

A month or so later, they were going out. Her name was Bonnie Vitello. She was two years older than Kevin, and had already been married once, and was on the verge of being married again. Still, she was curious about Kevin, whose bulk, at that time, did not cast a slender shadow. But he seemed smart and serious and good humored—he gave out a big laugh when he heard she worked at GTE, one of the local phone companies serving the LA area. Talk about a match made in heaven. It must have felt like destiny.

It wasn't long before Bonnie's engagement was off, and her new friend Kevin was living with her in her small apartment in Thousand Oaks.

✛

A week before they were supposed to get married, Bonnie's apartment was searched by police. The computer, modem, floppy disks, manuals were all seized. It seems Kevin had been messing around again—this time he'd been prowling inside the computer of a software company called Santa Cruz Operation, a fast-growing company which sold a version of the Unix operating system designed to run on personal computers. System administrators were worried that he might steal a copy of the company's proprietary software. What if he sold it to a competitor? What if he did something really nefarious like plant a bug in the software that nobody would notice until it was too late? For Santa Cruz Operation, hundreds of thousands of dollars could be at stake. Not to mention the reputation of the company.

Of course, Kevin hadn't stolen anything yet. *But he might.*

System administrators at Santa Cruz Operations had several options. They could have beefed up security so that Kevin (and others like him) couldn't access their computers. Or they could have taken their valuables off-line, where they would be safe. Instead, they reported Kevin's activities to the police. It was fairly easy to trace his calls back to Bonnie's apartment in Thousand Oaks. A few days later, an investigator from the Santa Cruz police department flew up to LA.

Until now, Kevin still had a clean adult record.

He was charged with unauthorized access to a computer—a felony. His lawyer got it knocked down to a misdemeanor, for which Kevin was sentenced to thirty-six months' probation. He also had to agree to meet with a system administrator for Santa Cruz Operation, who wanted to know about the holes he'd found in their system. Kevin told him, but he wasn't gracious about it.

✢

Kevin and Bonnie were finally married on June 9, 1987, in Woodland Hills. They had a small reception at her mother's house. Despite his troubles, he seemed happy. Bonnie brought out the best in him. He seemed more confident and self-assured. You can even see it in his driver's license photo, which was taken not long after the wedding. He was twenty-three years old, stood five eleven, weighed 240 pounds (a good 70 pounds overweight, which was about average for Kevin). Clean shaven. There's a kind of optimism in his blue eyes, as if he still had some hope for the future.

5

Kevin once again seemed serious about going straight. To save money, he and Bonnie had moved into a small condo in Panorama City with Kevin's mother, who was still working as a waitress at Fromin's deli. Bonnie worked 9 to 5 at GTE, and Kevin spent his days trying to get a real job. A part of him, at least, wanted to build a life.

Kevin's defenders argued that all he needed was a chance to prove himself. All he needed was a decent job, a way to find some value in his life beyond hacking, and he would have turned the corner. Others argue that Kevin had proven himself to be dangerously untrustworthy, that he did not understand—or did not care about—the rules of the game, and that until he did something to demonstrate otherwise, he should not be indulged.

One thing is clear: he certainly tried hard to get a real job. He sent out dozens and dozens of query letters, most of them with the same rough pitch: "Having over two years of education and experience in the Data Processing field, I am willing and able to put my talents and skills to work for [name withheld] and assist the company in attaining its goals . . . I am looking forward to utilizing the knowledge and ability I have acquired in a productive way and would appreciate the opportunity to meet with you for a possible job placement."

On the attached resume, he listed his education and experience, as well as the alphabet-soup of computer software and operating systems he could operate ("VM/CMS, OS/VS1, DOS/VSE, MS-DOS, RSTS/E, VAX/VMS, UNIX, TOP-20 . . ."). Under the heading, "Objective", he wrote: "Pursuing a computer programming career."

With Bonnie's help, he was hired at GTE in October 1987—only to be escorted to his car a week later by a security officer when GTE found out about his criminal history. Convicted computer criminals, Kevin discovered, are like convicted child molesters. You can do your time, but you are not forgiven.

✢

A few months later, Kevin got a break. On a long shot, he had applied for a job as an electronic funds transfer consultant at Security Pacific Bank. He dutifully filled out the application is his large, messy, almost childlike handwriting. In a sign of either desperation or deceit, when the form asked if he had ever been convicted of a criminal offense, he checked "no."

To his surprise, he got a letter from the bank's personnel office telling him he had the job. He was thrilled. He and Bonnie went out to dinner to celebrate. The salary for the job was $34,000—in Kevin's eyes, a ton of money. It would have been the first good job he'd ever had in his life.

Again, Kevin's reputation preceded him. Donn Parker, a computer security consultant at SRI, a high-tech think tank in Palo Alto, heard the news that Kevin was about to be hired by a bank. The idea horrified him. He called executives at the bank and let them know a little about Kevin's history. Jim Black, an LAPD computer crime detective, did the same.

The day before Kevin was to start the job, the offer was rescinded.

✢

A couple of weeks later, a press release was issued to the media indicating that Security Pacific had lost $400 million in the first quarter of 1988. It was an official-looking release in every way, well written, with the correct corporate jargon. Had the news gone out over the wire, it could have caused Security Pacific serious damage. But luckily for Security Pacific, the wire services called the bank for a comment before sending the story out, and discovered it wasn't true. It was apparently somebody's idea of a prank—or a way, perhaps, of getting revenge.

✣

One day Donn Parker, who only a few months earlier had helped get Kevin's job offer rescinded, picked up the phone in his office at SRI—"Hello Donn," a voice said. "It's Kevin Mitnick."

Parker couldn't have been more surprised. But after talking with Kevin for a couple of minutes, Parker realized that Kevin didn't want revenge, he wanted a job (Kevin apparently had no idea of the role Parker had played in getting him canned at Security Pacific). Parker was struck by how professional and confident Kevin sounded. He was courteous and good humored. He seemed to know a lot about what Parker was working on—the information security reviews for various companies, the research into computer crime for the Department of Justice. But Kevin was very cool about it, very low key.

It was no surprise that Kevin sought out Parker. The large, balding security guru was a kind of parental figure for many young hackers. If he took a shine to you, he could get you a job as a highly paid security consultant at a cool company, someone who actually got *paid* for messing around with computers all day. He was the hacker equivalent of a Nashville record producer who, if he liked your sound, could sign you up and make you a star. Or at least get you a decent job—something that, to a hacker, was almost as good.

This reputation was largely a myth. Yes, he hired kids sometimes who showed particular aptitude for computers, but he demanded more than just smoke and mirrors. "A lot of young hackers have this idealistic and juvenile idea that if they do something outrageous enough as a hacker, it will get them fame," Parker says. "Then they figure they'll be able to do glamorous consulting work without having to go to school, and without having to do the hard work of really getting educated."

Kevin put the question to him directly: "I'm looking for a job as a consultant in information security. Would SRI be interested in hiring me?"

"No, I don't think so," Parker said, sounding, as always, both thoughtful and firm. "SRI only hires people who are already experienced and who have proven themselves." He told Kevin the same thing he told every hacker who approached him: "Go back to school to get a degree in computer science or business administration. Then get a job, stick with it for a few years, build up some trust, prove to me that you are serious and committed. Then come and talk to me again, and we'll see what we can do for you."

Kevin took the news with aplomb. He thanked Parker for the advice. Then he said good-bye and hung up.

Several months later, after Kevin's computer was seized in an arrest, Parker figured out how Kevin had been so well-prepared for his interview: prior to their conversation, Kevin had apparently broken into his computer and stolen several weeks' worth of e-mail.

6

The turning point in Kevin's life came on December 9, 1988, when Lenny DiCicco ratted him out to the Feds. Over the years, Kevin and Lenny had developed an odd relationship: Lenny was, at various times, his apprentice, slave, partner, and confidant. Lenny saw the worst side of Kevin's character—the meanness, the vindictiveness, the desire for revenge against his accusers, the arrogance, as well as Kevin's paradoxical and infuriating capacity to tell lies but demand total truth from others.

Kevin and Lenny had been on some serious hacking expeditions. For months they had been deep into Easynet, Digital Equipment's internal computer network. They were after the source code for VMS, the operating system software for Digital computers, and a highly valued hacker trophy. VMS runs on millions of computers around the world—at banks, research institutions, universities, even in some air traffic control systems. If they got ahold of this, it would truly be like having the keys to the electronic castle.

It was scary, but it was also amusing. Here they were, two lost kids in the San Fernando Valley chomping on greasy burgers and sucking down Cokes, journeying into the electronic heart of one of the largest and most sophisticated corporations in the country. As the months passed, Kevin and DiCicco became more and more daring, even reading the e-mail of the Digital security sleuths who were trying to track them down. Apparently, Kevin was confident that even if they did get caught, Digital would never prosecute them. The security breaches were too deep. The revelations would be too embarrassing. It was one of many things Kevin was wrong about.

DiCicco had watched Kevin become more and more obsessed in recent months. Kevin was badgering DiCicco at his job, he was lying to Bonnie about where he was and what he was doing, he was hitting DiCicco up for money, then never paying it back. He demanded that DiCicco let him into his office where he worked so that he could hack freely at night. Then one day, as a joke or because he was pissed off or who knows why, Kevin called up DiCicco's boss and pretended to be an agent with the Internal Revenue Service and asked him to hold DiCicco's checks because he "owed Uncle Sam some money."

That was the last straw. DiCicco called Digital and spilled his guts. Digital put him in touch with the FBI, and next thing he knew, the FBI and Digital security experts had set up an elaborate surveillance net. One night, DiCicco wore a wire and talked to Kevin while he hacked. The next night, DiCicco lured Kevin out to his car, then waited for him to grab his red duffel bag out of the trunk—it was where he carried all his papers and computer disks and hacking junk—and then signaled for the agents to make the arrest. They quickly moved in and slapped the cuffs on Kevin.

Startled and betrayed, he looked at his friend: "Why did you do this to me?"

"Because you fucked me over."

❖

Kevin was taken to Terminal Island Federal Correctional Institution in San Pedro to be booked. Like everyone who is booked at San Pedro, Kevin was fingerprinted and photographed. At the time of his arrest, he and Bonnie owned two cars, a 1988 Honda Civic worth $5,000, and a 1984 Nissan worth $1,500, and had $2,377 in their savings account. If Kevin was profiting from his hacking adventures, it sure didn't show.

The photo taken at Terminal Island makes a striking contrast to the one taken about a year earlier, just after his wedding day. Here, Kevin is unshaven and scruffy looking. He's wearing large owlish glasses. He looks defeated and angry and fat. It is easy to imagine this face lurking in the shadows of cyberspace, thuggish and vengeful and mean.

He was held without bail in a maximum security cell. He was not allowed to use a telephone, presumably out of fear that he'd start World War III by whistling into the receiver. At the bail hearing, Judge Mariana Pfaelzer called him "a very, very great danger to the community."

✛

Kevin fit right into the *Wargames* paradigm. "Kevin Mitnick doesn't have a college degree, never owned a computer, and, by his mother's account, is not very smart," began one story in the *Los Angeles Daily News* not long after Kevin's arrest. "But his computer-science teacher at Pierce College said Mitnick, 25, could perform magic with a computer."

This was hot copy. Newspapers and TV stations jumped all over it. Digital added to the hype by claiming that Kevin had done $4 million worth of damage to their computers, an absurd number that presumably included a good portion of the development costs of the VMS software. Many excellent reporters, including John Markoff, went with this figure. The *Los Angeles Times* was one of the few papers to question it. They went with the more reasonable figure of $160,000, which included the lost computer time and human labor.

In an effort to define his powers, Kevin was inevitably called a "wizard" or "magician." Of course, so far as most newspaper readers (and writers, for that matter) were concerned, *anything* that had to do with computers was magic in those days. For all but the most up-to-date, computers were still strange new pieces of technology, foreign objects in our lives. If Kevin could "break into computers"—the very phrase suggests gloves and lock-picking tools—at USC, or at his old high school, or even at Digital Equipment, well, it wasn't much of a jump to imagine him starting World War III.

Not that computer security wasn't a legitmate problem. Security had always been an afterthought in the design of computer software and networks. Many of the building blocks of network communications were designed at a time when academics and scientists were the only ones using it. It was a system built, fundamentally, on trust. Computer security meant locking the doors to the computer lab on your way out of the building. No one had predicted the tremendous rush of people who would soon be gallivanting around in cyberspace with their one-hundred-dollar mail-order modems—many of whom were more than willing to exploit the fundamental openness of the system.

But hacker paranoia is rooted in something more basic. Hackers exploit primal fears. They exist beyond physical reality, in the netherworld of bits and bytes. They are spirits who can enter your life and perform black magic. In a sense, the growing fear of these ghostly beings is a measure of the alienation in modern life. We use cars and telephones every day—how many people understand how they work? Computers just deepen the mystery. No one knows what strange creatures lurk in the electronic wilderness. It is the terror of the unknown and the unknowable, of the terra incognito.

It's not unlike what the colonists had faced when they confronted the vastness of our unexplored continent. To give shape to their fear, they embodied it in a single creature: Satan. Soon Satan was dancing everywhere in the woods and hollows of New England. It grew horns and a forked tongue. Salem witches were "confessing" they'd embraced Satan before they were burned at the stake. Here it was, the enemy. The fear they had all felt so deeply had been given a face. It had been given a name.

And now they could go out and do battle against it.

7

Beit T'Shuvah means "House of Repentance" in Hebrew. It sits on a hill in the Echo Park section of LA, facing east toward the rising sun. In the 1920s and 30s, Echo Park was a fashionable place to live, but now this landscape of grand Victorian homes and Spanish-style bungalows has fallen on hard times. The streets are littered with mangy cats and watery-eyed kids and cyclone fences and large yellow and black signs bolted to telephone poles every hundred feet or so: "Warning! Narcotic

Abatement Surveillance and Enforcement Area. You are being photographed!"

Beit T'Shuvah is one of the largest houses on the block, a once-proud turn-of-the-century mansion that's tumbling toward ruin. It's painted a tasteful but depressing beige. The large front porch is furnished with a tattered Naugahyde couch and a couple of rickety wooden chairs. On the day I visited, a couple of tough-looking, shaggy men leaned against the wall, talking quietly and glancing out at the view—yellow-gray smog, the distant purple silhouette of the San Gabriel mountains.

Life inside the house is chaotic and crowded. Just to the right of the entrance is the office of Harriet Rossetto, the director of Beit T'Shuvah. Even within the general hustle and bustle of the house her office stands out as a busy, disorderly space. The walls are crammed with various religious artifacts, as well as a large poster of Albert Einstein, with a quote written below: "Great spirits have always encountered violent opposition from mediocre minds."

Rossetto, a licensed clinical social worker, has the wise and tired manner of a woman who has seen everything and is not easily fooled. On the day I met her, she was wearing a bright purple jacket with an angel pin on her lapel. She founded Beit T'Shuvah in 1988 when she saw that Jewish ex-convicts with addiction problems had no place to go after their release from prison. Beit T'Shuvah offers a classic twelve-step Alcoholics Anonymous program, combined with the teachings of Judaism. Rossetto welcomes all kinds: sex addicts, drug addicts, alcoholics, gamblers—to her, they're all variations of the same sickness.

Just behind Rossetto's office is the community kitchen. It's not an appetizing sight. Linoleum is bubbling off the floor, food is stacked on wire racks, pots and pans soak in the rusty sink, the air smells of last night's meal. In the TV room—the only common room in the house—there are a couple of sofas with foam popping out of them, several worn-out chairs, and, usually, a few open sleeping bags, where some recent guest has crashed out.

Meetings are held outside, in the small backyard. There is a canvas canopy over the patio, a circle of chairs beneath it. This is where the men come to sit and tell their stories—of alcohol addiction, drug addiction, sex addiction, whatever it may be. This is where they come to find understanding, to bond, to grow, to redirect their lives.

Upstairs are the sleeping quarters. The second floor has a few bedrooms which are jammed with beds. The third floor is open, like a giant barracks room, with beds—their mattresses sagging—pushed up against each other, peeling paint, posters on the wall. These are close quarters. It's a room that is overwhelming in its maleness. This is a place where others smell every fart, where the conspicuous masturbator is known by all, where no dark mutterings in the night go unheard or unremarked upon.

This is where Kevin landed in December of 1989. It was where he was supposed to renounce his prowess at the keyboard and become an ordinary, law-abiding citizen.

✤

Kevin had gotten off fairly easily. Prodded by media headlines, the judge wanted to crack down hard, but Kevin's attorney, Alan Rubin, hit upon the innovative notion of computer addiction. At the time, many considered it a clever bit of legal maneuvering. Whatever it was, it served Kevin well: he spent eight months in jail in LA, four months at Lompoc Federal Prison Camp, then six months in a halfway house. Lompoc is a minimum-security facility, complete with its own tennis courts and outdoor patios. When Kevin arrived in the summer of 1989, it was the home of Wall Street's fallen angel, Ivan Boesky, as well as dozens of other white-collar criminals.

In prison, Kevin kept to himself. He wrote letters to Bonnie. His mother, Shelly, brought him treats and tried to offer him encouragement and consolation. He survived. On December 8th, precisely a year after he was arrested, he moved into Beit T'Shuvah, where he was assigned a bed on the third floor.

His days were strictly regimented. He was up early, ate breakfast in the community kitchen. Like everyone else, he had daily chores. One of Kevin's was to clean the third floor bathroom.

He also met regularly with Rossetto. From the beginning, she saw in him the classic addictive personality. "In many addictive personalities, there is talk of a void, of the emptiness inside," Rossetto says. "The high is in the chase, the planning and the pursuit." She saw Kevin's hacking addiction as similar to gambling: "For Kevin, there was an adrenaline rush, an almost physiological charge. When he is in action, he isn't depressed. He does not feel the void." She believes his hacking had nothing to do with money or greed. "He was hacking to feel better. He was doing it to prove that he was *somebody*."

Why computers?

"For someone who had so little control over his life, and who was unbearably lonely, with no friends and no support from his family, computers were a constant for him," Rossetto says. "Technology was something he could control. It also got him into a social set, and it was an area of adequacy and competence. When he was behind a computer, he was not a fat boy with glasses. He was someone people looked up to, who they wanted to be like."

But there were few signs of Kevin the cocky hacker at Beit T'Shuvah. "Here, I saw a very private, closed, isolated person. He was fearful of rejection. And stand-offish." He had great difficulty during the group sessions; he was never happy to talk about himself, and did not bond easily with strangers. And although he clearly had a powerful brain, his interests were very narrow: he rarely read books, for example, even the cheap paperbacks that were floating around.

Still, he made progress. He went on a rigorous diet, eating mostly vegetables and grains. He attended Overeaters Anonymous. He went on long walks with the group, and spent a lot of time in the backyard with the weights and the stationary exercise bike. His weight dropped precipitously— he lost over 100 pounds during his stay at Beit T'Shuvah. He made a few friends. He was starting to loosen up in the group meetings.

And then, by chance, Uncle Mitchell arrived.

⁜

Mitchell Mitnick is Kevin's father's older brother, and by all accounts, he's had a wild life. He had left Detroit and moved out to California in 1966—"I immediately fell in love with Beverly Hills," he says. He went into the real estate business, and during most of the 1970s, he was living high. "I lived on Broad Beach Road in Malibu," Mitchell boasts. "My neighbors were Buddy Hackett and Ali MacGraw."

He also developed a heroin habit. "I was a fool for drugs," he frankly admits. He blew his money and destroyed his real estate business. He also crossed the law. Between 1981 and 1989 alone, Mitchell had been arrested fifteen times, often for drug-related crimes, including sales of contraband substances, but also for grand theft and burglary. It was just coincidence that he ended up at Beit T'Shuvah at the same time as Kevin.

Almost immediately, Kevin stopped hanging out with the group and started huddling with Uncle Mitchell. "He bonded with me like a father," Mitchell says proudly. Rossetto was not so happy about it—"as soon as Uncle Mitchell arrived, Kevin withdrew from the group. They were always off by themselves. They formed their own little clique."

Bonnie was a regular visitor. She and Kevin met with Rossetto to talk about their marriage. Bonnie wanted out; Kevin didn't. She had been shell-shocked by his arrest—she had known he messed around with computers, but she had had no idea how deeply into it he was. She had stuck by him while he was in prison, and now, according to Rossetto, she'd had enough. Perhaps as a way of rebelling, she had started going out with Kevin's best friend, Lewis De Payne (later, they lived together for a short time). Kevin, for his part, was obsessed with her—he wanted to know what she was doing, where she was going, who she was talking to. Rossetto tried to help patch things up, but she didn't have much hope.

During the last month of Kevin's six-month stay, Rossetto focused on helping Kevin get a job in the real world. It wasn't easy. His probation prohibited him from touching a computer for three years. And yet, it was the only real skill Kevin had. So Rossetto intervened and got the terms of his probation changed so that he was allowed to search for computer work, but was prohibited from using a modem.

The idea that Kevin might be able to turn his weakness into a strength appealed to Rossetto. "T'Shuvah," after all, could be translated as "turning your life around." What better way to do it than to turn a vice into a virtue? Rossetto helped him prepare a resume. She coached him on how to best present himself. She contacted friends who might be able to place him. She offered opinions on the kind of clothes he should wear to interviews.

All to no avail. "People were terrified of him," she recalls. "I thought it was very shortsighted. I thought somebody would see the value of turning him into an ally." And she still believes it would have worked: "If he would have gotten some respect and some dignity, I think he would have turned it around."

Instead, along with Uncle Mitchell, he went to work for his father, Alan, who had given up his career as an independent record promoter and was now in the construction business.

✣

The Cuckoo's Egg probably didn't help Kevin's chances of finding a job in the computer business. The book was the real-life account of Clifford Stoll's search for a hacker which began with a seventy-five-cent accounting error on a computer system at Lawrence Berkeley Laboratories and ended a year later with the capture of a West German hacker who was selling classified U.S. military data to the Soviet KGB. The book was published in December of 1989, just about the time Kevin was arriving at Beit T'Shuvah, and it was still hovering around the best-seller list six months later when he was released.

The book was a big success for many reasons—the folksy, low-tech charm of Stoll's writing, the dramatic spy vs. spy narrative, and futuristic technical details. But more important, it was the first non-Hollywood manifestation of hackers as a threat to national security. Here was proof: a West German hacker had penetrated military and defense computers. Never mind that the KGB didn't think the information was worth much. It still smelled of international intrigue, of cold war maneuverings, of the looming fear, born and bred in the nuclear age, that technology was a false religion that would bring on Armageddon.

At the same time, cyberspace was booming. Computer bulletin boards were springing up all over the country, there was talk of telecommuting and electronic commerce and digital money. Bank records and health records and credit reports were all held in computers. When we wanted cash, we went to an automatic teller. When we wanted to make a phone call, more and more people were dialing cellular phones. The electronic web was growing. And with it, so was our anxiety, and our sense of vulnerability.

✛

Meanwhile, Kevin's life rapidly fell apart. In September of 1990, Bonnie filed for divorce. Kevin's job with his father only lasted a few months. He moved to Las Vegas, presumably to be near his mother and grandmother, who had recently moved to the area. He enrolled at the University of Nevada at Las Vegas for a short time, taking courses in nutrition and racquetball and dietary counseling—he was apparently thinking about a career as a personal fitness trainer or a certified physical education teacher. To keep in touch with a support group, he was tempted to attend Alcoholics Anonymous meetings, but couldn't bring himself to stand up in front of a crowded room and say, "My name's Kevin, and I'm a hacker." Maybe he was ashamed, or maybe he thought it wouldn't do any good (and maybe he was right). He got a job at a company called Passkey Industries, where he did low-level computer work, and tried to abide by his probation restriction that forbid him to use a modem.

For kicks, he looked up Susan Headley, who happened to be living in Las Vegas and trying to make it as a professional poker player. She was also running an escort service on the side. They hung out some, and engaged in pranks like using a ham radio to intercept the drive-through mike at fast food joints and yelling "Fuck you!" to customers.

Until the spring of 1991, he was fairly clean. But then his past came back to haunt him.

8

Katie Hafner had a lot at stake with *Cyberpunk*. She had recently left her job as a writer at *BusinessWeek*, where she covered the weekly ins and outs of the high-tech biz. Now she wanted to do something more ambitious. At the time, she was married to John Markoff, who had just taken his job as a business writer at *The New York Times*. A book about the computer underground was a natural for them. It was a new, unexplored culture, one with wide-ranging implications for the future, and one that, as the success of *The Cuckoo's Egg* showed, plenty of book buyers were interested in.

Markoff's own involvement in the book was, at best, distant. Although they had intended to write it together, Markoff's job at the *Times* took first priority. It was the top of the ladder for him, the satisfying payoff after more than a decade as a journalist in Silicon Valley. He grew up in Palo Alto, not far from Stanford University—his father was a piano teacher, his mother was a professor at San Francisco State. During the 1980s, when Silicon Valley was booming, he had bounced back and forth between trade industry magazines and local newspapers like the *San Jose Mercury* and the *San Francisco Chronicle.* Now he was living in New York and covering what amounted to a cultural and technological revolution for the most influential newspaper in the country.

In the winter of 1989, Hafner plunged into the book. Kevin's story, which had been splattered all over the papers a few months earlier, was just what she was looking for. She spent months tracking down and interviewing Kevin's old gang—Lewis De Payne (who appeared under the pseudonym "Roscoe"), Susan Headley (who used the pseudonym "Susan Thunder"), Steve Rhoades, Lenny DiCicco, and others. Kevin, who was in Lompoc at the time, then at the Beit T'Shuvah, refused to talk with her without being paid.

Cyberpunk was published in July 1991 (the title

referred to a genre of science fiction popularized by writers like William Gibson, Vernor Vinge, and Neal Stephenson). The first third of the book, subtitled "Kevin: the Dark-Side Hacker," is devoted to Kevin's exploits. It's a lively, detailed, straightforward trip through his lonely world, with a lot of page-time given to the cops and security experts who chased him down. *"Cyberpunk* makes the very important connection between rampant technology and dissatisfied youth, hungry for love, power and revenge. In the view of the authors," Walter Mosley wrote in his review in *The New York Times*, "virulent teenage emotions combined with the vast capabilities of modern technology create a truly frightening situation."

To publicize the book, Hafner made the usual rounds, including readings at bookstores and appearances on TV and radio talk shows. Markoff's mother hosted a book party at her home in Palo Alto. It was a happy occasion, with a mix of friends and admirers, computer industry types, and fellow journalists. Also present was a quiet computational physicist from San Diego who would loom large in Kevin's future: Tsutomu Shimomura.

✢

For Kevin, fame was a bargain with the devil: it gave him recognition he both craved and loathed. On the one hand, he is a very private person. The idea of having his life laid out in public like that must have been akin to walking through a crowd naked. Even worse, Hafner and Markoff were making money off it. Kevin also knew very well that the book ended any chance he had of putting his crimes and misadventures behind him. He would forever be known as "Kevin: The Dark-Side Hacker." He and his friends started referring to the book as "Cyberjunk" or "Cyberpuke."

On the other hand, fame gave him status. He was, in his own small way, a star. How many other kids from Panorama City had had books written about them? Not many. He was perfectly capable of complaining loudly about inaccuracies in the book in one breath, and in the next, speculating about who would play him in the movies.

Not long after *Cyberpunk* was published, Kevin published a commentary on the book in *2600: The Hacker Quarterly*. It began: "I am sad to report that one part of the book *Cyberpunk*, specifically the chapters on 'Kevin: The Dark-Side Hacker' is 20 percent fabricated and libelous." He went on to complain that, because he had refused to talk to Hafner, "the authors acted with malice to cause me harm." Interestingly, he didn't deny any of his exploits, except to quibble about little things, like the fact that he hadn't been eating in the computer room at the Computer Learning Center of Los Angeles when he met Bonnie. Mostly, he just seemed angry because Lenny DiCicco, his friend-turned-rat, seemed to come off better than he did (an arguable interpretation). "This bias rewarded Lenny for his participation but robbed the readers of the real truthful facts!"

More revealing was a brief encounter Kevin had with Hafner while she was a guest on Tom Snyder's nationally syndicated radio talk show. Kevin happened to turn up during a call-in segment. He sounded nervous and was disarmingly polite:

TOM SNYDER: Here is Kevin now in Las Vegas—
KEVIN MITNICK: Hello?
TOM: Yes sir.
KEVIN: My name is Kevin Mitnick and I'm one of the subjects of the book and I have some comments and questions for Katie Hafner.
TOM: Okay.
KATIE HAFNER: Hi Kevin.
KEVIN: Thanks for the Lonesome Dove book. That way you can authenticate that I'm who I say I am, since I've never talked to you before.
KATIE: Mm-hmm.
KEVIN: The question I have here is, in your book, while I believe that eighty percent of the information you have here is accurate, but twenty percent of it is inaccurate—
TOM: That's probably everything she wrote about you.
KEVIN: No, I'm talking about the two chapters that were written on me. I'm saying that eighty percent of that was accurate. My question is, basically, for instance, early in this show, you've portrayed that the

way a secretary's password was gotten was by using a loginout patch [software code often installed by hackers to steal passwords as users log in and out of a system].

KATIE: That's right.

KEVIN: But that's incorrect in itself. And while I'm sure we don't have enough time to go into how that particular stunt was done, I do want to stress that I believe that this book that you've written was unfairly slanted to make me look like I was the leader in this, and to make Lenny look like the errand boy.

KATIE: Well I appreciate your calling in and saying this. One thing I'd like to say is that I tried to get you to talk to me for more than two years. I sent you many, many letters to try to get you to tell your side of the story, and you turned me down many many times. And now after the fact you're saying these things, which maybe you could have straightened out back then.

KEVIN: That's true, you did try to contact me. I told you at that time that I didn't feel comfortable talking to anybody unless I was compensated for my time. My main questions are surrounding—

TOM: You know Kevin—and by the way, I appreciate your attitude, and I don't quarrel with your attitude— but if everybody demanded compensation for everything they said nobody would ever say anything and no book would ever get written.

KEVIN: Well, right now I'm not being compensated, I'm just calling out of interest.

TOM: Let me ask you a question. I tell you what. You

raise a number of areas of great interest to me, and I'm sure to Katie, so can you hold through a commercial break here?

KEVIN: Sure.

[Commercial break]

TOM: Okay, we're back. Now is it still your turn Kevin? I forget where we were.

KEVIN: I have a few questions, and I have one comment.

TOM: Oh yeah, okay.

KEVIN: My first question is, Katie, in your galley copy you mentioned how Lenny was going to be a computer security consultant for Digital. Digital was offering him to consult in restitution for what the California court ordered. Why was this piece of information eliminated from the real copy that was published by Simon and Schuster?

TOM: And by the way, Katie, who is "Lenny" that he talks about?

KATIE: Lenny DiCicco is Kevin's friend who eventually, at the end, turned Kevin in to the FBI. He had been breaking into computers along with Kevin. That was my mistake, Kevin. I had been told this in confidence, and mistakenly put it into the book, and then realized I had made a mistake and took it out.

KEVIN: Oh, okay, I was just wondering—

TOM: Kevin, Kevin, Kevin. Can I ask you a question?

KEVIN: Sure.

TOM: You don't deny that you broke into computers, right? You did that, right?

KEVIN: Yes, I did.

TOM: Why'd you do that? I was going to ask Katie this, but as long as you're on the phone, what better source than somebody who was involved. What is the thrill or the motivation for doing this sort of thing?

KEVIN: Basically, the fascination of learning more about computer systems. See, they didn't offer that kind of in-depth exploring in an educational environment.

TOM: Yeah, they didn't, and the reason they didn't was because those programs were owned and copyrighted by Digital Equipment!

KEVIN: What programs? You're asking what motivated me to take one particular program, or are you talking in general?

TOM: No, I'm just saying, when you're breaking into a system, do you know you're doing wrong, or do you feel you have a right to access these things?

KEVIN: Oh, I know it's wrong. That wasn't the question I thought you were asking. I thought you were asking, in general, why does a hacker hack, what are the motivations behind it.

TOM: So you say the motivation is to learn more, because the kinds of information you have access to when you hack is information that is not available to you otherwise?

KEVIN: That's not necessarily true. It's basically to learn more about the operating system and computer systems. It's basically the fascination of learning about the computer itself, not necessarily the information the computer contains.

TOM: And when you were hacking, what was your

intent with the information that you gleaned? What were you going to do with that information?

KEVIN: Well, there have been so many incidents of my hacking, you'll have to come up with a specific incident.

TOM: I can't do that, I don't have the full list in front of me.

KEVIN: You can ask Katie. Go ahead.

KATIE: Well, one thing that interested me actually is why you were interested in VMS source code.

KEVIN: Basically, to learn from the sources how the operating system worked. To learn what other security flaws were within the operating system. Basically, as you quoted in the book, to "learn how the system ticks." Can I ask another question?

TOM: Sure. But let me just ask one thing of you. Once you learned how a system ticked was that the end of it, then you moved on to something else?

KEVIN: Not really, because there's always more knowledge to be gained. But I learned not to use the bad judgment I have learned in the past to come to that end [sic].

TOM: All right, one more for Katie then I gotta move on.

KEVIN: Okay, basically Katie, let me see, since I only have one more, I have it written down . . .

TOM: I'll tell you what, Kevin. Stay there, I'll come back to you.

[Commercial break]

TOM: Kevin, I got less than a minute for you, go ahead.

KEVIN: Okay, I'll just make my comment then. The problem isn't with the operating systems not being secure. Digital did a very good job in manufacturing a system that if just the front line people, the front line managers, were to use the tools that Digital makes available, and to read the information in the security guides that Digital puts out for its customers, they would run much tighter systems and wouldn't be as vulnerable to attack—

TOM: Okay, Kevin—

KATIE: That's a good point. He's making a good point.

TOM: Okay, I appreciate your calling, Kevin, and I thank you for joining us.

KEVIN: Thank you.

KATIE: Thanks, Kevin.

TOM: And by the way, Kevin, if you're unhappy with the book, you'll be happier when the movie comes out. Your act will be cleaned up like you can't believe.

9

About six months after *Cyberpunk* hit the bookstores, Kevin attended a conference hosted by the Digital Equipment Computer Users Society (DECUS), an influential organization with about 110,000 members worldwide. Digital, of course, had been the target of Kevin's deepest penetrations, and their security personnel had been involved in Kevin's arrest. Although Kevin had done his time at Lompoc and at Beit T'Shuvah, he was still on probation and forbidden to touch a modem—the digital equivalent of being under house arrest.

If he was genuinely trying to go straight, it's understandable why Kevin would want to attend this gathering. If he were going to make it in the computer security world, this was the crowd he was going to have to win over. Digital was the system he understood best—and since he had succeeded in hacking the system, he presumably knew details about its weaknesses that might be valuable to anyone whose job it is to keep Digital computers safe.

On the other hand, slipping into a DECUS event was the kind of trick that the old Kevin might have tried to pull off. Not that there were any corporate secrets on display. It was sublter than that. He could just drift around, matching faces to names, eavesdropping on conversations—who knew what valuable tidbits he might scoop up?

Kevin would later claim that his intentions were honest and sincere. In later years, he would often look back on what happened at the conference with bitterness. Perhaps it was the moment it became clear to him that he would never live down his past.

"At approximately nine-fifteen P.M. I walked into the South Hall registration area with the intent on registering for the entire DECUS symposium," Kevin later wrote in a security industry newsletter. He filled out a registration form, using his real name but omitting the name of the company he was working for "due to the fact that my employer did not want it publicized due to the sensitivity of my past." When he filled out the form, he "mistakenly" omitted signing the Canons of Conduct (which said, in essence, "thou shall not hack at this symposium") which most attendees are expected to sign. Kevin's explanation: "At that time, I was basically in a rush, since there were people behind me and I had to go work out."

On his way out, he bumped into Ray Kaplan, a computer security consultant he was friendly with. Kaplan, trying to make him feel welcome, asked if he wanted to meet a few people. "Hesitantly I agreed," Kevin wrote, "since I knew a lot of people were not happy with my past actions."

About an hour later, after Kevin had worked out in the hotel gym, Kaplan led him on a tour of reception. He shook a few hands, said a few hellos. "I just wanted to maintain a low profile and blend in without causing any controversy," Kevin wrote. One DECUS attendee, whom Kevin called "Mr. X," knew of Kevin's past exploits, and seemed "shocked" to be introduced to the infamous hacker. "I told Mr. X I am not interested in hacking his company's system anymore and that whatever information I could offer, I would be happy to talk to him." After that, Kevin left the reception and went to bed.

The next morning, he returned to South Hall. When he checked in at the registration desk, he was met by three DECUS officials—two men and a woman. One of the men asked Kevin his name, and he told them. "Then he asked me for identification, so I pulled out my California Driver's License. He looked at it and said, 'You can't attend here.'

"I asked why.

"He said, 'You know why.'

"I said, 'No I don't. Why?'

"He just repeated, 'You know why.' "

With that, Kevin's DECUS credentials were confiscated and he was escorted out of the building.

Ray Kaplan later appealed to DECUS officials on Kevin's behalf, arguing that Kevin had broken no rules. If he'd wanted to deceive them, he could have easily attended the symposium under an alias, and no one would have known the difference. But he hadn't done that. And if they were so fearful of ex-hackers, why wasn't anyone screaming about Lenny DiCicco, Kevin's former partner in crime, who also happened to be attending the conference?

The argument fell on deaf ears. Kevin was not allowed to return. To him, the message was clear: you will not be trusted. You will not be forgiven.

✣

Less than a month later, Kevin was hit with a second blow. His twenty-one-year-old half brother, Adam, was found dead in a parked car on January 7, 1992. The cause of death, according to the police report, was "methadone intoxication." A heroin overdose.

On the surface, Adam and Kevin had very little in common. Adam was seven years younger than Kevin. They never lived in the same household together. Whereas Kevin was fat and lonely and nerdy, Adam was thin and stylish and popular. He had been a wild punker in his high school days, but as he got older, he mellowed out. Like his father and his Uncle Mitchell, he was in the construction business, and had recently gone off on his own to specialize in selling and installing window blinds. Adam was his father's favorite son. He lavished Adam with as much attention as he withheld from Kevin.

Still, Adam meant a lot to Kevin. He and Kevin would often go to the gym and work out together; they would talk at family get-togethers. Screwed up as Kevin's family was, it meant a lot to him. It was the only thing he had to hold on to.

Kevin was in Las Vegas when he got the news that Adam had died. He returned to LA for the funeral. In his usual paranoid fashion, he had a lot of questions about Adam's death. But for once, his paranoia seemed justified. According to Kevin's friends, Adam's body had been found in the passenger seat of a car in the Echo Park neighborhood of LA. It didn't take a lot of detective work to figure out that someone had probably been with him, someone who had most likely gotten high with him, then maybe seen that things were going wrong, freaked out, and abandoned Adam in the car to die.

According to Kevin's friends, Kevin soon heard that Uncle Mitchell, his pal and confidant at Beit T'Shuvah, had been one of the last persons to see

Adam alive. And Mitchell, everyone knew, had had a long romance with heroin. It was hard not to wonder if there was a connection. Mitchell denies it. "It was terribly sad," he says. Nevertheless, a rift developed between Mitchell and his brother Alan. After Adam's death, Alan stopped talking to him.

A few days after the funeral, Kevin dropped in to see Harriet Rossetto. She was surprised and happy to see him, but also concerned. She thought he looked bad, obviously upset and shaken by this family tragedy. He flopped on the brown corduroy couch in her office and they spoke for an hour or so. He told her about Adam's death (in a sad irony, his body was found only a short distance away from the halfway house). He told her he was starting to hack again, that things were falling apart. "I'm slipping," he told her. She encouraged him to check himself in to Beit T'Shuvah again. She knew it wouldn't be easy—"This is not exactly the Ritz-Carlton."

"I'll think about it," Kevin said to her. Then he left.

She never saw him again.

10

By the early 1990s, at least a few people in law enforcement had come to the conclusion that it takes a hacker to catch a hacker. The only way they'd caught Kevin in 1988 was because Lenny DiCicco turned him in. The only reason Cliff Stoll had been about to catch Markus Hess, the West German hacker in *The Cuckoo's Egg*, was because Stoll knew as much (or more) about computers than he did. In 1991, when Dutch hackers had been caught poking around in U.S. military computers during the Gulf War, they were tracked down by a crew of private security experts, including Tsutomu Shimomura.

Law enforcement's own attempts to crack down on hackers had been disturbing and, for the most part, unsuccessful. In the late 1980s, their basic strategy was to kick down doors and indiscriminately seize the computer equipment of anyone who was suspected of electronic crimes. Some of these raids were legitimate, but many were not. The resulting outrage led to the founding of the Electronic Frontier Foundation, as well as inspiring an excellent book about the early days of the battle for law and order in cyberspace, *The Hacker Crackdown* by Bruce Sterling.

So it's no surprise that law enforcement would have wanted to try a new angle. Why not hire another hacker—in effect, turn one into a double agent? It was a tried and true strategy of law enforcement. They did it on narcotics cases, they did it with the mob, they did it with Russian spies.

The character they apparently chose was a mysterious, troubled, troubling one-legged criminal named Justin Petersen.

✛

Unlike Kevin, who never lived a very colorful or lusty life, Justin Petersen liked the fast lane. In the 1980s, he'd been a fixture on the club scene in Hollywood, hanging out at places like the Roxy and the Whiskey and Gazarri's. He'd lost the lower portion of one leg when a car made a left turn in front of him as he was cruising down Sunset Boulevard on his Harley. But somehow the limp and the prosthesis just made him more interesting. He always had a babe on the arm, he knew where to score a little blow, and he drove a nice little Porsche. A nice little *stolen* Porsche.

He also knew his way around the phone system. One of his best-known hacks was inspired by Kevin Poulsen, Petersen's sometime-friend and cohort who was living underground at the time. Poulsen was wanted for, among other things, swiping what were supposedly classified military documents while he was working at SRI in the late 1980s. In 1990, Poulsen rigged up an elaborate scam to win a radio station contest. By controlling the phone lines, he and others were able to score cash prizes, two Porsches, and a trip to Hawaii. Following in his friend's footsteps, Petersen later nabbed $10,000 from a similar radio contest. It was the kind of out and out criminal fraud that Kevin Mitnick had never even attempted.

Petersen, who often went under the alias "Eric Heinz," eventually fled to Texas to avoid arrest. His crime spree continued. He began living off credit cards—other people's credit cards.

Then an interesting thing happened. According to court records, Petersen received an unusual call on April 10, 1991, from Special Agent Richard Beasley of the FBI. According to Petersen, he confessed to Beasley that when he was in California, he had stolen Pacific Bell equipment, and then used the equipment to illegally gain access to the Pac Bell computers. He also confessed to illegal telephone taps and gaining access to TRW credit reports.

Perhaps he said a few things about Kevin Poulsen, too.

Because the next day—despite the fact that Justin Petersen was a wanted man, a hacker with clear criminal intent—no gang of FBI agents appeared at his door. Instead, strangely enough, Kevin Poulsen was arrested.

⁜

Not long after that, a small army of law enforcement officials who were not affiliated with the FBI, including U.S. Postal Inspectors and the Dallas Sheriff's Department, showed up at Petersen's door. He was eventually indicted on eight counts, including illegal computer access, mail fraud, credit card fraud, and possession of a fake Social Security card. He was also indicted for possession of a stolen vehicle—his Porsche—which he had transported across state lines.

Again, the FBI intervened. He pled guilty to the Dallas crimes, was released on bail, then returned to California. It's not clear exactly what arrangements were made, but on October 18, 1991, the FBI gave Petersen a polygraph test, presumably to test his trustworthiness as an informant. Later that day, Petersen and his attorney spoke with David Schindler, a U.S. Attorney in Los Angeles. A week later, they spoke with FBI agent Stanley Ornellas.

Then it was time to go hacker hunting.

❖

According to Petersen, the FBI went all out. They set him up in a safe house in West LA and paid him two hundred dollars a week, plus expenses. He bought new clothes and ate in nice restaurants. In return, he put his technical expertise to work chasing computer criminals.

His first task: find Poulsen's computer, which had been stashed somewhere for safekeeping by Poulsen's friend, Ron Austin. The FBI believed the computer contained classified documents stolen from SRI, where Poulsen had worked for a short period. (It did, but they weren't as juicy as they'd hoped.) Petersen earned his keep: he found Austin, who eventually led him to the storage locker in Tarzana where he had hidden Poulsen's computer. Austin was busted, the computer was confiscated.

Then Petersen moved on to his next project. "It would be a real feather in your cap if you could help us catch Kevin Mitnick," Petersen claims an FBI agent told him one day. Apparently the FBI had reason to believe Kevin was up to his old tricks again. Petersen agreed to look into it—why not? Although he had never met Kevin, he had heard plenty about him. To help him learn more, an agent gave him a copy of *Cyberpunk.*

Kevin's job with his father's construction business hadn't worked out. There was too much tension between them, too many buried emotions. Besides, Kevin was good at only one thing—computers—and those skills weren't in high demand at a construction site. So Kevin quit and took a job as a "researcher" with Teltec, a private investigators' firm near where he was living in Calabasas. He had been hired as a favor to his father, who apparently felt bad about letting his son go, and who was friendly with one of Teltec's owners. According to De Payne, it was a pretty dull job—Kevin's day consisted of going through databases looking for real estate transactions and divorce filings. De Payne, doing his best to sound like a loyal friend, claims Kevin wasn't doing any hacking at Teltec—"maybe a little social engineering." Or maybe a little more than that.

In any event, in June 1992, Teltec got into trouble. The owners were arrested on suspicion of tapping into TRW computers to get financial records. As part of their plea bargain, they pointed the finger at Kevin—who promptly vanished. The FBI, eager to make a high-profile bust, wanted Justin Petersen to help them find him.

When Petersen began tracking Kevin in the summer of 1992, Kevin was still wounded by Adam's death. He was not happy with the LAPD's inability to track down the person who had abandoned Adam in the car in Echo Park—in effect, leaving him alone to die. Maybe Uncle Mitchell had had something to do with it. Or maybe not. It wouldn't have been unlike Kevin to turn to hacking to try to find the answers.

Petersen put the word out to some of his hacker pals that he was looking for Kevin and before long, they were talking on the phone. Using the name Eric Heinz, he gained Kevin's trust in a particularly canny, and perhaps cruel, manner. According to Kevin's friends, he told Kevin that he and Adam had once dated the same woman, a mysterious character named "Erin." This may or may not have been true. Justin and Adam had traveled in the same circles—the LA club scene—so it was certainly within the realm of possibility.

At the time, Kevin was hanging around with his old friend De Payne. Justin tried to ingratiate himself with them. He would invite them over to his apartment in Hollywood and try to goad them into causing trouble. He would talk about the many wiretaps he'd put on people's phones, or he'd dish out some secret about a Pac Bell computer that he had picked up somewhere. It didn't take Kevin and Lewis long to catch on to what was actually happening. They were less disturbed than amused—the hacker-working-for-the-Feds-to-catch-a-hacker scenario played into their spy vs. spy fantasies.

Before long, they decided to start building a case against Petersen. It seemed to Kevin and De Payne that he was more dangerous than they were—he was committing crimes, after all, in the name of the law. After consulting a lawyer, they began taping his phone conversations. Now they were goading *him* to talk about his adventures. They followed him to Studio One, a nightclub off Santa Monica Boulevard in LA, where Petersen regularly put on a dance party called "Midnight Mass" ("lots of cheap gals in elegant dresses," De Payne quips). Over a span of several months, they toyed with Petersen, logging his every move, trying to draw him out, trying to get *him* to commit crimes.

Petersen claims Kevin's "investigation" of him bordered on harassment. At one point, Petersen says, "He once called up my father and said he was an administrator at a local hospital. He told my father that my mother had been seriously injured in a car accident, and that he needed to get a little financial information from him. And my dad, you know, he was so shocked. He just fell for it. He told Kevin everything he wanted to know—Social Security numbers, bank accounts, whatever."

✢

In September of 1992, based largely on what they had learned from Petersen about Kevin's whereabouts, the FBI raided Kevin's apartment, as well as De Payne's. Kevin was either lucky or well-informed—he wasn't home. In November, an arrest warrant was issued, accusing him of violating probation by illegally accessing Pac Bell computers.

By this time, Kevin and De Payne were onto their friend Eric. They had figured out that, while he was working for the FBI, he was also committing fraud. They learned that he had apparently hacked into DMV computers and adopted the identity of a dead person, Eric Heinz, and was now collecting Social Security benefits in the dead man's name. Someone—it's not hard to guess who—tipped off Eric Heinz, Sr., the dead man's father, to what was going on. It wasn't long before administrators at the Social Security office had launched an investigation into who Eric Heinz really was.

The FBI couldn't have been too happy at the way their investigation had gone awry. Kevin had not only eluded their trap, he had made them look ridiculous by exposing their informant as a criminal. As usual, Kevin had managed to piss off the wrong people.

And as usual, he didn't stop there. It was Eric Heinz, as well as one of the FBI agents involved in the case, that Kevin was investigating when he hacked into the DMV and asked that the documents be sent to Kinko's in Studio City. He undoubtedly believed that the ends justified the means, that the crimes Petersen had commited in trying to track him down were far greater than anything he'd ever done, and that, therefore, this wasn't a serious matter.

As usual, he was wrong.

11

It wasn't long after Kevin's escape from Kinko's that detectives from the Glendale Police Department made a chilling discovery. In the process of questioning a woman named Michelle Brooks for a variety of minor charges, including possession of a false driver's license, she apparently got spooked. While the detectives listened with slack-jawed amazement, Brooks spilled her guts about a long-forgotten murder that happened more than ten years earlier. It had been committed, she claimed, by her ex-husband, Mitchell Mitnick.

The murder had happened around 1981, Brooks told the detectives. The victim was a black man Mitchell and a friend had dumped over the side of the road somewhere above Malibu. The detectives did some checking and found out that, yes, in 1981, the Malibu Sheriff's Department recovered a body that had been dumped over the edge of Topanga Canyon Road. A black man in his thirties. Single gunshot wound to the face. Pockets turned inside out. No wallet, no ID, no keys. Through fingerprints they were able to determine his name: Robert Allen.

At the time, the Malibu Sheriff's office did some poking around. They were pretty certain Allen had been murdered, but they had very little evidence to go on. Allen was poor and black—not exactly the kind of victim the Malibu Sheriff's Department was going to lose any sleep over. Could have been a drug deal gone wrong. Or a family dispute. They had no idea.

Brooks told the Glendale detectives to talk to a guy named David Spire, a former friend and accomplice of Mitnick's. So that's what they did. In March of 1993, Detective Tom Kuh sat down with Spire, hoping to get some information out of him. Spire wasn't a tough nut to crack. After a little prodding, Spire said, "I can pretty much tell you what happened."

Spire told Detective Kuh that he and Mitchell were driving around west LA in a gray Volvo station wagon. It was the middle of an afternoon in

July 1981. They were high. They decided to stop at a fast-food place—he thought it was Mc-Donald's, but he couldn't remember for sure—just off Western Boulevard near the Santa Monica Freeway. As they were walking in, they met a black guy. He had a big stack of money in an envelope, and he was talking about how he wanted to get a hooker. He had a Jamaican accent.

Spire claimed Mitchell knew what was going down. The guy was going to pull what's known on the street as a Jamaican switch. He'd show them a big stack of cash and try to get them to go in with him on the hooker. Then when they gave him money, he would put it in the envelope, then switch envelopes. The second envelope was filled mostly with dollar-bill-sized paper, with only a few bills up front to make it look good. Then at some point, he'd take off with the envelope full of real money, and leave the phony one behind.

According to Spire, Mitchell didn't take kindly to being scammed.

Spire told Detective Kuh: "So [Mitchell] tells me, get in the car, we're going to drive this guy to where he wants to go. Whatever. And when he's going to do the switch, we're going to end, you know, ending up with his money instead of him ending up with our money. Basically, that was the program. So I get in the front seat and the black guy gets in the front seat. Then Mitchell goes . . . to the back of the car . . . and comes out with this piece and just tells the guy to shut up. You know, say nothing. And tells me to drive and as I start driving away, the guy starts talking, he like starts to panic, and the Jamaican accent's gone and he starts, ahhhhh, and you know I didn't do nothing, and Mitchell, he's like this, and he goes, he tells the guy, 'Don't move, don't move. I don't know what the guy did, but evidently he moved a little bit and Mitchell shot him . . .

"I said, 'Oh, fuck.'

"And then he tells me, 'Drive, drive, get out of here. Go!'

"And I go, 'What did you do?'

"And he goes, 'Just get out of here . . .' "

"What happened after that?" Detective Kuh asked.

"Drove to Topanga Canyon. I drove. Topanga Canyon. He pulled the body out there. Just left it up there."

"Did you bury it?"

"No."

"Cover it? Did Mitchell bury it? Well, what do you mean you don't know if the guy was dead? Where did he shoot him?"

"He shot him in the head."

"Okay. So—was the guy walking, talking, breathing?"

"He was breathing."

"He was?"

"Yeah."

"A labored breathing?"

"He was, he was just breathing. Well, I'm sure it was labored."

"Was he saying anything?"

"No."

"So at the point you dumped him out of the car, he's breathing?"

"Yeah."

Later in the interview Kuh asked him, "Did you ever hear about the body being found or anything?"

"Nope. Never heard anything about it."

"Weren't you afraid that if he was still breathing, didn't he mention that, you know, we should finish this guy off? I mean was there any question about him surviving?"

"I know he didn't shoot him again."

"And you never asked him why he shot the guy? I would think—that would come up."

"Oh yeah, I was scared to death. I thought he was going to shoot me."

"Did he say why he'd shot him?"

"That's what I said to him a bunch of times. I said, 'What did you do, Mitchell? What made you do it?'"

"What was his response?"

" 'I told him not to move.' That was his response. That's what he—that was his response, his exact words. 'I told him not to move.' I said, 'Jesus Christ, all he did was move?' I thought, 'God damn.' But up until right now, I didn't know the guy ever died or, you know, for sure or anything. I just—"

"You never looked in the papers?"

"Never, never. Never, never. Never had anything to do with it again. I was scared stiff."

✣

Detective Kuh testified that Brooks told him that, on the day of the murder, Mitnick and Spire returned home between 9:00 and 10:00 P.M. They locked themselves in the bathroom—Brooks told Kuh that she believed Mitnick was doing drugs, and had hidden himself in the bathroom so he wouldn't be seen by his ten-year-old daughter.

Brooks knocked on the door, and Mitnick let her in. She saw drugs and syringes, as well as a black wallet. "When she asked about the wallet," Detective Kuh testified, "she was told by Mr. Mitnick that he had just killed a person, a black man, in Los Angeles."

According to Kuh's testimony, she asked to look at the wallet. She looked inside and saw some papers. She also saw a driver's license and a photo of a middle-aged black woman with a baby, apparently about one year old.

She asked where the wallet had come from. Mitnick told her it was from the black guy he'd shot.

"Where is the guy now?"

"We dumped the body in the canyon earlier," Mitnick told her.

"At that time," Kuh testified, "she saw Mr. Mitnick take the wallet, or the contents of the wallet, and burn them in the fireplace of the residence."

✛

These accusations must have been a blow to Kevin. This was, after all, the guy he had bonded with "like a father" at Beit T'Shuvah. This was the guy he had trusted to get him on the road to recovery. Now, while Kevin was wondering if his uncle had been involved in Adam's death, his uncle was being charged with murder.

Unlike his nephew, however, Mitchell was able to hire first-class lawyers to represent him in court, including Harry Weiss, an aging Beverly Hills attorney who was known around the courthouse as "the Lawyer to the Stars." By raising questions about the police investigation, as well as pointing out the lack of witnesses, he was able to get the charge reduced to manslaughter. Mitchell plead guilty, and received the minimum sentence allowable under federal guidelines: four years in jail.

To this day, Mitchell maintains that prosecutors lied under oath, and that he took the manslaughter plea just to get the case resolved. He claims that it was his partner, Spire, who really did the killing. "I did not shoot that man," Mitchell says in a tone that leaves no room for misunderstanding. "I am one hundred percent innocent."

III

THE CHASE

1

After Justin Petersen self-destructed, law enforcement was back to square one. Kevin was gone,
and they had no good idea where. There were reports that he was in Las Vegas, that he was in Denver, that he was still in Los Angeles. He lived in
the ether, calling friends like De Payne at all hours
of the night, but refusing to disclose where he was
or what he was doing. He communicated with other
friends via Internet Relay Chat or on ham radio.
He was invisible and untraceable, a ghostly spirit
on the move.

For the FBI, help came from an unlikely source. A few months after Kevin's escape from Kinko's, a software engineer in England named Neill Clift received some puzzling e-mail. His correspondent claimed to be an engineer at Digital Equipment named Derrell Piper. In the message, Piper explained that Digital was recruiting engineers and wanted to know if Clift was interested. Clift didn't hesitate—he was *very* interested.

Clift, a stocky, muscular guy with metal-rim glasses who was in his late twenties at the time, had grown up in a small place called Brownhills in the West Midlands of England—it was about as far away from the epicenter of the digital revolution as you could get. He had intended to study chemistry at Leeds University, but then like so many others of his generation, he fell through the looking glass when he got access to his first mainframe computer, an old Digital Vax 11/750. He became fascinated with the software that ran the machine, and eventually made a reputation for himself as an expert at finding the holes in Digital's VMS operating-system software.

Now here was Digital, the third largest computer maker in the United States, knocking on his door.

He and Piper began exchanging e-mail. Clift knew that Digital was going through hard times, cutting thousand of jobs and restructuring departments in order to keep up with Hewlett-Packard and IBM. Not exactly the moment you expected to be wooed for a new job. But Clift wanted to believe. And why shouldn't he? To draw him in further, the man who called himself Derrell Piper offered Clift a lot of information that he recognized as proprietary to Digital. Before long, Piper had his complete trust. He asked for—and got—nearly every security flaw that Clift had discovered in previous months.

After several weeks of this, Clift got a whiff that something funny was going on. He began to ask his correspondent a few pointed questions. When he seemed slightly adrift, Clift grew suspicious. He probed the path the mail was taking, and saw that it wasn't going to Digital at all, but was being forwarded to a computer at the University of Southern California. With a little probing, Clift discovered that the software on that machine had been patched to allow access to any user name with a special password of #ME#.

Fuck!

Clift knew he'd been hustled. And he knew who it was, too. His old pal Kevin Mitnick.

✛

Kevin had gotten to know Clift back in the late 1980s, when he would frequently try to wrangle information from Clift on the latest Digital security info. They never had any real-time contact—no face-to-face meetings, no phone calls. It was strictly e-mail. In fact, it was Clift's machine that Kevin was logged onto when he was busted in 1988 for computer fraud. When Kevin was shipped off to

Lompoc to serve out his sentence, Clift thought he'd heard the last of him.

Apparently not. How had Kevin tracked him down? That was what Clift wanted to know. He had changed jobs, moved to a different city. In the months that followed, Clift would piece it together. It was a typical tale of Kevin's ingenuity and persistence.

According to Clift, Kevin first called the office at his old job, trying to figure out where he'd gone. He managed to wrangle the detail out of someone that he'd moved to the Manchester area. Kevin then tried the Post Office to see if Clift had left a forwarding address—he hadn't.

So Kevin turned his attentions to British Telephone, assuming that one of the first things Clift would do was have a phone installed. He first called British Telephone and pretended to be Clift. He said he wanted to verify the installation date of his (Clift's) phone service. He then told them that he wanted to be contacted at work should any problems arise and, sure enough, he managed to get Clift's company name and work phone number. On the day the phone was to be installed Kevin again pretended to be a British Telephone engineer and managed to get someone in the office to tell him both the unlisted numbers Clift was having installed.

Then Kevin hatched the second phase of his plan. Within Clift's first few weeks at his new job, Kevin rang him up and said he was a Digital engineer named Mark Pilant. According to Clift, one of the first things Kevin said in the telephone conversation was, "It's been a long time since I talked to you." Clift knew he had never spoken to this guy, and so alarm bells went off immediately. Then Kevin used the same ruse he'd use later: "We're recruiting some people in the engineering group— would you be interested?"

When "Mark Pilant" called him at home the next day, Clift started to get suspicious. He called Digital. Yes, there was an engineer at Digital named Mark Pilant. No, he hadn't called. Then who was it? The person had a distinctive voice. Clift called up Ray Kaplan and asked him to send a copy of the tapes of the security conference where Kevin had spoken. It was just a hunch— Clift hadn't kept up with the news in Kevin's case, he didn't know if Kevin was out of jail or not, if he'd gone straight or was back to hacking.

He put the tape in the player and there it was. That voice. It was Mark Pilant. It was Kevin Mitnick.

✛

Having been hustled once by Kevin a few months earlier, it was doubly troubling that he was hustled again via e-mail. And this time, he'd fallen for it hook, line, and sinker. Worst of all, Clift had to go into this new boss and explain that he had been snookered—Kevin had gotten all this latest security info out of him. Then to make matters worse, Clift had to call engineers at Digital and tell them what had happened. For a security expert like Clift, it was worse than embarrassing. Another engineer might have tried to bury it; not Clift. He took his lumps.

And then he set out to get his revenge. He was tired of all the trouble Kevin had caused him, all the humiliation, all the hassles. God knows how many hours he'd spent trying to keep the guy out, trying to reconfigure his machine, close up this hole, close up that hole. . . .

Clift knew by now that Kevin was on the run. He knew he was a wanted man. So with the help of his pal Michael Lawrie, a systems and security manager based at the Loughborough University of Technology in Leicestershire, he began to lay a trap. He figured that if he could lure Kevin into his system, he might have a good chance of figuring out where he was living, and that might, in turn, help get Kevin arrested.

So the first thing he did was write special software that he could install on the system and that would log every detail of Kevin's activities. That was no easy feat, since Kevin was shrewd enough to easily spot any routine surveillance software. But once it was set up, it basically logged every keystroke onto a secret file—in effect, making a record of his every move on the keyboard, a kind of musical score of hacking.

Now, Clift just had to entice Kevin into visiting his system. To do this, he relied on friendship. He sent Kevin e-mail, suggesting that he was welcome to come into the site and look around. And Kevin, taking kindness wherever he could get it, fell for it. He and Clift struck up an e-mail correspondence. Clift listened to Kevin brag about the systems he gotten access to, the newest bugs he'd found. They began chatting about their lives. Clift and Lawrie pretended to turn a blind eye when Kevin wandered around in their system, poking and prodding, to see what new information he could glean.

Unbeknownst to Kevin, Clift began feeding everything he learned to Bob Lyons, a corporate security consultant for Digital Equipment in Maynard, Massachusetts. And Lyons began feeding it to the FBI.

2

It wasn't much help. Clift gave the FBI reams of information about Kevin's activities—the exact times he was logging onto Clift's computer, how long he was hanging around—but it didn't do much to pinpoint Kevin's location. It's too easy to cover your footsteps in cyberspace, too easy to get lost in the electronic shuffle. Sure, the Feds wanted to catch him, because they were always looking for ways to make statements about electronic crime, but it wasn't like they could justify putting a team on the case—or even a single agent—full time. If they were going to find him, they were going to have to get lucky.

And that is exactly what several agents thought happened in March 1994. As a matter of routine, they happened to be attending the Computers, Freedom, and Privacy Conference at the Palmer House Hilton in Chicago. CFP is an annual event, a big, sprawling, eclectic get-together that attracted several hundred hackers, crackers, wireheads, cyberpunks, computer cops, academics, lawyers, and businesspersons. For three days, the best minds in the computer culture wrestled with the Big Questions of the day: how can we insure privacy in electronic communications without restricting freedom of speech? How should exisiting copyright laws be revised to cover digital information? What exactly is the Clipper Chip, and how can it be stopped?

In the midst of all this, one of the agents happened to notice a tall, quiet, dark-haired young man who looked surprisingly like . . . Kevin Mitnick. Was it possible? Well, it wasn't inconceivable. Maybe Kevin thought CFP would be the last place FBI agents would look for him. Maybe he thought he'd get lost in the crowd. Maybe the FBI had gotten lucky.

Early on the morning of Friday, March 25th, agents made their move. They had figured out which hotel room the suspect was staying in, and at 8 A.M., they pounded on the door. There were four FBI agents—three men and a woman. They heard vague rumbling behind the door, as if they had just woken someone—or several persons—up from a deep sleep.

A voice through the door: "Who is it?"

"FBI."

Muffled panic.

They knocked again.

A young, dark-haired kid opened the door—Kevin, agents thought. He was in his underwear. Behind him, luggage and clothes and computer gear were spread all over the floor.

"You're Kevin Mitnick," one of the agents said.

He blinked and looked confused. "I'm not Kevin Mitnick," he told them. "I'm Lee Nussbaum."

The agents believed that "Lee Nussbaum" was an alias Kevin had been using recently. "We know all about the aliases. You're Kevin Mitnick."

"You've got the wrong guy," the young man insisted.

The agents asked him to put his clothes on and take a walk to FBI headquarters a few blocks away. The young man didn't complain. He got dressed. Then the agents slapped handcuffs on him.

In fact, FBI had reason to be suspicious. They didn't have many good photos of Kevin, except for the mug shot after his 1988 arrest. But from what they could tell, it looked like this "Nussbaum" character could be their guy. Same height and weight. Same dark hair and glasses. He was certainly geeky enough. The only way to find out for sure was to take him downtown.

At the same time as they thought they were busting Kevin, a different crew of FBI agents knocked on the door of another possible outlaw. Apparently, the agents thought they had tracked down Justin Petersen, who, after failing to help nab Kevin, had gone AWOL and vanished. Investigators had reason to believe he had been going by the alias "Agent Steal." And one of the conference attendees, they noticed, was named Robert Steele. Coincidence? Four agents knocked on his hotel room door. "Room Service," one of them said.

"I didn't order anything," came a baritone voice from inside the room.

"FBI."

A burly middle-aged man with a beard pulled open the door. He wore nothing but a towel over his privates. He did not look amused.

"Are you Justin Petersen?" one of the agents asked.

"No, I'm Robert Steele."

The agents figured out pretty quickly that something was wrong. Steele was forty-something; Petersen was in his late twenties. Petersen had a bum leg; Steele's, they could see, were both operational. And Steele was not behaving like a man on the lam. In fact, he was staring them down pretty good.

Although the agents didn't get the joke at the

time, there was delicious irony in the fact that the
FBI mistook Robert Steele for a hacker. Steele was
an ex-CIA operative who now runs an information
services company called Open Source Solutions,
Inc. One of the main notions of his business is that
the intelligence community is mired in the cold-
war ideology, a dinosaur of past generations. He is
also one of the few people in the security establishment who sees hackers as a valuable presence.
"Hackers are a national resource," Steele says in
his stock speech, which he repeats at computer security gatherings all around the country. He sees
them as pointing out flaws that might otherwise be
exploited by hardcore criminals, and often berates
his peers for their hacker paranoia.

The FBI agents at the door knew none of this.
They just knew that this big burly dude didn't
match their description of Justin Petersen. They
quickly apologized and departed.

"Nussbaum" was a different story. The agents
marched him in handcuffs down the hallway, into
the elevator, through the hotel lobby, out the front
doors into the mild spring morning air, and several
blocks down the street to FBI headquarters. Their
suspect didn't say much, he had stopped protesting
his innocence, he was just going along with it,
walking silently along. Innocent or guilty, he was a
cool cucumber.

Once they were inside FBI headquarters, agents
took off the cuffs. They photographed and finger-

printed him. They offered him coffee; he asked for water instead.

A half hour later, the fingerprint ID came back from Washington. The suspect's real name was Lee Nussbaum. He was a student at Columbia University in New York City. Agents questioned him briefly: he had no idea how or why Kevin was using his name. As far as he knew, he had never met Kevin Mitnick, talked to him, or exchanged e-mail with him. He just happened to look a lot like him.

Red-faced agents cut him loose.

✛

In fact, Kevin had spent much of the winter and early spring of 1994 in the Denver area. He was spotted by a technician for Colorado SuperNet, an Internet provider in the Denver area, who claims Kevin had been hired by a local company to help them set up an Internet connection. The technician had no idea it was Kevin at the time—it was only later, after he saw a poster that had been prepared by the U.S. Marshals Service, that he realized who it had been. And that surprised him, because the Kevin Mitnick he'd known hadn't been real savvy about setting up the connection to the net, and would sometimes page him five or six times a day to ask fairly ignorant questions. Later, after he realized that this ignoramus was in fact Kevin Mitnick, he wondered if the dumb questions had been some kind of ruse. If it was, he didn't understand the point of it. If it wasn't, then Kevin's reputation was much exaggerated.

At around the same time, Colorado SuperNet was having problems with an intruder in their system. They believed he had gained root access, which meant that, if he chose, he could have caused a great deal of damage. He didn't. He mostly just read private e-mail and used the system for free net access. Later, system administrators suspected it might have had something to do with Kevin's presence in the area, but they couldn't say for sure. The method of intrusion was fairly simple—again, it was not what they would have expected from someone with Kevin's reputation.

For a large Internet provider like Colorado SuperNet, which was trying to capitalize on the tremendous boom for Internet access, security comes down to economics. In general, the more secure a system is, the more awkward it is to use—and the more expensive it is to operate and maintain. Most providers have better things to spend their money on—like expanding their customer base. Was it really worth it for them to spend thousands of dollars building elaborate walls just to keep a few kids from getting free access to their system? As long as a hacker doesn't do something really dumb like knock out their system (which costs them serious money and damages their reputation) or get caught reading private e-mail (which could be embarrassing), he can often go unnoticed for months.

One might argue, in fact, that many of these large Internet providers enable hackers like Kevin to thrive. They're not interested in really stopping hackers, because that would detract from the bottom line. What they want, instead, is for the hackers to be good boys and behave.

Kevin also spent a lot of time logging on at smaller Internet sites run by universities. Many of them make no pretense about having a "secure" system. They can't afford it, and don't really want it. These systems are not run for profit, but to share information. They are the last vestiges of the open community spirit that once defined the computer revolution.

Nyx, a small Internet site at the University of Denver, is a good example. It is run by Andrew Burt, lecturer and software analyst at the university. He has no money for elaborate security—nor does he have the time to administer it. Nyx is an "open" system, designed to be used easily by outsiders. If they put in elaborate security, public access would be serverely restricted. Besides, Burt believes that until every message on the Internet is automatically encrypted, "the phrase 'Internet security' will remain an oxymoron."

Potential crackers at Nyx are asked to read a personal note from Burt: "To start, let me say I am not personally against hacking; indeed, I learned a lot of what I know about computer science as direct and indirect results of hacking (past tense—consider me, shall we say, 'retired'). I don't have any desire at all to chase hackers off Nyx; as long as you don't threaten Nyx, or act stupid, hey, have fun. In fact, I don't like to waste my time chasing stupid people, it just ticks me off that I have to. In other words, I'll only go after you if you're being stupid, inconsiderate, obnoxious, selfish, destructive, etc."

In April 1994, when Burt discovered that Kevin was prowling around in the Nyx system, he didn't panic. He asked Kevin not to damage anything, and he didn't. They exchanged files. They tolerated each other. Kevin apparently read a notice Burt had once posted about how he felt the words "hacker" and "cracker" were not very poetic words to describe intruders into computer systems. Burt preferred the term "spider."

"Think about this," Burt wrote. "Spiders sneak in through the tiniest holes, which you often don't even know you have. Spiders get in no matter how hard you try to keep them out. You don't see spiders most of the time—but they're there. Many people are unnecessarily afraid of spiders. They're annoying, but most spiders don't harm anything. Spiders don't like to be exposed. Some spiders are poisonous, but most aren't. It's hard to reason with a spider; they just see things differently. Spiders often spin intricate webs to continue their existence (to catch food, passwords, etc.). One spider may lay eggs, bringing you more spiders. Spiders are mostly solitary. Some spiders think they're freedom fighters (ah, um, Spiderman). Spiders have a mostly bad reputation. Most people try to squish spiders when they discover them."

3

Whatever fantasies Kevin might have had about quietly disappearing into the woodwork ended abruptly on July 4, 1994. That was the day Kevin's photo—the old 1988 photo from the Digital arrest, the one that made him look like a menacing thug—first appeared on the front page of *The New York Times*. It was accompanied by a story titled, "Cyberspace's Most Wanted: Hacker Eludes F.B.I. Pursuit" by John Markoff.

Since the publication of *Cyberpunk*, life had changed for Markoff. He and Hafner had split up, and he had moved back to California to become the *Times'* Johnny-on-the-spot in Silicon Valley. It was a big beat—he covered everything from corporate buyouts to industry trends to technological breakthroughs. He was an ideal man for the job, with an easy, unpretentious manner and a sharp sense of the important trends in the computer industry. His stories were smart and timely, and what they lacked in context and literary flair he more than made up for by developing top quality sources within the industry. He regularly beat the pants off the competition.

With all this activity, Kevin Mitnick was hardly at the top of his agenda. But then in early 1994, he found a piece of his private e-mail posted in a public newsgroup. For someone like Markoff, a top-flight reporter who makes his living by having better information than his competitors, the notion that his private e-mail was being skimmed by a stranger was not to be taken lightly. When he called friends to tell them about what was happening, one name leapt to everyone's mind: Kevin Mitnick.

At the same time, Markoff started hearing from various cellular phone companies that they suspected Kevin was poking around in their internal computer systems, presumably looking for copies of the software that runs cellular phones. Because of *Cyberpunk*, he was considered a Kevin Mitnick expert—he sometimes made a little extra pocket money by giving what some called his "Cyberpunk speech" to various companies and computer security conferences (it's a common—and controversial—practice of many top journalists). So it's not surprising that if people in the computer security world suspected Kevin was causing trouble again, the news would filter back to Markoff.

Markoff's story, written in textbook *Times* style, was at once detached and authoritative. There was no mention of the fact that Markoff had suspected Kevin of reading his e-mail, nor of any possible bias that might result from that. Instead, the story reiterated the standard view of Kevin as a national menace. It repeated many of the crimes of his youth, and repeated unquestioningly Digital's assertion that Kevin caused "$4 million in damage to computer operations at the company and had stolen $1 million in software." The story also touched the *Wargames* hot button: "As a teenager, he used a computer and a modem to break into a North American Air Defense Command computer, foreshadowing the 1983 movie *Wargames*."

Whether this is true or not has long been a matter of dispute. According to De Payne and others, it's pure myth. Steve Rhoades, one of Kevin's pals in the early days, claims that yes, Kevin did mess around with NORAD. Neither offer any evidence. Back in 1989 and '90, when Hafner was working on *Cyberpunk*, she spent a great deal of time trying to nail this down—to no avail. She omitted the detail from the book. If Markoff had uncovered new evidence about NORAD since then, he didn't cite it.*

The only news in the *Times* story—besides the fact that the FBI hadn't caught him yet—was that Kevin was "now suspected of stealing software and data from more than half a dozen leading cellular telephone manufacturers." How they knew it was Kevin, and not any of the hundreds of other hackers and phone phreaks out there who saw cellular phone manufacturers as interesting targets, was not disclosed. Nor were there any questions raised about why the cellular phone companies' computers were so vulnerable to intrusions, or why Kevin's actions were more of a threat to the cellular business than, say, Mark Lottor, who openly sold software that allowed cellular phones to be hacked, and whom Markoff had celebrated in the premiere issue of *Wired*.

The fact that this story ended up on the front page, even on a typically slow news day like July 4th, reflected, perhaps more than anything, the *Times'* own worries and suspicions about the rise of

---

*A confession: in my article about Kevin in *Rolling Stone,* which was written shortly after he was arrested in 1995, I trusted Markoff's reporting and, after checking with Rhoades, decided to include the fact that Kevin had broken into NORAD in my article. I now believe that it's probably a myth, and regret having included it.

a new information culture that was destabilizing the newspaper business.

But to some of Kevin's friends in the computer underground, it looked like Markoff was trying to get even.

4

Kevin's mug appeared on the front page of about 1.7 million copies of *The New York Times*. The photo was in every airport and train station and newsstand in America. It accompanied thousands of families on their holiday barbecue. It undoubtedly sparked hundreds of conversations about the dangers of this new thing called the Internet. Overnight, Kevin's sullen mug became the living symbol of electronic terror.

It was undeserved. Kevin could be mean, petty, vengeful, crude, and frightening. To people he decided to harass, he was an electronic nightmare. He was spooky. He was incorrigible and compulsive and did not seem to care that what he was doing was wrong. He broke into computers. He copied proprietary software. He was breaking the law, no doubt about it.

But he was not Jeffrey Dahmer. He did not kill people and eat them. He was not a serial rapist or a terrorist bomber or a preacher of hate. And he was not Ivan Boesky or Michael Milken, men who reaped billions with questionable trading practices on Wall Street. By all accounts, Kevin wasn't profiting from his escapades. He wasn't interested in destabilizing the U.S. economy or delivering secret military documents to Saddam Hussein. What he wanted, among other things, was the cellular phone source code that would allow him to hack cellular phones. A crime, yes. But did that make him a menace to society? Hardly. In fact, Kevin's boldest move—and his stupidest—was to make an enemy out of John Markoff, the one man with the means to put him on the front page of the most powerful newspaper in America.

Predictably, the *Times* story perked up the hunt for Kevin Mitnick the way a bolt of lightning perks up a dozing cow. The *Times* is read like the Bible by every government pooh-bah and law enforcement honcho in the country—the collective response was *I don't know who the hell this Kevin Mitnick character is or what he's up to but he should be stopped. Now.*

The story also brought old enemies out of the

woodwork. One such person was Sandy Samuels, a ham radio operator in Mission Hills, California. Samuels called the FBI on July 7th and told them that someone—he believed it was Kevin—was hassling him on his ham radio. It made sense. Kevin had been a ham radio buff as long as he'd been a phone phreak—his call sign was "N6NHG," the last three letters of which supposedly stand for "Nation's Hacker Great." Samuels told the FBI that because of the closeness of the radio calls, he believed Kevin might be staying in the area—perhaps at a relative's house.

Law enforcement was more than eager to check it out. To help with the case, the FBI alerted the U.S. Marshals. Like the FBI, the U.S. Marshals Service is a division of the Department of Justice. It is the oldest law enforcement agency in the country, dating back to 1795. They're purebred hunters. Their main job is to track down criminals with existing warrants and haul them in. Sometimes it takes years. In LA, the sixty U.S. Marshals spend most of their time going after big-time drug dealers and violent felons; to them, a computer hacker was an interesting change of pace, but not necessarily anything to get worked up about.

The case was assigned to Deputy Kathleen Cunningham and Deputy Jeff Tyler. They had both joined the U.S. Marshal's office three years earlier, in 1991, but Deputy Cunningham, forty-one, is the more experienced of the two. Before moving to LA, she'd been a Vermont State Trooper for eight years, and had also been with the U.S. Border Patrol. She's from eastern Massachusetts, a tall, strong woman with auburn hair and freckles and large, powerful-looking hands with fingernails that look as if they've never been touched by nail polish. But there's a gentleness about her that belies her rough-and-tumble job. On the first day I met her, she told me about a dog she'd rescued from South Central LA. She'd seen it on the street, a mangy puppy covered with fleas and with half its hair falling out. She rescued it, brought it to the vet, and was worried that she'd end up taking it home to her two other dogs. Her desk in the Roy Bal Building in downtown Los Angeles has dozens of dog pictures under her glass tabletop, including photos of a Dutch Shepherd, a rare breed of dog which she owned while she was with the Border Patrol.

Deputy Tyler, twenty-seven, is a quiet man. He's an inch or two shorter than his partner, but he has big arms and shoulders and a thick neck. He has a kind of clean-cut all-American-boy handsomeness—if he told you he was a running back for UCLA, you'd believe him (he wasn't). He's also from the East Coast; he went to high school near Saratoga Springs in upstate New York. He worked at the racetrack during the summer—parking cars, doing cleanup, as a security guard. But from the time he was a kid, when he played cops 'n' robbers with his brother, he knew he wanted to be a cop. He majored in criminal justice at the State University of New York in Albany, then worked for the

Internal Revenue Service for a while before he joined the U.S. Marshals.

Tyler and Cunningham spent the first few weeks of July checking out Mitnick's known addresses in the LA area. They discovered that his mother and grandmother had moved to Las Vegas. They stopped in to see Kevin's birth father, Alan, who was living in a condo in Calabasas, a fairly undeveloped community on the northern edge of the San Fernando Valley. Alan struck them as a cool, distant presence. "I'm sorry, I don't know how to help you," he told them. "I don't know where Kevin is right now."

"We think it would be in Kevin's best interest if he turned himself in," Cunningham told him. "He's going to get caught sooner or later. If he turns himself in, it's easier to convince the judge to go easy on him. If he gets caught committing another crime, he could be in serious trouble."

"I'm sorry, I can't help you," Alan repeated.

Cunningham didn't believe it. She was sure he knew plenty. But she couldn't blame him for not wanting to rat on his own son.

✢

A week or so later, Cunningham and Tyler drove to Las Vegas in their government-issue Crown Victoria. It was a long, hot, dull eight-hour drive across the desert. As they approached the house where Kevin's mom, Shelly, lived in a nice residential neighborhood on the outskirts of town, they decided to do a quick drive-by first, just to get the lay of the land. They were surprised to see a black Nissan Pulsar in the driveway—Kevin's car.

Cunningham thought, Maybe today's our lucky day.

They drove past the house and parked around a corner, out of sight. If Kevin was around, they had to be careful not to spook him. Unlike Shirley Lessiak, who had let Kevin slip through her fingers, Cunningham and Tyler were expert fugitive-grabbers. If Kevin was in the house, they were going to get him.

They settled on a plan. There had been a big storm in the area the night before, and a utility crew happened to be in the area, working on the wires and cleaning things up. Cunningham approached one of the workers—a woman—and flashed her badge. "I want you to do us a favor," Cunningham told her. She asked the worker to knock on Shelly's door and ask whoever answered it if they'd had any problems due to the storm. Cunningham instructed the woman to take note of who answered the door, and then to report back to her. Meanwhile, Cunningham and Tyler remained a discreet distance away.

The worker knocked on the door—no answer.

Cunningham and Tyler didn't know what to make of this. Maybe Kevin was off in another car. Maybe he had spotted them and was hiding in the house. They had no idea.

Before they got out and checked around, they

radioed for a backup unit. They were told it would be about twenty minutes—the only other available marshals were out on a call. They'd just have to wait.

But then a few minutes later, Shelly's garage door opened. A man in a nice shiny Honda Accord drove out. What the hell was this? It didn't look like Kevin. But you never know. They knew Kevin's weight fluctuated wildly, and it was not hard to imagine him putting on a mask or some other disguise in order to make a getaway.

They followed behind the Honda for a short distance then decided to pull it over. Since they were in an unmarked car, they had no light or siren. So Cunningham, who was behind the wheel, pulled up beside the car and Tyler flashed his badge and motioned for the driver to pull over. He was a small, older man. Definitely not Kevin.

He pulled off to the side of the road. Cunningham approached the driver's side window and asked for ID and registration. The car, it turned out, was registered to Shelly.

"I'm a friend of Shelly's," the man explained.

"Where is she?"

"At work."

"We'd like your permission to go inside the house and look around."

"No, I can't do that. It's not my house."

"Where are you going right now?"

"I'm on my way to meet Shelly," he said.

"Is she at work?"

He nodded.

"Will you tell her to come home right away? We'd like to talk to her." Cunningham gave the man her pager number and told them to tell Shelly that if she couldn't come right away, to be sure to call. "It's important."

They let him go. He promised to relay the message to Shelly.

✣

While they waited, they checked out Shelly's house. They walked around the outside, peering in through the windows—they wanted to be sure no one was hiding in there. They were surprised by how nice it was: nice furniture, clean, well kept.

They also talked to the neighbors. They showed pictures of Kevin around, asked if they'd seen him lately. One neighbor said she'd seen him about a month earlier. He'd arrived in a brown van. Shelly wouldn't let him into the house, the neighbor told them, so Kevin slept in the van.

✣

Shelly never showed up or called, so Cunningham and Tyler decided to pay her a visit at work. They drove downtown to the sagging old Sahara casino, which is on the unfashionable end of the strip, far from the imposing black pyramid of the Luxor or the ivory and gold towers of the Mirage. When they arrived, Cunningham and Tyler contacted the Sahara's security office. They told them who they were, and that they wanted to talk to Shelly Jaffee. It was a simple precaution—they were in plainclothes, but they were carrying their guns and didn't want to go wandering through the casino looking for Shelly and possibly alarming gamblers or scaring her off.

The security officer returned a few minutes later and said, "Sorry, Shelly doesn't want to talk to you."

"You don't understand," Cunningham said firmly. "This is not a question of what Shelly wants to do."

The security officer, sensing perhaps that he was out of his league, agreed to take them to her.

They found her in the coffee shop, where she was working as a waitress. She was not happy to see them. "I can't talk to you, I'm busy," she said, brushing past them with an armful of food.

The restaurant supervisor interrupted, however, and said the staff would cover for her.

Reluctantly, Shelly led Cunningham and Tyler into a hallway in the back of the restaurant.

"We're here to talk to you about Kevin," Cunningham said, trying to be as gentle as she could.

Shelly immediately launched into a heated defense of her son. She started yelling about how he was a good kid, how he had never done a lot of the things he had been accused of—he had never broken into a military computer, he had never fled to

Israel, he wasn't a serious criminal. "He gets accused of all this stuff, and none of it's true," she cried.

Cunningham tried to reason with her. She told Shelly that it would be better for everyone if Kevin just turned himself in. Then she added, "Your son is not well. He needs help."

That's when Shelly blew up. "My son is not mentally ill!" she shrieked. "He does not need help!"

At that point, Cunningham and Tyler realized it was hopeless. Maybe they'd have better luck with grandma.

✛

Reba Vartarian was the only thing close to stability in Kevin's life. She was a busy, articulate woman who had married several times, divorced, and now had enough money to live comfortably in a new antique-filled house. She was known for her unorthodox views—she was something of a sexual libertarian, for example. More than once she has told visitors that prisoners in U.S. penitentiaries are entitled to sexual relief. If the state hired prostitutes to relieve their tensions, apparently prison would be a more civilized place. Some friends felt that Shelly and Kevin were really more like sister and brother than mother and son, and that Reba, the grandmother, was the real matriarch of the family.

She was also shrewd, as Cunningham and Tyler found out.

When they knocked on Reba's door that afternoon, she answered it immediately. Cunningham and Tyler identified themselves and flashed their badges.

Reba went pale and grabbed her heart.

"We'd like to talk to you about Kevin," Cunningham said.

"Oh, you scared me to death," Reba said, gathering her composure. Apparently she'd thought they were ready to haul her in. She invited them into the foyer.

"We're here about the warrant," Cunningham explained.

"What warrant?"

"Kevin violated his probation. A warrant has been issued for his arrest."

"I don't understand," Reba said, looking confused. "What kind of a warrant is it?"

Cunningham explained.

"So what did he do?"

"Like I said, he violated his probation."

"What do you mean he violated probation? I don't understand."

So Cunningham explained again.

"So now you have a warrant?"

"Yes."

"What kind of a warrant is it?"

Cunningham explained. Her patience was growing thin.

"I don't understand," Reba said with complete sincerity. "How does this warrant work?"

"We just want to know if you've seen Kevin lately."

"No, I haven't."

"Have you talked to him?"

"No."

"Do you know where he is?"

"I have no idea."

"Excuse me, but I know you have a close family. You're Kevin's grandmother. I have a hard time believing that you have not spoken to him recently."

Reba just shrugged. "I can't help you."

5

A week later, Las Vegas was a hacker mecca. Hackers and crackers and cyberdudes of all stripes emerged from their sun-blocked bedrooms and cubicles to attend DefCon II, a hacker convention that was held, coincidentally enough, at the same casino where Shelly worked—the Sahara. By day, speakers discussed privacy on the net and computer viruses and the hacking scene in Europe. By night, they gathered in hotel rooms and at casino bars to swap tales of hacking prowess, to dump on the new and clueless, and to argue about (among other things) the current celebrity status of Kevin Mitnick.

Thanks to the recent article in *The New York Times*, it was a hotly debated topic. For a few, of course, Mitnick's celebrity was itself evidence of his skills. To others, particularly the elder tribesmen in the hacker clans, it was evidence that Mitnick was a real wanker—the mere fact that his name was so well-known was proof that he was a second-rater. The best hackers, the argument went, are by definition invisible and unknown.

Then there were others who just thought Kevin was a terminally immature jerk and foul-mouthed character who brought disgrace and bad vibes to the very word "hacker."

Some of the more politically oriented DefCon attendees were disappointed that Kevin never seemed to have any revolutionary ambitions. He didn't talk openly about the injustice of the information culture, he didn't publicly mock the rich and powerful. Unlike others, he didn't parade around at hacker conferences with the Hacker's Manifesto silk-screened on a T-shirt in tiny, almost unreadable print:

the conscience of a hacker

did you, in your three-piece psychology and 1950's technobrain, ever take a look behind the eyes of a hacker? did you ever wonder what made him tick, what forces may have molded him?

I am a hacker, enter my world . . .

. . . the world of the electron and the switch, the beauty of the baud. we make use of a service already existing without paying for what could be dirt cheap if it were not run by profiteering gluttons. we seek after knowledge and you call us criminals. we explore . . . and you call us criminals. we exist without nationality, without religious bias . . . and you call us criminals. you build atomic bombs, you wage wars, you murder, you cheat and lie to us and try to make us believe it's for our own good.

yet we are the criminals.

yes, I am a criminal. my crime is that of curiosity. my crime is judging people by what they say and think, not what they look like. my crime is that of outsmarting you. something that you will never forgive me for.

I am hacker and this is my manifesto. you may stop this individual, but you can't stop us all . . .

the mentor

In short, nobody at DefCon knew quite what to make of Kevin. He was too nasty to be a martyr, too complicated to be a hero, too persistent to be dismissed, and too famous to forget.

✛

Talk about a coincidence. On the first day of the conference, DefCon's organizer, Jeff Moss, a.k.a. Dark Tangent, was downstairs in the coffee shop at the Sahara with three pals. It was Saturday morning, and Moss, a fresh-faced entrepreneur and ex-hacker, was eating his usual eggs, toast, bacon, and chocolate milk.

One of the waiters walked by and happened to notice their DefCon name tags. He stopped at their table and asked out of the blue: "Who's the most famous hacker of all?"

Moss and his friends tossed out a couple of names: "Kevin Poulsen, Kevin Mitnick, Agent Steal [a.k.a. Justin Petersen] . . ." They debated it for a moment, then decided that Poulsen was number one.

"Who's after that?"

"Probably Kevin Mitnick," Moss said.

"He used to be my roommate," the waiter said proudly.

What?

At about that time, a waitress walked by. Moss remembers her as an older woman, straight dark hair, maybe five eight in height, energetic, but with the tired look of a person who'd had a tough life.

"That's my son," the waitress said.

"Who?" Moss asked.

"Kevin."

"You're kidding."

"I'm not kidding."

Moss and his friends were shocked—the last person they'd expected to run into at DefCon was Kevin's *mom*.

They talked for about ten minutes. She told Moss she hadn't talked to her son in six years. He asked if she had ever read *Cyberpunk*—she said she hadn't, she wasn't interested in learning the details of what her son was doing. Mostly, she seemed concerned about how Moss and his friends were going to end up. "I hope you boys aren't like Kevin," she said sadly. "You should be careful. Don't do anything wrong, don't break the laws. Don't turn out like my Kevin—that's no way to live your life."

Moss, who had recently finished his first year of law school, assured her he would be fine.

✝

When Winn Schwartau took the podium at DefCon, he faced a sea of motley faces. Schwartau, a noted computer security expert and self-promoter, was no beauty queen himself: curly hair in need of a trim, mustache, wire-frame glasses, and a ball-busting manner. His talk covered his usual theme: Information Warfare. How the technology was changing the face of war. The computer hacker as information warrior. HERF guns and EMP/T bombs (don't ask). It was Schwartau's boilerplate speech, the one he gave to computer security groups around the country, and which made up the backbone of his book, *Information Warfare: Chaos on the Electronic Superhighway.*

When he was done, he paused for the usual questions. John Markoff's voice rose out of the crowd. "How come you did it?"

"Did what?"

"You know what."

Guffaws from the crowd. What was he talking about?

A woman chimed in: "How come you flamed Lenny DiCicco?"

Schwartau was stunned. "When did I flame DiCicco?"

"On the WELL."

"I don't know Lenny, and I don't have an account on the WELL," Schwartau said.

Conversation moved on. But later that evening, Schwartau logged onto the WELL and discovered what Markoff was talking about:

```
From: miles@well.sf.ca.us (Winn Schwartau)
Newsgroups: alt.2600
Subject: Kevin Mitnick
Date: 16 Jul 1994 02:02:47 GMT
Organization: The Whole Earth 'Lectronic Link,
Sausalito, CA
Lines: 84
NNTP-Posting-Host: well.sf.ca.us
X-Newsreader: TIN [version 1.2 PL1]


Lenny, your a low-life piece of shit scumbag
sucking snitch. I am getting _real_ tired of
hearing the stories you and Steve Rhoades fab-
ricated in the [sic] 1988 that are now being
printed as fact.

If you continue to slander me I _will_ expose
your recent activities that should result in a
```

```
revocation of your probation. All I will say is
the name ''Andy''. Now you know I know.
```

The post went on to accuse DiCicco of various crimes (all of which he later denied), including faking job references, eavesdropping on his boss, and helping himself to petty cash.

```
I could go on and on and on, but what's the
point? You would turn in your own mother if you
could benefit by it.
```

```
KDM
```

Of course, Schwartau had no idea if it was actually Kevin who posted this outburst in his name. No doubt he held a grudge against DiCicco, and maybe his own exposure on the front page of *The New York Times* provoked an outburst to try to get revenge. It sounded like him. But mail spoofing is a common enough trick among hackers—it could easily have been posted by someone who wanted everyone to believe it had been posted by Kevin. It was impossible to know for sure.

Before he left DefCon, Schwartau called the WELL and talked to one of the system administrators. Schwartau had once had an account on the WELL, but it had long been canceled. The administrator checked her records—they showed he had logged on to the system on July 15th at 18:54

PST for twenty-eight minutes and left this nasty rant.

"How could this have happened?" Schwartau asked. Her reply, he later wrote, "could be the headline for much of corporate security:"

" 'Oh, it's simple,' she said. 'We have no security.' "

6

By late summer, Kevin had become the ghost in the electronic attic. He was everywhere and nowhere, familiar yet unrecognizable, a spirit whose adventures were exaggerated with every retelling of the story. His fearsome reputation had far outgrown his crimes.

There were rumors that he might visit or was living in the San Diego area, and system administrators in the area were on full alert. At the University of California, they had "wanted" posters of Kevin in the computer labs, and administrators were told to keep an eye out for him, lest he wander onto the campus and start using one of the Macintoshes in the lab that were hooked up to the net. At Qualcomm, a wireless telecommunciations and engineering company in the area, someone had wandered into the lobby and stolen a copy of the company's monthly newsletter, which contained names and short biographies of new employees—a valuable resource for someone who preferred social engineering to computer cracking, and people at Qualcomm wondered whether Kevin had anything to do with this. Another Internet provider in the area had a Kevin Mitnick dartboard hanging in the office. Others wore Kevin Mitnick masks.

Then there was the San Diego Supercomputer Center. Tsutomu was well aware of Kevin's long hacking history—in fact, several years earlier, Kevin had called him up and, with typical bluster, demanded that Tsutomu give him some cellular phone software that he was after. Tsutomu refused. Now Kevin seemed to be trying to get it in some less direct way. Tsutomu's machine, always a juicy target for hackers, had received a few pokes over the summer. Nothing too serious, but Tsutomu apparently suspected Kevin might be behind it. In addition, he knew all about Markoff's suspicions that Kevin was reading his e-mail. He knew about the worries at Qualcomm and other companies in the cellular phone industry that Kevin was after their software. And it was pissing Tsutomu off.

Tsutomu's friends at the Supercomputer Center

shared his feelings. But a few of them had a sense of humor about it. At a national conference for Unix system administrators that was held in San Diego at the end of September, several of Tsutomu's pals altered their convention badges to play off the Kevin paranoia. Andrew Gross, a graduate student and Tsutomu's protégé at the Supercomputer Center, became "andrew mitnick@netcom.com." Tom Perrine, manager of workstation services at the Supercomputer Center, became "tom mitnick@netcom.com." Several other local system administrators joined in the fun, and before the convention was over, there were a dozen or so Mitnicks wandering around. One system administrator even wandered into the Qualcomm hospitality suite with his Mitnick nametag. The company reps didn't think it was too funny.

❖

John Sweeney, a feature writer for the London *Observer*, knew a juicy story when he saw one. After reading a small item about Kevin in a British newspaper, Sweeney flew to California and tried to dig up an interview with Kevin. Unlike many of his American counterparts, Sweeney had no problem with the idea of paying sources a little cash to talk to him. He talked to several of Kevin's friends, including Bonnie, who characterized Kevin as a kind of martial artist: "he has the ability to kill but he doesn't."

Still, money didn't buy him an interview with

Kevin, whose fear of the media was, understandably, quite keen. And so like other journalists on Kevin's trail, Sweeney went home empty-handed. "I went to drown my sorrows in the Coach and Horses near the *Observer*'s offices," Sweeney later wrote. The Coach and Horses is a London pub. His cellular phone rang. "A breathy American voice came on the line: 'You'll never guess who this is?'"

Kevin, of course. Before he left LA, Sweeney had given one of Kevin's pals a hundred bucks and his cellular phone number and asked him to forward it to Kevin. But he never really expected Kevin to call.

Sweeney asked him about the "scumbag sucking snitch" message that had been posted in Schwartau's name.

"Somebody spoofed me," he quoted Kevin as saying. "It sounds like it was written by a kid." Kevin then complained about "sensationalist press coverage that had made him out to be like 'Carlos the Jackal,'" Sweeney wrote. He asked him about the 1988 photograph that made him out to look like an electronic terrorist. "That picture was taken three days after I had been arrested," Kevin told him. "No shower for three days. I felt pretty scummy. They have made me out to be John Dillinger or a desperado, but I'm just an excellent prankster. I have never profited from it."

What was prison like?

"They kept me in solitary confinement for eight months and gave me a hard time because of those stupid phone restrictions," Kevin said. "They wanted to punish me. The sanitary conditions were disgusting. I got assaulted a couple of times. It was hell."

Sweeney asked him what it was like being on the run.

"I feel like a fucking murderer," Kevin said, "and I wouldn't harm a fly."

✜

Deputy Cunningham and Deputy Tyler had plenty to do over the summer besides hunt for Kevin. They handle between 75 and 100 cases at a time, most of them violent felons. That summer they devoted many hours to tracking down a convicted drug dealer who, seven years earlier, had escaped while being transported to a federal penitentiary in Indiana. They chased rapists and murderers, crackheads and absentee fathers. Still, they kept a close eye on Kevin's case, and tried to speak to some of his more distant relatives—without much luck.

Coincidentally, on September 27th, she and Tyler were called to transport Justin Petersen from the Metropolitan Detention Center in downtown LA to a clinic that looked after his prosthesis. After going AWOL as an informant, Petersen had finally been arrested in August of 1994 after failing in an elaborate electronic ruse to steal $150,000 from a bank in Glendale. Now he was sitting in his jail cell, awaiting trial.

For Cunningham and Tyler, this transporting prisoners was a routine part of their job. They knew plenty about Petersen—he had called their office twice offering to help them catch Kevin, but Cunningham, wary of his reputation, had never returned his calls.

Before Cunningham left her office, she got word from David Schindler, the U.S. Attorney who was partly responsible for engaging Petersen in his short, unhappy career as an informant, that they were not to speak with Petersen about the Kevin Mitnick case. It was an odd request, and arrived with no explanation. Cunningham guessed that Justin's identity as a former informant probably had something to do with it.

As Tyler and Cunningham drove Petersen to the clinic, he tried to give them information about Kevin that he thought would be helpful. In any other circumstance Cunningham would have listened; this time, however, she told him not to speak about it. When Petersen asked why, Cunningham, visibly frustrated, explained those were the orders she'd been given from Schindler.

"If you have any problems with it," Cunningham told him, "talk to your attorney and to Schindler's supervisor."

7

As the summer passed, Kevin's old friend in England, Neill Clift, was losing patience. For months now, Clift had been talking to Digital and to the FBI, feeding them reams of computer logs that marked Kevin's every move. Still, they seemed no closer to catching him than they ever had. In a fax the FBI sent to Clift over the summer, they frankly admitted that they didn't think they had much of a chance of catching Kevin with electronic sleuthing. If they were going to have any luck at all, it was going to be the good old-fashioned way: by wearing out shoe leather.

So Clift took it to the next level. For the first time in their bizarre, six-year-long relationship, he decided to make personal contact with Kevin. One day when he knew Kevin was logged onto the machine, he left little messages where he knew Kevin would find them: "Ring me up my friend." Then later: "Come on play the game. Ring me up mr Mitnick." Later still: "You might find something to your advantage."

But Kevin logged off instead of responding. So the next day, Clift replaced all Kevin's programs on the machine with a message: "You're not as careful as you used to be. . . . Ring Neill!"

Kevin called him at 1 A.M. that morning just after he got the message. Then he called Clift again at work at 9 A.M. . . . and so on, several times a day. It lasted for over a month. It was typical of the relationships he had while on the run—completely electronic, via e-mail and phone. It was a kind of tortured male camaraderie, marked by one-upsmanship and braggadocio, as well as lies and manipulation.

They talked mostly about technical stuff—Kevin had a great deal of respect for Clift's skills and wanted to learn what he could from him. Technically, Clift discovered, Kevin was not very skilled. He could use code to exploit security weakness, but he had no real idea how it worked. He used programs cookbook style. At first, he seemed to want Clift to teach him tricks about how to find security holes—"he didn't seem to realize that it takes a great deal of hard work," Clift recalls. He then asked Clift to teach him all about VMS internals so he could find the bugs himself. Clift agreed, knowing that it would take at least a year of hard work to get up to speed. Kevin even used a chunk of money from the *Observer* interview to buy the bible on VMS internals, *VAX/VMS Internals and Data Structures*. He asked Clift to point out which parts he should read first. It seemed to Clift that the book came to signify for Kevin his investment in technical skill—"as if owning the book showed how commited he was," Clift says. At one point when Clift accused him of only wanting to learn how to break into systems, Kevin shouted: "Well, I bought the fucking book, didn't I?"

They spent hours going over the many security programs Kevin had snatched from Clift and Digital over the years. Clift confronted him directly: those programs had been meant for the engineers who fix the problems and no one else, Clift told him. Kevin said it didn't matter that he took them because he didn't sell them. That attitude amazed Clift: "Just because Kevin made no direct profit from his labors he thought it okay to hound me for years on end using every possible method of attack just to get a look at them."

Conversation often moved beyond technology. They talked about bicycling (Kevin had a mountain bike), and how they'd both managed to lose a lot of weight in recent years. They talked about weight training and diets. Clift asked if he was religious and Kevin said he was Jewish but he only did religious things on very special occasions (Kevin joked that if he got the chance to log onto his machine on a Saturday he'd take it). Clift's girlfriend came up, and Kevin asked a lot of questions about his family—Clift got the sense that he was trying to see if they came from the same background. Clift was shocked to hear that Kevin's mother didn't really understand all the trouble he was in.

To Clift, Kevin didn't seem vulnerable or moody. He didn't seem down except when money was running low. He thought he had a good sense of humor, except for a few immature sexual remarks about women, which Clift found embarrassing. He frequently brought up two key incidents in his life: *Cyberpunk* ("don't believe it," Kevin said), and the DECUS incident ("I was really trying to go straight. . . .").

All in all, Clift thought of Kevin as a very intelligent person who must spend a great deal of time thinking his way around obstacles. "For Kevin, hacking was like a real job. He got up in the morning and went to work trying to break into places," Clift recalls. But Clift was startled by Kevin's lack of ability to put himself in anyone else's shoes— he had no concept of how much trouble he caused anyone. For example, Clift told him how he feared for his job at one point when the phone calls were coming regularly at work as Kevin tried to con his way into the system. All Kevin said in response was that he was sorry about the problems but that it was "nothing personal."

"That was his stock answer to everything—'Nothing personal,'" Clift recalls. "Somehow that makes it all a game and he is not responsible for what happens."

❖

"Why don't you just turn yourself in?" Clift asked.

Kevin claimed that he didn't trust the authorities. He said he didn't have the money for a good lawyer and that without a good one the law would come down hard on him. Clift thought he was scared. Really scared. He spent a great deal of time trying to justify to Clift what he did—he said it wasn't destructive, it caused only minor irritation. In fact he described himself as very good at irritating people when he went after them because he was very good at what he did.

He often talked about coming to England. He thought it would be nice if he and Clift could actually meet face-to-face. He asked a lot of questions about the IRA, apparently because he'd just seen *In the Name of the Father*. Also, he worried about the standard of living, which was considerably lower than in the United States. And he was afraid the UK authorities would arrest him and wondered if it was better if he went somewhere else in Europe.

Another draw was a nineteen-year-old Israeli woman named Shimrit Elisar, who was working as a systems administrator at an Internet provider in England that Kevin hacked into. He'd been reading her e-mail, and apparently liked what he saw. He developed a kind of cyber-crush on her—even though they'd never met or exchanged a word. He talked increasingly with Clift about going to Israel, and Clift wondered if that was why he was interested in her, because she could provide some kind of entrée for him. . . .

Clift was never sure if Kevin really wanted to be friends, or if he was just using him for information. Kevin claimed to have friends that he went out with at night and who knew nothing about his hacking but Clift doubted it, he spent so much time hacking.

As time passed and they grew closer, Clift felt bad about giving him up to the FBI. But on the other hand, he felt like he didn't have much choice. Kevin had been messing with his life for too long.

❖

Clift was never sure how he found out. Kevin made it sound like it had come from some personal connections, but Clift wondered whether he'd been reading the e-mail of his pal Michael Lawrie.

Anyway, Kevin found out that Clift had been

talking to Digital, and he knew they were passing it on to the FBI.

Kevin sent Clift this e-mail in reply:

```
From: HICOM::KEVIN 23-SEP-1994 17:13:32.38
To: HICOM::NEILL_CLIFT
CC:
Subj: RE: You


You are a paranoid bastard. I have no reason to
harass you yet. The reason I wont call you any-
more is because I don't have any reason to talk
to stool pigeons regardless of what they have
to say (bugs, etc..) I am_not_going to harass
you unless you harass me. Thanks a lot for con-
tacting DEC and informing on me about Isael
[sic]. You really underestimate my contacts. I
know more than I let on. Too bad we can't be
friends, that would have been nice, but all you
want to do is help them bust me.

Thanks loads . . .
```

After this, Kevin must have known that his days were numbered. But strangely enough, his next brush with the law had nothing to do with Neill Clift or the FBI.

8

Kevin Pazaski is a fraud analyst for McCaw Cellular Communications (which was recently bought out by AT&T, and is now called AT&T Wireless Services) in Kirkland, Washington. Visiting McCaw's glassy four-story building in Kirkland, one gets the sense that the world is changing faster than we can assimilate it: there's an old wooden barn across the street, still in good condition, as if the cows were due home any minute. But just behind the barn is an eight-lane highway. And just beyond the highway is another office building, this one occupied by Microsoft, the all-powerful software company that is controlled by Bill Gates, the richest man (or the second richest, depending on how Warren Buffet's stock holdings happen to be doing) in America.

Pazaski's office is on the fourth floor. It's a small cubicle, no windows, just a modest L-shaped desk pulled up against the wall. There's a photo of his daughter on the left, near a large street map of Seattle. Pazaski fits nicely into this small space—he's a thin, wiry guy with a big nose, a mustache, and a baritone voice that seems to tuba out of his oversized Adam's apple. He has wandering eyes, always flitting over your shoulder to see who is passing behind you in the hallway. He dresses casually at his job, usually in chinos and loafers, a polo or rugby shirt. He grew up in Washington, and had been working at McCaw for five years. Until July of 1994, he had supervised accounts receivable in the fraud department—basically, a desk job. Then he got promoted to more active duty. Now he's in charge of tracking any illegal or fraudulent use of McCaw Cellular Service in the Rocky Mountain and Pacific states—what McCaw calls the "Pac-Rock region."

That sounds like a huge area, but unlike New York or Los Angeles, where drug dealers are constantly using cloned phones and there are well-established "call-sell" rings operating, there was very little cellular fraud in this area. In fact, this position had been newly created for Pazaski. Before then, they hadn't had anybody watching.

Most cellular fraud involves using modified cellular phones to steal free airtime. It's not a difficult trick. Cell phones are basically radios that send signals to nearby towers, which then route the phone calls over land lines to their destinations. Every phone has two identifying numbers that are automatically sent out over the airwaves with each call: one is the phone number itself, and the other is the Electronic Serial Number (ESN), a semi-permanent serial number that is programmed into each phone by the manufacturer. When a call is placed, the cellular phone carrier's computers that route the call automatically check the phone number and the ESN—if they match the cellular carrier's records, the call goes through.

To make free phone calls, an outlaw "clones" a phone—that is, reprograms the software in the phone so that it behaves like someone else's phone. It takes a fair amount of technical know-how to do this, as well as special software and a laptop computer. The trickiest part of the process, however, is not technical: it's getting someone else's phone number and ESN. The ESN is (supposedly) known only by the owner of the phone and cellular service provider. And it is (supposedly) closely guarded by both.

There are, however, various ways of getting around this. One way is to grab the numbers out of the air with a scanner—it requires an expensive piece of equipment, however, far beyond the means of most small-scale hackers. Most hackers use social engineering. He or she might call a dealer and pose as an employee. "They could call someone in the main office and say something like, 'Hi, I'm Dave in the activating department,'" Pazaski explains. "'We're having a problem with activation, and need to know the last five numbers you activated.' And boom, they'd give them to him."

Cellular phone fraud is difficult to track down—and expensive. Until recently, many providers have not bothered—they've written it off as a business expense. But now they're starting to pay closer attention. In 1994, the cellular phone industry claimed that it lost a whooping $1 billion in revenues due to fraud. Many providers are installing complex computer systems designed to catch irregular usage patterns and shut it down before it gets too large. This works fine if the outlaw is making three-hour calls to Pakistan. But with a quiet hacker, just using the phone for personal use, making sure to clone a new phone every week or so, the chances of getting caught are almost nonexistent.

Or so Kevin Mitnick must have thought.

✢

Pazaski had literally just moved his papers into his office last July when he got a call from one of McCaw's representatives in Oregon. The rep had reason to believe that somebody was using an Oregon-cloned phone in Washington, and asked

Pazaski to look into it. Pazaski checked the call detail records of the suspicious phone calls. By checking in which "cell" the calls were logged in— that is, which cellular tower received them—Pazaski could come up with a rough approximation of the caller's location.

The fraudulent calls started on the 27th of June, in Albany, Oregon. Apparently the user was heading north, because the line of calls traveled straight up Interstate 5 to Salem, and then to Portland, and then finally into the Seattle area. Then on the 28th, he switched to another number. It is a common trick used to avoid detection. Many phreakers think that if they just keep switching numbers, they'll never get caught. In this case, Pazaski noted that the phreaker switched to a different number on July 2nd. He used that number for five or six days, then switched again. Later, when Pazaski went back to reconstruct what had happened, he noted that the phreaker seemed to grow more confident, because the intervals between switching phone numbers grew progressively longer: eight days, then eleven days, then sixteen days.

But Pazaski couldn't just run out and arrest him. For one thing, you can't go to the police with $500 in losses. They'd just laugh at you. He had to wait for the dollars to get big enough for law enforcement to get interested. As a rule, the Secret Service, which has jurisdiction over most cellular phone fraud, won't touch a case with losses under $10,000.

Besides, tracking down a phone phreaker takes a lot of time, and it's not worth it unless there is a lot of money involved. Often, if it's a drug dealer or a call-sell operation, the user can run up thousands and thousands of dollars of calls in just a few days. But that was clearly not the case here. By looking at the numbers the guy was calling, Pazaski could see that he wasn't a big-time criminal (the vast majority of cellular phone criminals, like the vast majority of hackers, are male). In fact, by looking at the numbers the person was calling, it was pretty clear the person was a hacker. He was dialing up a lot of Internet providers around the country. There were only a few personal calls—mostly to movie theaters, the bus line schedule, and taxi service. There were also few to the Showboat casino in Las Vegas.

To Pazaski, this was a problem, but not a big problem. Sure, the guy was stealing free phone service, but he wasn't running up thousand-dollar calls to Bangladesh. In fact, in New York or LA, no one would have ever noticed this low-level stuff. Unfortunately for this hacker, this wasn't New York or LA. In Seattle, even a small amount of misuse stuck out like a sore thumb. Plus, Seattle had a fraud investigator named Kevin Pazaski who was new at his job, and kinda bored.

So Pazaski just waited and watched. He half expected the hacker to get scared and quit. He'd seen that happen a lot—they used a cloned phone for a few weeks, maybe a month, then they got nervous.

This guy apparently wasn't getting nervous. The bills accumulated. Then in the beginning of October, when Pazaski estimated the total fraud loss neared $15,000, he went out and hired a private investigator.

Time to go hacker hunting.

9

Todd Young has that David Caruso thing about him. The redheaded machismo, the tough-guy charm, the 9mm SIG-Sauer semiautomatic weapon he keeps under the front seat of his car. But while Caruso, the former star of *N.Y.P.D. Blue*, swaggered in fantasyland, Young lives in the real world. He's a private investigator who specializes in cellular phone fraud for the Guidry Group, one of the largest private investigation firms in the country. They handle everything from bodyguards for CEO's and foreign dignitaries to tracking down wayward husbands. Young works mostly the West Coast, LA to Seattle. Typically, he is hired by cell phone providers when they have something particularly dangerous or unusual on their hands. He goes after drug dealers in South Central who are using cloned phones, or the Russian mafia. Lone hackers are small potatoes for him, nothing to get too excited about, but he's essentially a bounty hunter—you pay him, he'll chase 'em.

In fact, earlier in the year, a high-tech company in the LA area (Young won't say which one) had hired Young to see if he could find Kevin Mitnick. Young spent several weeks poking around, but turned up nothing. Had the company been willing to put more money into it, Young has no doubt that he might have been able to track him down. But when Young told company officials that finding Kevin was not going to be an inexpensive endeavor, they told him to drop the investigation. When Young heard about the hacker Pazaski was monitoring, the name Kevin Mitnick didn't even cross his mind. He assumed Kevin was still in the LA area.

For Pazaski, the decision to hire Young was simple. With a small-time crook like this, Pazaski knew it would take months of prodding to get the Secret Service to go after him—they did, after all, have more important things to do than crack down on small, nonviolent crimes like this one. And the local cops, well . . . The only group with an interest in getting him stopped was McCaw, which was losing valuable airtime to the hacker. The only way Pazaski was going to stop him was to hunt him down on his own, find his name, address, and other vital info, then serve him up on a silver platter. And because of insurance and liability problems, McCaw wasn't eager to have their own employees running around in the streets playing Columbo.

So Pazaski called Young. They had known each other for five or six years—they'd both worked together at another telecommunications company, U.S. West, then split and went their separate ways. They reunited one afternoon around a table in one of McCaw's conference rooms. Pazaski had determined that the hacker was using a cloned mobile phone with the number 206-619-0086. Then he ran a computer report on all the calls the hacker had made from that number and discovered that most of the calls were coming through two cell towers in central Seattle. That meant that the hacker was probably calling from the same location—or very near the same location—each time he dialed. This made Young and Pazaski's job fairly simple. Had the hacker moved around every time he called— had he been, for example, in a car driving all around Seattle—it would have been virtually impossible to pinpoint him. As it was, all they had to do was take out a map of Seattle and draw an X to mark the location of each tower. One was on a hill just above Green Lake near Interstate 5, while the other was atop the University Hospital on the campus of the University of Washington. They then drew a loose circle around the area where the two cell towers overlapped—it was an area roughly fifteen blocks wide and three blocks deep in the heart of what Seattle folks call the U (University) District. That was the target area where their hacker was operating.

Besides narrowing the search dramatically, the target area told Young and Pazaski several things. This was no Russian mafioso; he was probably a college student. He obviously had a lot of time on his hands—he was on the phone five or six hours a day. He was definitely a hacker—almost all the calls were to Internet providers or PBX systems. Given the location, he was probably operating out of his apartment. To Young, he was just another geek who thought himself beyond the reach of the law.

✣

On the afternoon of October 7th, Young drove to Pazaski's office in Kirkland in his green Jeep Cherokee. From the outside, it looked just like any other Cherokee—except for a small, dish-shaped antenna on top, which was partly hidden by ski racks that Young keeps on the roof.

Inside, however, it was high-tech deluxe. The centerpiece was a TSR CellScope 2000, which was hooked up to a Toshiba laptop. The CellScope was essentially a radio receiver that honed in on cellular telephone calls more or less the way a radio tuner hones in on a radio station. Attached to the receiver was a small white box that sat on the dashboard, which took the cellular phone signal coming in from the antenna and displayed it in a circle of red LED lights. When a call was being tracked, one of the LED's lit up, signaling the direction from which the call was originating. All Young had to do was to lock on to the signal and then drive in the direction of the LED light—if it pointed left, drive left. If it pointed straight ahead, drive straight.

Young and Pazaski headed out at about 1 P.M. It was a cool, clear autumn afternoon. It was decided that Pazaski should drive so that Young would be free to fiddle with the equipment. For Young, this was another day at the office. For Pazaski, it was a thrill. He wouldn't usually go on this kind of adventure, but because Young was a friend, and because the hacker was in the U District (not exactly a frightening neighborhood), he felt comfortable tagging along. Besides, he liked the adventure of it, the high-tech sleuthing.

It was a short drive across the Evergreen Point Floating Bridge into Seattle. The highway off-ramp deposited them on the outskirts of the U District. Then they pulled off on a quiet residential street and talked strategy. They knew the phone number the hacker was using, but there were some forty or fifty channels in this cell site that the call could be going out on. Young set the scanner to jump from channel to channel at brief intervals. Scattered voices filled the car as the scanner roamed the channels—talk of business deals, of missed appointments, the mundane day-to-dayness of regular conversation, punctuated by short bursts of static (imagine slowly twisting the tuning knob on your car radio). They knew most of the hacker's calls were to Internet access points, so they listened for the characteristic fuzz and screech of a modem. They also knew that he didn't usually come on the air until 5:30 or 6:00 P.M.—presumably after he got home from work.

So they had some time to kill. They drove along the boundaries of the area they had marked out on the map. They pulled over frequently and listened to the scanner, laughing at little bits of conversation they picked up (cellular phone carriers and agents in their employ are exempt from laws that forbid electronic eavesdropping on cellular calls).

An hour or so later, they broke for lunch. They bought some bagels at a grocery store, returned and ate them in the Cherokee. Then they drove some more. They parked for a while on a street at the edge of the U District, where the shabby student neighborhood gives way to broken windows and urban despair. As the shadows grew, they watched a drug deal go down not fifty feet from them. That spooked them a little—the thought occurred to Young that some wacked-out crackhead might think they were cops and take a shot at them. So they drove on. They motored up to a more affluent neighborhood at the top of a hill overlooking Interstate 5. Lights of Seattle began to glitter below them. It was 6:20 P.M. They had already spent more than five hours in the car together—they were tired, bored, cranky, ready to call it a day.

Then they caught some male voices on the CellScope. Talking about accessing some files. Yucking it up. Young checked the receiver—the call was coming from 206-619-0086. This was their guy! Pazaski felt a shot of adrenaline. Young locked the receiver onto the call. The LED swung to the left, indicating that the call was coming from the southwest, somewhere down in the heart of the U District.

"It's coming from down there!" Young said, pointing to the neighborhood below them.

Pazaski gunned the throttle. They headed left down Ravenna, a major cross street. Traffic was heavy, time was precious. They had to find the hacker before he hung up. Every red light was traumatic. Young beat on the dashboard: "Come on, let's go!"

As they headed down Ravenna Avenue, Young watched the signal strength and the LED's on the CellScope. They turned east on Roosevelt, until the signal strength grew weaker. As they reached 50th Street, the signal strength increased. They could hear the voices of the two guys—Pazaski was struck by their cockiness. They were talking about accessing files and destroying data. Sounded like they were out to get somebody. Young listened closely, picked up a few place names. It sounded like the person they were after lived in Denver—

"This guy is a fucking terrorist!" Young said.

Meanwhile, they were stuck behind another traffic light. "God damn, God damn! Let's go!"

When the light changed, they headed up Brooklyn Avenue. They only went a couple of blocks when the dot swung rapidly to the left . . . hey, we got something here. They looped around the block, and when they drove down the street again, the dot did the same thing. The signal seemed to be strongest as they passed a tired, flimsy-looking, 1950s-style apartment complex called the Lyn-Mar. Okay, this must be the place. They took one more pass to be sure. As they drove by the Lyn-Mar, the red dot swung wildly, and the signal strength maxed out. No question about it.

Young was a little dismayed to see that the guy lived in an apartment complex. It would just make it tougher to pin him down. The CellScope worked great to indicate the immediate area of a caller, but identifying the exact room or apartment the caller was in was the toughest part. Young started by doing a little old-fashioned footwork. He got out of the car and walked up to the front of the Lyn-Mar. He found a row of gold mailboxes built into the wall in a shallow hallway on the ground floor. He was relieved to see that there were only twelve units in the building—it shouldn't be too difficult to narrow it down, he thought. The last name of each resident was attached to the front of the mailboxes with blue tape. Young just started reading off the names, left to right, starting with apartment one: "Merrill." Apartment two . . .

Before he even read the next name, he heard a voice through the thin stucco wall. A male voice. He listened more closely . . . it was coming through the door of apartment one, just a few feet to his right. He moved closer, then stooped down below the peephole and listened . . . it was the same guy he had heard on the CellScope! It's him, the hacker! Young could hardly believe his luck. "I laughed inside. I thought, 'God damn, I can't believe this.' "

He ran back to the Cherokee and said to Pazaski, "Kevin, Kevin, you're not going to believe this. I found him. I heard his voice . . ." And while he was talking to Pazaski, the voice of the hacker was still audible on the CellScope. "That's him," Young said, confirming the voice.

For Pazaski, this was damn exciting. For Young, it was damn satisfying. Never one to be modest, Young said, "I hope you're impressed with me." The whole thing had taken five to ten minutes at most.

The call stopped soon after. Thinking they were finished for the day, Young got out a notebook and walked back across the street and to take notes for the affidavit he'd soon have to write up to get a search warrant. He was just starting to write when he heard a door open—the door to apartment one, the hacker's door! Young watched the door open, and there he was, he walked right out. Young ducked behind a van, and watched him lock the door—to Young, this was a crucial detail, because it established that the guy he had seen lived there, that he wasn't just a friend or visitor. Young rushed back to the Cherokee and told Pazaski, "He just came out!"

Young's first impression: the guy was not the college freshman that he'd expected—he was older, maybe a grad student. Young thought he looked like an overweight Weird Al Yankovic. Big guy, chunky, not fat. Small mustache. Longish black hair. Silver metal-rim glasses. Leather jacket. Carrying a green, black, and purple gym bag over his shoulder.

They flipped a U-turn and followed him up the street. They watched the man they would come to know as Brian Merrill walk several blocks to the Safeway at 52nd Street and Brooklyn Avenue. When he entered the store, they pulled into a parking lot across the street. Pazaski jumped out and continued the chase into the Safeway. He watched Merrill buy a jug of mineral water; Pazaski picked up some Arizona iced tea and bananas. Pazaski stood right behind him in line at the checkout counter. Merrill said nothing to anyone, just smiled at the clerk, paid for his water, and headed out up the street to the dingy little YMCA, where he frequently worked out.

Pazaski returned to the Cherokee, where Young was waiting. Enough excitement for one night.

✧

The next night, Young returned—this time without Pazaski. Young was nothing if not thorough—he wanted to be sure no mistakes were made. He sat outside Merrill's apartment for over an hour, listening to the fuzzy sound of modem tones on the scanner.

Young took a night off, then returned at about 6:30 P.M. on Monday, October 10th. He parked on the street not far from Merrill's apartment, turned on the scanner—nothing. About ten minutes later, he saw the same Weird Al Yankovic character walking down the street with a white plastic grocery bag. He watched him walk into the apartment. Two minutes later, the scanner trapped a call to an answering machine in Denver—the caller hung up before leaving a message. A minute after that, the same person called a voice mail system in Denver, and again hung up. Then there was yet another call to an answering machine—this time, Young heard him leaving a message. It began, "Hey dude, it's me." It was Merrill. He said he was sending "two password entries," and asked the person to get back to him about how the person's "Cracker" software works. He asked if Cracker uses the "full *Webster's Dictionary*" or if it's able to "run permutations of words." Merrill ended the call by saying "I'll check back later."

Five days later, Young was back again. He and his wife had been on their way to see a movie called *The Browning Version* at a nearby theater. After they bought their tickets, they realized they had some time to kill, so Young brought his wife over to see the hacker he was tracking. She also worked in the cellular phone business, and so had more than just a passing interest in the case. He parked the Cherokee in the usual spot, and sure enough, at just after 6 P.M., the calls began. They listened to two brief calls to the LA area. Then the door opened and Merrill walked out. He was wearing jeans and a leather jacket again. Except this time he was carrying his cellular phone. Young and his wife watched him dial—bickering at the same time about what kind of phone he was using. Then he put the phone to his ear, and there was the voice coming off the scanner again. Young started up the Cherokee and followed Merrill down the street towards the Safeway, listening to him yak as they idled along behind him.

After dinner and the movie, Young and his wife returned. They fired up the scanner. This time they just heard modem tones. But after about twenty minutes, Merrill again stepped out of his apartment and headed down the street with his cellular phone. He made another call to Denver. Young and his wife drove ahead of him a block or so and parked in the lot near a Taco Bell. They watched him walk straight toward them. He got closer and closer. It was an unsettling moment. For a split second, Young wondered if Merrill was on to him. For cover, Young leaned over and kissed

his wife. It was like a scene out of an Alfred Hitch-
cock movie. Merrill walked within five feet of the
car, and right into the Taco Bell. He never even
glanced at them.

10

At about 6 P.M. on Thursday, October 27th, Young and Pazaski arrived at Seattle's North police precinct. They met with several police officers, including Detective John Lewitt, who was part of the Seattle Police Department's Fraud and Explosives Unit. Busting a hacker is not exactly an everyday occurrence in the SPD. Like other cops, they tend to see crime as something that involves guns or drugs or hookers. But hey, if the boss wants this guy arrested, they'll do it. To get a feeling for what they were getting into, they watched a short video about computer hackers—what they do, how to arrest them, how to properly seize their equipment. They learned, for example, that it's very important to turn the computer off—don't just walk in there and yank the cord out of the wall. Otherwise, valuable information might be lost.

When the video was over, Lewitt slipped his bulletproof vest on under his sport coat. It was police department procedure to wear one anytime an officer served a warrant. A few minutes later, Young and Pazaski left in the Cherokee, while Lewitt and the other police officers took the bomb truck, which doubled as an evidence collection truck, as well as several unmarked cars. They had assembled quite a crew—four detectives, two sergeants, one captain, and two officers. Four Secret Service agents followed in another car.

It was about 7:15 when they arrived in the U District. The cops all assembled in the parking lot of a nearby Burger King, while Young and Pazaski drove past Merrill's apartment—they noticed the lights were on inside, an encouraging sign—and then parked along a side street about one block north. Young turned his scanner on, hoping to trap one of Merrill's calls. If possible, they wanted to catch him in action, actually using the cloned phone. He would then radio the police, and they would go in and bust the hacker. Young had spent enough time monitoring Merrill that he knew his behavior patterns pretty well. He was *always* on the phone around this time of night.

Except tonight.

They waited half an hour; nothing happened. The cops sat in the parking lot at Burger King, drinking hot chocolate and coffee, bitching about the previous Sunday's Washington Huskies football game (they'd lost to the University of Oregon, 31-20). Another half hour passed. The cops started glancing at their watches. What was going on? This was supposed to be a quick in-and-out. Nobody was in the mood to waste the entire night. This guy was just a two-bit phone phreaker.

Of all nights for him to take a vacation, Young thought. He had been sitting there for an hour and a half now. If Merrill wasn't home, why were the lights on? Had Merrill been sitting in his apartment the whole time, watching TV, maybe? Young doubted it. From what he'd learned about Merrill's life, if he was home, he was on the phone.

Young's frustration grew. He'd put a lot of work into this case. Besides the hours he'd spent doing surveillance, he'd also taken several days to write a detailed affidavit. Then he'd had to lobby hard to find someone to take the case. Local police didn't want it because they were too busy. The Secret Service, who usually have jurisdiction in cellular fraud cases, wasn't interested because the dollar amount of McCaw's losses was too small. It was only when Young took it to Ivan Orton, a smart and progressive King County prosecutor, that he finally got any action. With Orton's help, they were finally able to convince the Seattle police to go out and make the bust.

Young had a police radio in his Cherokee, but because they were afraid Merrill could be monitoring it, they didn't use it. Young and Pazaski sat in the dark, waiting. They speculated about where Merrill might be. They made sarcastic comments about the kooks who walked by. They tapped their fingers on the dashboard. They yawned. They waited some more.

At about 9:00 P.M., after almost two hours of tension and apprehension, the police radio crackled to life: "Okay, we're ready to do the warrant."

Young politely suggested they wait a little longer.

The suggestion was denied.

✛

An unmarked police car pulled up a hundred feet or so from Merrill's apartment. Lewitt and Tom Molitar, a Secret Service agent, as well as several other cops, jumped out. They moved swiftly and silently towards Merrill's front door, careful to keep out of view of his windows. If he was home, they didn't want to spook him.

Lewitt positioned himself on one side of the door, Molitar on the other. Another cop stood watch behind them. There were cops watching the windows, cops watching the rear exit, cops in the street. They pretty much had the place surrounded.

Lewitt knocked. "Seattle police."

Nothing.

He pounded again. "Seattle police. We have a search warrant."

Still no answer.

"Let's go in," Lewitt said to Molitar. They both took their guns out of their holsters—standard operating procedure on a forced entry, when you never know what you might find behind the door. It's one of the spookiest moments a cop faces, and statistically, one of the most dangerous.

"Ready?"

Lewitt and Molitar each put a foot on the door and gave it a kick—a shove, really. The flimsy wooden door immediately collapsed.

Inside, they found a sparsely furnished, dreary, cavelike apartment. The only thing that made it any different from every other sparse, dreary, cavelike apartment in the world was the rat's nest of technology: a Toshiba T4400SX laptop, several modems, cell phones, manuals. The furniture was shabby—"Goodwill furniture," Lewitt called it. To him, the place seemed lonely and impersonal—no photographs on the walls, no posters, hardly anything personal. He noticed an X ray of what appeared to be someone's colon on the kitchen table; also medical bills and a prescription for Zantac, a drug often prescribed for stomach problems.

After checking the bathroom and the closets to make sure no one was hiding out anywhere, Lewitt and the other officers got down to work. They pulled the bomb truck around to the front of the apartment—a mistake, Young thought, since it advertised to the world that the cops were there—and proceeded to go over Merrill's apartment with a microscope. They shot seven rolls of 35mm film. They confiscated 150 items, including his computer, several cell phones, three modems, and every wire, plug, battery charger, and diskette they could lay their hands on. They also grabbed Merrill's Aerosmith and Red Hot Chili Peppers CD's, copies of money orders, scraps of paper out of his nightstand, a tube of ChapStick, his checkbook, medical records, as well as a fat book called *VAX/VMS Internals and Data Structures.*

When they were done, about the only things left were some clothes and a few pots and pans and a clunky old mountain bike. They left a copy of the search warrant on the kitchen table.

✠

While the police were searching the apartment, David Drews, the manager of the Lyn-Mar, fixed Merrill's door as well as he could. He was surprised that Merrill was in trouble. He hadn't known him very well, but he seemed like a decent enough guy. Merrill had moved into a one-bedroom, partly furnished apartment four months earlier, in June of 1994. He paid his rent, $490, and security deposit in cash. Drews knew that he had a job at Virginia Mason Hospital in downtown Seattle—he'd sometimes see him leaving for work in the morning, heading toward the bus stop with the cellular phone pressed to his ear. "It was like it was attached to him," Drews recalls. But cell phones are common enough among students in the U District—Drews thought nothing of it.

He had also noticed that Merrill was a night owl. Because Drews's apartment was directly above Merrill's, he would sometimes hear the screech of modem tones as Merrill logged onto his computer late at night. Other times he would blast Aerosmith or the Red Hot Chili Peppers. Once, Drews had to go downstairs at 3 A.M. and tell him the music was keeping him awake. Merrill was apologetic, and immediately turned it down.

It was about 11:30 P.M. when Drews finished fixing the door. The cops were just finishing up. Drews returned to his apartment and went to bed. He heard the evidence truck drive off just as he was falling asleep.

Maybe two minutes later, there was a knock on his door. Probably a cop, Drews thought.

It was Merrill. He looked flustered. Drews would later conclude that he had been on his way home from the gym when he saw the police vehicles parked outside his apartment. He had waited until they were gone, then snuck around the back alley into the complex.

"Sorry to bother you," Merrill said politely. "Did you let somebody into my apartment?"

"No, they kicked in the door," Drews told him.

"Who's 'they'?"

"The Seattle police, the Secret Service."

"Oh fuck," Merrill said, and disappeared into the night. Drews never saw him again.

11

The next morning, Kevin Pazaski received a phone call. The caller identified himself as a Seattle police officer. He said he had been along on the raid of Brian Merrill's apartment the night before, and said it was very important that he find out if any videotape or photographs of Merrill existed.

"Who did you say you were?"

The caller repeated his name.

Pazaski was suspicious. "What did you say you look like?"

He told Pazaski he was six feet tall, mustache, dark hair. A fairly generic description.

"Okay," Pazaski said.

"I really need to know if you have any photographs or videotape of the suspect," the caller asked. "It's important information. It's really critical to our case against him."

"Well, if you were there last night, you should know exactly what we have," Pazaski said. He was suddenly suspicious of the call. "Is there a number where I can call you back?"

"Sure," the caller said. He gave him a number.

"I'll check it out."

"I really need to know this information."

"Well, maybe you should call Ivan Orton. He's the one in charge of this case," Pazaski said.

As soon as he hung up, Pazaski dialed the callback number. It connected to the Seattle police, but there was no officer there by the name the caller had given. Pazaski hung up. He felt uneasy.

A short time later, it hit him: Merrill. That was him.

✢

That same Friday morning, King's County prosecutor Ivan Orton perused the box of stuff confiscated at Merrill's apartment. He examined the computer, the half-dozen cell phones, the E-PROM reprogrammer. He figured it was a little cellular phone operation, some college kid who was having fun making free phone calls.

On the following Monday, however, Orton got a call from Ken McGuire, an FBI agent in Los Angeles. He told Orton that the FBI had received a tip that Kevin Mitnick was complaining that his apartment in Seattle had been ransacked. Did he know of any search warrants that had been served to anyone who might fit Mitnick's description?

Orton didn't have to think too hard. "Yeah, as a matter of fact, we do have something interesting here," he said. He told McGuire about the recent bust and promised to look through the confiscated materials and see if he could find anything that might link Brian Merrill to Kevin Mitnick. Back in 1992, Orton had attended a law enforcement convention in Colorado Springs. Katie Hafner had given a speech about hackers, and Orton remembered her talk about Kevin. He was intrigued.

That night, Orton tried to examine the software on the confiscated laptop. The files were unreadable—they were all password-protected—but he was able to open the backup disks. Some of the files were encrypted, but Orton managed to examine quite a few documents. He scanned files of e-mail—much of it was to (or from, Orton couldn't be sure) Neill Clift in England. The name meant nothing to him. One file named "KDM.WAVE" was an audio recording that mimicked the AT&T's corporate jingle: "Thank you for using AT&T," except it had been altered to say, "Thank you for using Kevin Mitnick." When he opened another file, a document flashed on the screen that said, "This software is registered to Kevin Mitnick."

Very interesting indeed. Orton spent almost three hours browsing through the files on the laptop. Like the cops who raided the apartment, Orton was surprised by the lack of personal details. There was no correspondence from friends, hardly any mention of any life beyond the technical manuals and computer code.

Orton's most remarkable find, however, was an ASCII file (a simple, easily read computer file that contains just words, no graphics) that was fairly large—almost one megabyte. He opened it, and was surprised to find a list of thousands of names. Beside each name was a long number, which Orton recognized as a credit card number, as well as an expiration date, and a charge for $25.70. Orton didn't know it at the time, but this was the subscriber list for Netcom, one of the largest and fastest growing Internet providers in the country. Orton had no way of knowing that this file had been floating around in the computer underground for months, and that dozens of hackers had copies of the same file.

To his credit, Orton didn't jump to any conclusion. He didn't assume that Kevin—or "Brian Merrill"—was engaged in credit card fraud. In fact, if this guy really was the infamous Kevin Mitnick, the überhacker, the demon in the cyberdarkness, Orton was surprised by how *little* trouble he'd caused.

"Given the knowledge and capability he had," Orton would later say, "he's really done very little."

Nevertheless, Orton did his job. The next morning, he called Special Agent McGuire and said, "I think we've found something you might be interested in here."

✢

For Pazaski, the weirdness continued. In the following weeks, he began getting strange phone calls at home. The phone would ring in the middle of the night—he'd pick it up, and there'd be no one there. His wife became worried. Who was this guy? What was he doing? When the news came that Brian Merrill was probably an alias for Kevin Mitnick, Pazaski called up and had his credit record blocked. He didn't know if Mitnick could actually gain access to it or not, but he wasn't taking any chances. Suddenly the phone line at his house seemed like an umbilical cord to the darkness. Who knew what spirits it could summon up?

And Pazaski wasn't alone in his fears. Detective Lewitt was warned to watch his financial statements for evidence of tampering. One day, not long after this, the bank called. They had not received his mortgage payment. Lewitt was sure he had mailed it weeks earlier.

He thought, "Oh God." The hacker's revenge.

Turned out the check was lost in the mail.

12

Lile Elam is not your typical wirehead. She has a big tumble of auburn hair, she wears colorful red-frame glasses, and is stylish in her own bohemian way. And unlike many veterans of the net, she is tolerant—even generous—with people who are just learning to feel their way around in cyberspace. And most unlikely of all, she is a fine artist. She paints big splashy abstractions (mostly watercolors now) that are suggestive of wind and sky and turbulent states of consciousness, the products of a life balanced at the intersection of art and technology.

For years it was an uneasy alignment. Since she was six years old, Elam had wanted to be a painter. But she also wanted to be able to pay her rent. So after high school, she attended the State Technical Institute at Knoxville, Tennessee, where she studied computer science for two years. She ended up moving to the center of the action, Silicon Valley, and eventually worked as a Unix systems administrator at Sun Microsystems, a manufacturer of high-end computer workstations. But she always kept painting. She didn't like the fact that her two lives were so separate. It felt schizophrenic.

To Elam, the Internet had long seemed a perfect medium for artists. It was visual, it could communicate to large numbers of people, it could break down the cloistered walls of the art world, which made paintings accessible only to people in big cities. Wouldn't it be great, Elam speculated, if someone built an art gallery and put it up on the net? Artists could "install" their paintings, and people from all over the world could visit by just clicking the mouse on their computer. To hell with digital commerce and on-line shopping and news on demand. *This* was what the Internet was good for.

In April 1994, she was displaying several new oil paintings in her studio, an abandoned police station in Redwood City. Friends came by to admire her work. One of them was Tsutomu's friend and cellular phone maestro, Mark Lottor. Lottor was particularly struck by one painting—a large moody watercolor, with great clouds of yellow and white bleeding down into darker colors.

Lottor eventually offered Elam a deal: in exchange for her painting, which he decided to call *Art on the Net*, he would give her an Internet connection for one year on Network Wizards' computers. With that, she could build her own web site, her own virtual art gallery.

Elam eagerly agreed, and went to work building the site. She already had a name for it, too: Art on the Net.

✢

By October, Art on the Net was a success, the kind of grass-roots project that characterizes the entrepreneurial spirit of the computer culture. Some sixty-five artists from all over the world had built their own exhibition sites on Art on the Net—poets, musicians, painters, sculptors, digital artists, and animators. It was becoming a Soho of cyberspace, a place for artists to show their work, as well as a place to hang around and bullshit.

Keeping the site running smoothly, however, took a tremendous amount of time and effort. Although the site was supposed to be a cooperative, with each artist maintaining his or her own space, most of the heavy lifting was left to Elam, who was desperately trying to juggle her time with Art on the Net and still keep her day job at Sun Microsystems. It was not unusual for her to work until 1 or 2 A.M. at the offices of Network Wizards in

Menlo Park, where the computer that houses Art on the Net is physically located.

Around 2 A.M. one night in late October, she was working with some collaborators, uploading and downloading images, when she noticed that an artist was logged into Art on the Net from Netcom. Ordinarily that would have been fine—lots of artists accessed Art on the Net from other sites. But Elam knew that this particular artist's account didn't have Internet access yet—so how could he be connected from Netcom? Elam thought about it for a moment, perplexed. That was so weird . . .

Then it occurred to her: maybe it wasn't the artist who was using the account. Maybe it was someone else.

Elam quickly dialed up Netcom and looked around. She could tell from the session logs which account was being used to access Art on the Net— it turned out to be someone named "gkremen." She checked the "gkremen'" account and realized it had been broken into. While she was reading the details of the account, which had been open to all, the permissions suddenly changed so that they could be read only by the owner of the account. It was an eerie moment: Elam knew the intruder had discovered that she was on to him.

She immediately logged off Netcom. She sat there in the dark, at 2 A.M., not sure what to do. Her palms went clammy. Who was this person? Why was he breaking into Art on the Net?

A moment later, she got a message on her computer screen. Someone wanted to talk to her.

It was him. Or her. The intruder.

Elam hesitated. How could he hurt her? He was probably miles away, just a ghost in her machine. Why not try to flush him out, see what he was up to? He sent her a message. It read: "I bet you're really pissed because I broke into your system and you don't know who I am."

"No, I'm not pissed," she wrote back. His tone seemed aggressive at first. She just tried to keep him talking. She wanted to draw him out, see what he was after. The idea that this person on the other end of her computer could be Kevin Mitnick hadn't crossed her mind. She knew plenty about him from Lottor and Tsutomu, but there were hundreds of crackers out there. Why would Mitnick be interested in Art on the Net?

After a few minutes of chatting, the intruder began to loosen up. She had recently been to England, so they talked about the weather in Europe. He seemed interested in that, for some reason— she thought maybe he was thinking about taking a trip there. She invited him to log onto the Art on the Net web site, have a look around. As they talked, it became clear to Elam that he didn't know what the web was.

Elam was incredulous: "You've never heard of the web?"

Nope, he'd never heard of it. In fact, he thought

it was a trap. He thought she was trying to lure him into some forbidden zone that he would never be able to escape. How could any hacker expert enough to break into her system not be familiar with the World Wide Web? Every newspaper in the country had been writing about it for months. Half the teenagers in America had their own web pages. Maybe it was a joke and Elam didn't realize it. Or maybe not. Maybe this intruder lived cocooned in a narrow corner of the electronic world, oblivious to the momentous changes that were going on around him, a hacker from an all-but-lost generation.

All in all, Elam and the mysterious stranger talked for nearly an hour. By the end of the conversation, he had put Elam at ease. She didn't think he was out to cause any trouble. He hadn't even intended to scare her. "I think he was just curious," says Elam. "He just wanted to come into my site and look around and see what was going on."

Later, a message was left on Lottor's answering machine, referring to the break-in at Art on the Net. A colleague had no trouble identifying the voice: Kevin.

13

Not long after the incident with Elam's computer, Deputy Kathleen Cunningham received an unusual phone call. The caller identified himself as Tom Perrine, manager of workstation services at the San Diego Supercomputer Center. "John Markoff at *The New York Times* gave me your number," he told Cunningham, who had no idea who Perrine was. "I have an idea about how to catch Kevin, and I thought we should talk about it."

Ordinarily, Cunningham was highly skeptical of calls she got out of the blue. But this call was different. Although she didn't know a lot about computers, she knew enough to know that some pretty smart people worked at SDSC. In early September, Markoff had called her and recommended that she bring in Tsutomu Shimomura to look for Kevin. He was an expert in tracking computer criminals, he told her. Markoff had given her Tsutomu's number at the San Diego Supercomputer Center. Cunningham, who had been busy with truly dangerous criminals at the time, never called him.

Now, here was Markoff again, and SDSC. What was it with these guys? Cunningham didn't know, but she was willing to listen.

So Perrine laid it out for her: he told her that he believed Kevin was trying to illegally access computers at San Diego Supercomputer Center, and that there were several people there who were willing to help chase him down. They were willing to offer their time and expertise, and they were confident that in a short time, they would be able to locate him.

Cunningham was intrigued. But she was also cautious. How did she know this person she was talking to was actually Tom Perrine? She had been around Kevin and his pals long enough to know that any one of them was certainly capable of spoofing her.

"Okay, let's figure out a time and place and get together and talk about it," Cunningham said.

The caller agreed, and said he would call her back soon.

She never heard from him again.

✣

In fact, the call *had* been from Perrine.

After Tsutomu heard about the break-in to Art on the Net, he had had enough. A few weeks earlier, Kevin had also tried to break into Lottor's machine—Lottor knew it was Kevin because Kevin had called him up and, with typical bravado, *told* him he was going to do it. As far as Tsutomu was concerned, Kevin had gone over the line. This was getting too personal. He had to be stopped. The question was, how?

Clearly Tsutomu wasn't going to get much help. After her encounter with the mysterious stranger on Art on the Net in October, Elam had called Netcom to tell them that someone was getting unauthorized access to an account on their system; they had told her they were too busy to worry about it— an attitude that justifiably pissed Elam off. And the cops certainly weren't going to round Kevin up— they had been after him for years, and nothing had come of it. It was time to try something else.

So the guys at the Supercomputer Center came up with a plan. It was a kind of sting operation, one that happened to be modeled on the SDINET ruse that Clifford Stoll had used in *The Cuckoo's Egg*. Stoll had created fake goverment documents referring to a secret project called SDINET, which Stoll also invented. He then used the documents as bait for the hacker, leaving them in various places in his machine in hopes that the intruder would stumble over a few of them. That would pique his interest, Stoll hoped, and he would start prowling around for more. And the more time he spent wandering around in Stoll's computer, the better chance he'd have to track him down. The plan worked, enabling Stoll to set up a monitoring system that traced the hacker's calls back to Germany, where he was eventually arrested.

A similar ruse, it seemed, might catch Kevin. The gang at the Supercomputer Center knew that Kevin was very interested in the source code for OKI cellular phones. Why not post information on the net somewhere, using a fictitious name, that they had stolen a copy of this much-coveted software? If they handled it right, if were they cool about it, maybe they could flush Kevin out of the woodwork. Once they made contact with him, they figured it would take maybe six months of careful communication to gain his confidence. Then they could set up a face-to-face meeting— and bust him.

So Perrine called Deputy Cunningham to run the idea by her. But the more Tsutomu and Perrine thought about it, the less appealing it seemed. It would take a huge commitment of time and a lot of delicate maneuvering. There were all kinds of legal issues—like entrapment—to worry about. And Kevin might not fall for it. Or he might get spooked at the last minute.

Also, in comparison with Markus Hess, the hacker in *The Cuckoo's Egg*, Kevin was messing around with cell phones, not military secrets. That was a crime, to be sure, but did it justify spending months and months to search him down? At least one of Tsutomu's close friends thought it wasn't: "Kevin was a pain in the ass, he needed to be stopped, but I don't think he belongs in jail. He is a tremendously creative person. In his own way, I think he's a kind of artist."

Tsutomu and Perrine eventually abandoned the plan. There had to be a better way.

✢

A few weeks after Perrine's call to Deputy Cunningham, Andrew Burt made an amusing discovery. He logged onto Nyx and discovered that Kevin had left him a gift—a strange little piece of doggerel, apparently inspired by Burt's earlier post about spiders. The message was full of Kevin's characteristic on-line bravado. He loved to play games of one-upsmanship with system administrators like Burt (in the note, Kevin calls him by his login, "aburt"). It was a takeoff on the Spiderman theme song, a popular Saturday morning cartoon of the 1970s:

Spiderman, Spiderman,
does whatever a hacker can.
Plants a bug, any size,
Catches passwords just like flies.
Hey there, there goes the Spiderman.

Is he strong? Listen, bud,
he can cause an IRC flood.
Can aburt lock him out?
No, aburt doesn't have the clout.
Hey there, there goes the Spiderman.

In the chill of night,
at the scene of the crime,
like a streak of light,
he cloaks himself just in time.

Spiderman, Spiderman,
friendly neighborhood Spiderman.
Welcome, then he's ignored,
fucking over aburt is his reward.
To him, life is a great big bash,
especially during the nyx crash,
you won't catch the Spiderman!

Spiderman, Spiderman
Hacking nyx like only a spider can
Spreads a web, any size
snatches passwords just like flies!
He's Spiderman!!

Spiderman, Spiderman
Fucking with aburt's plan
Bugging telnet and ftp
Lamer aburt will never catch me!
I'm Spiderman!!

The note gave Burt a chuckle. But playful as it was, there was also something perverse about it. The more Kevin was hunted, the more invincible he felt. There was the tangy smell of adrenaline in this silly rhyme. Kevin was on the run. He was *wanted*.

IV

ENTER THE SAMURAI

1

If you were a thief and you wanted to burglarize someone's house, you'd probably pick a time when the people who lived there weren't home. If you wanted to break into someone's computer, you'd probably do the same. You might pick a holiday—like Christmas Day. On Christmas, lights on the information highway are dim. Even the most dedicated computer wizards are likely to be away from the screen. It is a day for families, for eggnog, for mapping Santa Claus's progress across the sky.

Tsutomu Shimomura is not big on eggnog and

Santa Claus, but this Christmas, the intruder got lucky. Tsutomu spent the day in San Francisco with a woman he was seeing at the time, Julia Menapace. Menapace, a pale, plain-looking woman with long straight brown hair, had worked as a programmer at Apple Computer, and had a reputation for being quite brilliant herself. Menapace wasn't feeling too well that day, so Tsutomu spent most of the day playing with a new computer. Tsutomu collects computers the way Imelda Marcos collected shoes—he has thirty or so of them, each in various states of disrepair at any given moment. His newest traveling companion is a 2.4 gigabyte, 85 megahertz SPARC portable. It's the .44 magnum of portables, ridiculously powerful, a Dirty Harry machine.

The following afternoon, Tsutomu left Julia in San Francisco and headed down to Menlo Park to have dinner with Lottor when his cell phone rang. It was Andrew Gross, his understudy at the San Diego Supercomputer Center. Gross was home in Tennessee, where he was spending the holidays with his family. At some point, Gross happened to check his e-mail, where the log files that record the activity in Tsutomu's computer are routinely mailed to him. Instead of getting longer, like they were supposed to, the log files were getting shorter. That was not supposed to happen. Alarmed, Gross immediately called Tsutomu on his cell phone and told him about the log files. They both knew exactly what this meant.

Someone had broken into Tsutomu's computer.

⬦

Tsutomu lives in constant motion. Even his closest friends debate whether he owns a car or just rents one everywhere he goes. He seems to be constantly flying across the country from one conference to another, touching down for a few days in Silicon Valley, then jetting off to the beach or Lake Tahoe. He knows nothing about pop culture—once, when a close friend was watching a rerun of *I Love Lucy,* he walked into the room and looked at Lucille Ball on the TV and said, "Who's that?" He rarely comes into the office at the San Diego Supercomputing Center. He interrupts meetings. He keeps people waiting. He disdains lesser minds. When he works, he holes himself up for days or weeks at a time, hardly showering or eating. When he's done, he disappears.

Tsutomu and Kevin share a number of qualities: both relate better to machines than to other human beings. Both functioned poorly in high school. Both are highly intelligent. Both have large egos. Both can be obsessive. Both distrust authority. And both deliberately cultivate a sense of mystery about themselves.

This is surprising, because their backgrounds couldn't be more different. Unlike Kevin, Tsutomu's family is intact. When I began to research this book, I called his father, Osamu Shimomura, a world-renowned biochemist who lives and works in Woods Hole, Massachusetts. Osamu allowed me to visit him at the Marine Biological Laboratory, where he has been a professor since 1984. Osamu, a tall, thin, friendly, frail-looking man who, despite some thirty-five years in this country, still speaks broken English, led me into his lab crowded with test tubes and glass beakers. There are posters of jellyfish on the walls, and a small desk cluttered with papers and a laptop computer. The work of Osamu's life has been to study a rare phenomenon called bioluminescence in sea creatures (such as jellyfish and tiny shrimplike crustaceans).

Osamu introduced me to Akemi, Tsutomu's mother, who works as Osamu's assistant. She's a small, exceedingly polite woman who seems very at home in her white lab coat.

Osamu then gave me a demonstration of bioluminescence. He reached up on a shelf in his lab and grabbed a glass mason jar labeled "1944." Inside, he said, were tiny dried marine crustaceans called *Cypridina* that had been gathered in Japan during the war. He opened the jar and dumped some into his hand—they were tiny, about the size of peppercorns. "Now, watch this," he said. He walked over to the sink and turned on the water and passed his hand under it, dampening the shrimp. Then he opened his palm and used his thumb to mix the tiny shrimplike creatures around—and suddenly, his palm was glowing. It was as if he were holding a handful of black light. "Japanese soldiers were supposed to use this in the jungles on Iwo Jima," Shimomura explained. "They planned to wipe it on their backs, then moisten it with saliva, so they could follow each other at night without lights. The war ended, however, before they tried it."

Tsutomu's parents spoke of him with a mixture of affection and bewilderment. The last time they'd seen their son was when Tsutomu's grandmother had been sick three years earlier. As Osamu put it, using a bit of American idiom that may convey a different meaning than he intended, "I had to drag him kicking and screaming" to Japan to see her. Tsutomu was no closer with his sister Sachi, who is four years younger, working on a Ph.D. at Cornell in medieval literature. She hadn't spoken to her brother in five years.

In fact, the last time Osamu had talked to his son was in January of 1995, just a few weeks after the break-in to his computer. It was, as usual, a brief conversation. The next thing he knew, he was reading about his son in *The New York Times*. He seemed understandably proud.

While we talked about Tsutomu's background, I happened to mention Los Alamos National Laboratory, where Tsutomu had worked as a computational physicist. Osamu mentioned that he had been very close to Nagasaki when the bomb was dropped.

"How close?"

"About ten kilometers away."

I asked him what he remembered, and he said it was a very difficult subject for him to talk about. "I've tried to forget," Osamu said. Only recently, perhaps due to the publicity surrounding the fiftieth anniversary of the bombing, he found himself thinking about it again.

On August 9, 1945, Osamu was sixteen years old. He was working in a factory that built Japanese fighter planes in Isahaya, a small community in the hills about fifteen kilometers outside Nagasaki. At about 11 A.M. a warning siren went off, signaling the approach of American bombers. Osamu went outside to look—he saw a bomber very high in the bright blue sky, passing from north to south. He watched as the plane dropped three small parachutes—he saw no human bodies under the parachutes, so he was puzzled (in fact, they were guidance instruments for the bomb). A few minutes later, another bomber passed overhead, then the siren rang again informing them that the air raid was over. He went back into the factory—and saw a blinding flash of light. It was so bright his eyes were temporarily blinded. Less than a minute later came a thunderous explosion and a pressure wave that hurt his ears. Outside, the sky turned gray, and it began to rain. Osamu stumbled home, unhurt, through the radioactive cloud.

Tsutomu's mother, Akemi, had also been at Nagasaki that day. She was nine years old. Due to the constant bombardment of the city by American forces, her parents had sent her to live with friends in the countryside. She had been there for several months, helping with the harvest. Then on August 9, she happened to travel into Nagasaki to visit some relatives. When the bomb detonated, she was two kilometers away. Fortunately, there had been a large hill between her and the epicenter of the blast, so she wasn't burned. Her brother was not so lucky. He had traveled into the city that morning, and when the device hit, he was at ground zero.

2

As a child, Tsutomu's world was as fertile as Kevin's was barren. He was born in 1963 in Nagoya, Japan. The following year, his family moved to Princeton, New Jersey, where Osamu had been hired as a full-time professor. The Shimomuras never had a lot of money, but they lived comfortably in the confines of academia. Tsutomu spent most of his youth a stone's throw from Princeton's lovely stone buildings and walks shaded with oaks and elms. It was the spiritual home of modern physics, where Albert Einstein had spent the waning years of his life, and where his two-and-two-third-pound brain now rested in a jar of formaldehyde at Princeton Hospital.

In some ways, Tsutomu was just like any other kid growing up in the 1960s and 70s. When he was about ten years old, he read J.R.R. Tolkien's Hobbit books. There was never a computer in the house—personal computers didn't exist until the mid-seventies—but Tsutomu diverted himself in other ways. "Depending on what he was working on at the moment, his room looked like a disaster area or a chemistry experiment," his sister, Sachi, recalls. But to some of the kids in the neighborhood, he was an odd creature. When Sachi was about five years old, one of her friends asked, "Is your brother a genius?"

Sachi immediately ran to her mother. "Mommy," Sachi asked, "what's a genius?"

Summers had their own ritual for the Shimomuras. Every year from the time Tsutomu was seven or eight until he was about fifteen, Osamu would pack the family in the car and drive across country (in later years, they sometimes flew) to San Juan Island, near Seattle, where Osamu would do summer research on a particularly rare species of jellyfish called *Aequeorea*. Sachi and Tsutomu would spend hours out on the docks with a long pole that had a small net attached to the end. On a good day, they might catch 2,000 jellyfish, which they would then pour into buckets and tote over to the lab. While it could be fun at first, netting jellyfish was boring, tedious work. Osamu showed me a family photograph of Tsutomu, age thirteen, standing on the pier on San Juan Island, a jellyfish net in his hand, dressed in a checkered shirt and jeans, looking like he wanted to be anywhere but there.

For Tsutomu, high school was a joke. He had no patience for schoolwork he wasn't interested in. He had no respect for teachers he didn't believe were intelligent. Whether he was kicked out of high school or whether he left on his own free will is unclear—"basically, I was persona non grata," Tsutomu says. In any event, he never graduated.

Maybe that was because he'd found better things to do. By the time he was fifteen years old, he was hanging around the department of astrophysics at Princeton. He was a kind of child prodigy there, working on sophisticated projects like satellite image processing. When he was eighteen, much to his parents' relief, Tsutomu applied to the California Institute of Technology—Caltech—and was accepted. There he met his mentor, the physicist Richard Feynman.

Feynman was one of the more colorful characters in the history of modern science. He grew up in Far Rockaway, Queens, tinkering with radios and dazzling his colleagues on the high school math team, and went on to help build the nuclear bomb at Los Alamos and win a Nobel Prize for, as the Nobel Prize Committee put it, his "fundamental work in quantum electrodynamics with deep ploughing consequences for the physics of elementary particles." Meanwhile, he played bongo drums, seduced colleagues' wives, and impressed a whole generation of students with his brilliant, far-reaching, colorful lectures.

He was also a proto-hacker. At Los Alamos, while he was working on the bomb, he became fascinated by locks. He picked the locks on the Coke machine, on file cabinets, on safes in his colleagues' offices. Combination locks were the toughest—to crack them, he used a combination of psychology (he knew, for example, that many people left combinations on their desks, just as they do computer passwords today), and mechanical aptitude (he figured out that if the first number in a combination was 19, the tumbler was usually imprecise enough to recognize anything between 17 and 22. This dramatically cut the number of possible combinations). To Feynman, like to a hacker, a lock was an interesting problem, a kind of intellectual challenge.

When Tsutomu arrived at Caltech in September, 1983, Feynman was at the end of his career. He had already suffered one bout with the cancer that would kill him six years later. But Feynman took Tsutomu under his wing, and opened his eyes to the maverick possibilities at the intersection of physics and computers. Less than two years later, when Tsutomu was twenty, he was offered what amounted to a post-doctoral position at Los Alamos. It was quite an honor. Los Alamos was one of the premier computing and physics labs in the country—it was rare for them to offer a position to someone that young, and without a high school or college degree. It also had to be a little strange—here he was at the lab that built the bomb that vaporized his uncle and could have killed his mother and father. But if it bothered him, he didn't speak about it much.

At Los Alamos, Tsutomu worked in the "T" unit (for "theoretical"), which was, coincidentally, the same unit Feynman had once worked in. It was perhaps the most prestigious unit at the lab. Tsutomu's basic task was to take a complex problem in physics—say, hydrodynamics—and figure out a way to run it on a computer. It requires a rare ability to draw mental pictures of abstract equations, and then translate that picture into a language that a computer understands. This talent to literally "visualize" computer architectures and networks is Tsutomu's great gift. "Tsutomu is one of the few people I know who can 'see' cyberspace," says Larry Smarr, director of the National Center for Supercomputing Applications. "His mind can visualize all the complex data flows. He can 'see' it just like you or I can see a mountain range."

Los Alamos was too isolated for Tsutomu, however. The lab was in the middle of nowhere, everyone was older than him, the parties were boring. He much preferred life in San Diego, where he traveled in 1988 to work on a sabbatical at the San Diego Supercomputer Center, and then decided to stay. The San Diego Supercomputer Center is one of four computer think tanks founded by the National Science Foundation. It's affiliated with the University of California at San Diego, as well as numerous private companies, including many that are deeply involved in the defense industry.

Tsutomu found a house near the beach, and, when he wasn't out roller blading, worked on various computer modeling projects. He also made contacts with the National Security Agency, as well as the military, and helped develop software which, in time of war, might help analyze and penetrate enemy computer systems. It was experience that would come in handy when it came to tracking down hackers like Kevin Mitnick.

3

The first thing Tsutomu did after he learned of the break-in was to alert his friends and coworkers. He called Jay Dombrowski, the communications manager at the Supercomputer Center. He also called Dan Farmer, the outspoken, redheaded, motorcycle-boot-wearing computer security guru who was employed at the time by Silicon Graphics, a manufacturer of workstations and high-end computers. (Farmer has since moved to Sun Microsystems.) In his off-hours, Farmer had been working on a piece of software called Satan, which was a controversial point-and-click program that immediately highlighted the weaknesses in computer software (and which someone—Farmer thought it might have been Kevin—later stole a copy of).

At around midnight, Tsutomu turned up at a friend's office to borrow some computer equipment that he knew he'd need in the coming days. He was so upset-looking—he was shaking and distraught—that the security guard let him in without asking who he was.

"Tsutomu has a samurai sense of honor," says Brosl Hasslacher, a physicist at Los Alamos who worked with Shimomura. "He believes deeply in a kind of unspoken code of ethical behavior." He also has a samurai sense of humiliation. He didn't like the idea that his machine had been broken into, that his personal files might soon be spread all over the net. It certainly didn't do much for his reputation as a security expert. Even worse, he had a strong hunch who was behind it: Kevin.

Whoever it was, the intruder made off with a lot of goodies, including hundreds of megabytes of personal files and e-mail, as well as various security tools and cellular phone software. The intruder also grabbed a copy of Tsutomu's Berkeley Packet Filter, a surveillance tool developed under a research grant from the National Security Agency that can be slipped into a computer while it's running and can then snatch valuable bits of information as they fly by on the network. For a hacker, it's a stealth tool deluxe.

To Tsutomu, this was serious business. In his ongoing quest to test the limits of network security, he has, according to Hasslacher, written some of the most potentially destructive software in the world—what he calls Class 10 tools. "Tsutomu has built software that can literally destroy an alien computer," Hasslacher boasts. "They are essentially viruses that can, for example, tell a computer to sit in one register until it literally melts the circuitry in the chip or to command the hard drive to hit the same track 33,000 times—until it destroys the drive." Most computer security experts are highly dubious that such tools could work on anything but an old-fashioned PC, and suggest such talk may be more bluster than fact (Tsutomu, perhaps afraid of giving away his secrets, wouldn't talk about it). Fortunately, these weapons—if they indeed exist—were stored in a safe place.

By the next morning, Tsutomu was on a plane back to San Diego, where he began the tedious and complex process of sorting through his computer logs, trying to recreate the attack. It wasn't easy. Much of the data sources had been destroyed—"things were looking grim," he later told a security-industry newsletter. He began studying file access and modification times, which can reveal what someone did and when, as well as what kind of link the intruder had to the network. By correlating this data across about twenty gigabytes of information on four servers, he was able to determine the order in which the attack took place. But the mechanism of the attack was still unclear.

❖

By the beginning of the new year, a week or two after the break-in, Tsutomu had more or less pieced the puzzle together. On January 11th, he attended a computer-security conference at the Sonoma Mission Inn, a luxurious retreat in the Sonoma Valley frequented by celebrities and corporate dealmakers. The conference, called CMAD III, which stood for the 3rd Annual Workshop on Computer Misuse and Detection, drew a small, exclusive crowd of about seventy top academics, law enforcement officials, and industry reps. It was the Upper East Side of nerdsville, the elite guardians of the net.

Tsutomu made a Hollywood entrance. He'd been scheduled first thing that morning, but his presentation was delayed. No one had seen him around. Was he going to be a no-show? Word had gotten around that he had something important to talk about. Something big.

Just before noon, Tsutomu finally arrived. Even in this oddball crowd, Tsutomu was a sight: here it was well into winter, but he was wearing shorts, sandals, and a T-shirt. His long black hair was pulled back in a ponytail. Steve Lodin, a grad student at Purdue University who was attending the conference, knew immediately that something was up: "Tsutomu looked pretty agitated," Lodin recalls. Lodin watched him huddle around the table with a member of the Computer Emergency Response Team, a government center headquartered at Carnegie-Mellon University in Pittsburgh. There was electricity in the air. They shuffled papers and transparencies, trying to get organized. Then after a short break, Tsutomu's talk began.

He stood in front of the room and, in his rapid-fire, mechanical, thousand-word-a-minute style, he laid it out for them: how he had discovered on Christmas Day that his computer had been attacked, the complex and tedious search through his log files to try to figure out how it happened. By retracing the intruder's footsteps, he finally determined that his machine had been accessed by using a little-known and complex procedure called "IP spoofing."

What had happened, to put it as simply as possible, was that the intruder had figured out a way to mask an alien computer as a friendly face. It dialed up Tsutomu's machine and said, "Hi, I'm your friend X." Tsutomu's machine, thinking it was a pal, threw the door open and let it in. Once the intruder was into the system, he had root access—which meant he had the keys to every room in the house. He was then able to wander around as he pleased, opening drawers, inspecting the closets, rifling through the mail.

Of course, Tsutomu didn't have to explain the technical details to this crowd. The system's vulnerability had been known for a long time—two respected security experts, Robert Morris and Steve Bellovin, had published papers about it years earlier. But it was such an elaborate method of attack that it had rarely been used. In computer security lingo, it was "nontrivial." That meant it required a lot of time, a lot of patience, a lot of study, and a lot of guts.

Not only that, but much of the attack appeared to have been automated—that is, someone had written a computer program which had carried out the attack. That made the attack all the more alarming, because that meant it could be done by anyone with enough savvy to run the script—which meant, basically, that someone with slightly above average technical knowledge (by hacker standards, that is) like Kevin might indeed be able to pull it off.

Tsutomu's talk lasted about twenty minutes. Before it was over, he offered the crowd one last tidbit. He mentioned that shortly after the attack, two messages had been left on his voice mail, apparently in reference to the attack. He offered to play them back now. He turned the volume up on his computer as loud as it would go. The voices were a little fuzzy, but the people in the front of the room could hear it just fine.

"My technique is best," the first message began in what sounded like a mock-Japanese accent. "Damn you. I know sendmail technique. Don't you know who I am? Me and my friends, we'll kill you." Then another voice came on: "Hey boss, my Kung Fu is really good."

Then he played the second message: "Your technique will be defeated. Your technique is no good."

✢

The voices on the messages were too well disguised to be identifiable, but the taunting, disparaging tone was certainly Kevin's style.

There was another problem. If Kevin was involved in this, it was unlikely he was in it alone. At the very least, writing the code for the IP spoofing script required a technical expertise that even Kevin's friends agreed was out of his league. Technically, he was fine at exploiting simple holes in systems like the WELL or Netcom. They were big places, easy to get lost in. Tsutomu's machine was different. It had bells and whistles. Also, Tsutomu ran a Unix operating system, and Kevin's expertise was with Digital's VMS.

Did Kevin have a partner in crime? Or was he just a scapegoat? No one knew for sure.

✢

Two weeks after the CMAD conference, *The New York Times* sounded the general alarm. "Data Network is Found Open to New Threat," the front page headline read on Monday, January 23rd. "The new form of attack leaves many of the 20 million government, business, university and home computers on the global Internet vulnerable to eavesdropping and theft," John Markoff wrote. "For computer users, the problem is akin to homeowners discovering that burglars have master keys to all the front doors in the neighborhood."

That was true. It was also true that the key metaphor made the attack seem simpler than it really was. Also, the vulnerabilities to this type of intrusion could be greatly reduced by a simple change in routing protocols.

But the *Times* story was also a measure of how much things had changed in the computer culture. Two years earlier, a new vulnerability in the Internet would have meant nothing. But by 1995, the Internet was becoming America's spinal cord. To the established information order, it predicted a radically destabilizing future. The whole information industry was in turmoil: phone companies wanted to get into the cable TV business, the cable TV operators wanted to get into the phone business, new mergers in the software industry were announced every day, the old fiefdoms in Hollywood were crumbling. And no one was feeling it more than newspapers. Old kingmakers like the *Times* and *The Washington Post* saw their influence waning. To them, a hole in the net was welcome news. It reinforced what they already knew: that this was a world full of anarchists, thieves, and miscreants. Why not play it up?

✣

When Ron Austin saw the article in the *Times*, he knew Kevin was in trouble. Austin was the former hacker who had been busted, along with Kevin Poulsen, by hacker-turned-FBI-informant Justin Petersen. Unlike his two buddies, however, Austin is a decidedly nonthreatening character, at once thoughtful and trusting (both rare qualities in this crowd). Although Austin had no idea where Kevin was living or what he was doing, he had been in contact with Kevin for several months. Kevin would telephone him out of the blue, or they would leave messages for each other in Austin's account on Nyx, the hacker-friendly Internet provider at the University of Denver. Mostly, they exchanged information about Justin Petersen, who had betrayed them both, and for whom they shared a degree of bitterness.

They also talked about Kevin's life on the run. Like Lewis De Payne, who was also speaking to Kevin on the phone frequently, Austin would often urge Kevin to turn himself in—or leave the country. Austin says he went so far as to have his lawyer call the prosecutor's office and ask what kind of treatment Kevin could expect if he turned himself in. According to Austin, prosecutors refused to discuss it. When Kevin heard that, it only reinforced his fears that they would throw the book at him. It also redoubled his determination to keep running: "If that's how they want to play the game," Kevin told Austin, "then let them spend their money trying to catch me."

Austin knew that Kevin probably had something to do with the break-in to Tsutomu's machine. Kevin had mentioned Tsutomu's name several times, and Austin knew that in Kevin's search for the source code for OKI phones, Kevin had tried to get into Mark Lottor's machine. To Austin, it was natural that Kevin might go after Lottor's friend, Tsutomu, next.

Now, seeing this story about the break-in to Tsutomu's machine in the *Times*, Austin's worst fears were realized: the net was closing on Kevin. Even though there was no mention of it in the *Times* story, Austin knew that Markoff and Tsutomu suspected Kevin was behind it. Austin e-mailed Kevin a warning to be careful. He also phoned Markoff: "I bet the next thing you're going to write is a story about how it was Kevin Mitnick who did these break-ins," Austin told him. Markoff demurred— "I had no idea what I was going to write next, or how this was going to turn out," Markoff says.

As it turns out, Austin was right. Although like everything in this story, it wasn't quite that simple.

4

Charlie Pritchett picked up the ringing phone in his little office behind Hollingsworth Auto in Raleigh, North Carolina. It was January 4th, a chilly Wednesday morning. "U-Save Auto Rental," Pritchett said into the receiver, hitting the "U" hard, as if to emphasize that you really did save money renting from him.

"I'd like to get some information about renting a car," the voice on the other end of the line said.

"Local or long distance?"

"Local."

"Are you looking for any type of car in particular?"

"No, just solid reliable transportation. I've just arrived in town to look for a new job. I'm staying at the Friendship Inn in North Raleigh. Is that far from you?"

"No, not far," Pritchett said. "How soon do you need the car?"

"Right away. Tomorrow."

Pritchett checked to see what was in the yard. "I've got a Plymouth Horizon," he said. "Nice little blue four door. It'll get you around town."

"How much is it?"

Pritchett told him.

"That sounds like what I'm looking for. Do you require a credit card for a deposit?"

"Not if you're staying in the area and have a valid driver's license."

"No problem. Can you hold the car for me? I'll be down tomorrow."

"Sure. What's your name?"

"David Stanfill."

"How do you spell that?"

"S-T-A-N-F-I-L-L"

"Okay, it'll be here."

✣

In the rental car business, you deal with a lot of strangers. The strangers Pritchett meets are stranger than most. His customers are the people who can't afford to go to Hertz or Alamo. They don't have corporate expense accounts, and most of them don't have credit cards. They don't care what the car looks like, or if it has an auto-reverse tape deck, or if the fan belt squeaks. They just want cheap reliable transportation.

Pritchett is happy to oblige. U-Save Auto Rental is a one-man operation. His office is about the size of a freight elevator. There are stacks of used tires in the corner, it smells of grease and cigarette smoke. Still, it's not an unfriendly place. Pritchett has posters of Belize on the wall, and there's a Coke machine near the door. Pritchett himself is a gray man: short gray hair, gray eyes, a gray smoker's complexion. He's talkative and helpful. When customers come in to rent a car, he likes to yak. He'll tell you about his thirty years in the army reserve, where he was an operations sergeant. He likes to tell his customers how Capital Avenue—the road right in front of his shop—is old Route 1. "Just get on it and drive north," Pritchett likes to say. "It'll take you right to New York City."

Pritchett is also a booster for the city of Raleigh. Not that the city needs his help. Raleigh smells like a boomtown. The old tobacco-field languor is gone, replaced by Saturn dealerships and condo developments with names like "Quail Ridge" and cellular phone towers blinking at night on every hilltop. Everyone is from somewhere else. Thanks mainly to all the high-tech jobs at Research Triangle Park, the unemployment rate is about half the national average. The weather is mild, the beach is nearby, the mountains aren't far in the other direction. It's a paradise, of sorts. In 1994, *Money* magazine picked the Raleigh/Durham/Chapel Hill area as the top place in America to live. Visitors are greeted by signs along the highway: "Welcome to Raleigh/Durham. Top Place to Live in America. *Money* Magazine."

Nevertheless, Pritchett doesn't like to take any chances with strangers. You never know what kind of crazy shit somebody might pull. The world is full of kooks and weirdos and murderers.

That's why he keeps a 12 gauge pump-action shotgun under his desk. You can never be too careful.

❖

Pritchett thought he looked scruffy. He noticed him walking up through the used car lot in front of the U-Save office. Bushy dark hair. A couple of days' growth on his face. Carrying a nylon case on a strap over his shoulder—a laptop, Pritchett realized.

The bell above the door tinkled as he stepped inside. "Hi. I'm David Stanfill. I called you the other day about renting a car? I think you mentioned a blue Plymouth Horizon. . . ."

"Oh yeah, right," Pritchett said.

Pritchett makes it his business to size people up quickly. He doesn't want to rent a car to a nut, or to some lowlife who will leave it abandoned in a ditch. And when he looked at Stanfill, he liked what he saw. He seemed shy, friendly. He didn't seem to be in a hurry. Pritchett gave him a pen and a rental agreement form to fill out, and before he knew it, they were talking up a storm.

Stanfill told him that he was from Las Vegas. He said he'd worked at a company called American Information Technologies. He gave Pritchett his business card. It read: "M. David Stanfill. Systems Administrator. American Information Technologies, Inc. 3661 S. Maryland Parkway. Las Vegas, Nevada. 89109. 702-894-5418. Fax: 702-870-3411." It wasn't really a very professional-looking business card—it was cheaply produced, printed on flimsy white paper. But to Pritchett, it looked real enough. Stanfill told him that he was on leave from the company right now. He said he had come to Raleigh because he had just been through a messy divorce and he had to get away. He said he'd read about Raleigh in *Money* magazine, which rated it one of the best places in America to live, so he thought he should give it a try. He said he was looking for a job in the computer industry, something that paid around $30,000 or $40,000 a year.

That all sounded good to Pritchett. "Raleigh is a great place to live."

"It's a nice-looking town," Stanfill agreed.

"You ever had North Carolina barbecue?" Pritchett asked.

Stanfill said he hadn't.

"Well, you gotta try some while you're here."

"Where's the best place to get it around here?"

"Well, personally, I like to go to the Barbecue Lodge," Pritchett said. "It's just up the street a couple of blocks." He explained to Stanfill that North Carolina barbecue isn't like Texas barbecue or even South Carolina barbecue. "In North Carolina, we use only pork. There's no chicken or beef barbecue. And there's no tomatoes in it, either. Up here, it's vinegar based. It's completely different than anything you've ever had before."

By the time Stanfill drove off in the little blue Horizon, Pritchett had taken quite a shine to him. Ordinarily, before he let a car go off the lot without a credit card for security, he would have made a phone call and checked out Stanfill's references. In this case, he didn't. Why bother? He was obviously a decent guy. Pritchett felt bad for him, in fact. Going through a messy divorce, looking for a new job.

It's a tough world out there, Pritchett thought.

✛

A couple of days later, David Stanfill checked out of the Friendship Inn and moved to the Sundowner Inn. It's a no-nonsense, no-frills hotel directly across the street from Pritchett's U-Save Auto Rental. The marquee read: "Free Cont. Breakfast/HBO/Pool." The lobby was littered with brochures for local tourist attractions: "Visit a Real Tobacco Farm!" "The Smoky Mountains—a Vacationer's Guide to the Most Beautiful Spot on Earth."

Stanfill arrived in the middle of a busy afternoon. John Miles, the manager of the hotel, checked him in. Miles looks like a high school science teacher—short sleeve-dress shirt, glasses, durable trousers. He also noticed that Stanfill was carrying his laptop in a nylon case over his shoulder. He had one other small bag. Stanfill said he would be staying a few weeks, he wasn't sure. He wanted to pay day by day. That was fine with Miles. He charged him the corporate rate, $36.95 per night plus tax. Stanfill paid in cash.

Looking at the computer slung over Stanfill's shoulder, Miles thought about how much the world had changed. Computers were everywhere now. You could carry them around like a book. Not like the old days, when a computer was big and clunky and hard to use. Miles knew those days better than most. He had once run a small computer bulletin board out of his home. There were only a few hundred users on it. But he remembered one famed hacker who went by the name "The Condor." He had been a kind of celebrity. Miles wasn't sure, but he thought one time The Condor had logged onto his BBS. He didn't do anything, just poked around, checking it out. Miles hadn't thought about him in years. He didn't even know what his real name was.

For all he knew, it could have been David Stanfill.

5

What if Charlie Pritchett's comment about the highway outside his shop running all the way to New York City had piqued Kevin's curiosity? Suppose he was bored one afternoon, pixeled out and lonely, and decided to hop on Route 1 in that dumpy little Plymouth Horizon and drive north for about twenty hours, through Virginia; Maryland; Washington D.C.; Pennsylvania; then into New Jersey, and finally across the George Washington Bridge into Manhattan. He might have driven downtown on Broadway, past Times Square, past the Flatiron Building, until he hit Union Square, turned east at around 14th Street, and found himself sitting in front of a club called Irving Plaza.

If he had arrived at about 8 P.M. on the night of the January 12, he would have seen a crowd outside the front door, many of them pale, thin, their eyes hollowed out from too much time in front of a computer screen. He might have recognized them as kindred spirits. He might have seen a twenty-year-old kid get out of a car, trailed by reporters from *The New York Times*, *The Washington Post*, *New York* magazine. He would have seen flashbulbs and cameras and the undeniable excitement of celebrity in New York. He probably would have recognized the twenty-year-old kid in the center of it all as Mark Abene, a.k.a. Phiber Optik. Abene had just spent ten months in a federal prison for computer trespassing, and now he was being feted like Huey Newton had once been, a radical outlaw who had become the darling of fashionable New York.

Maybe Kevin would have gotten out of his car and followed Abene into the club and listened to him as he gave interviews to reporters and talked about cleaning toilets at the federal penitentiary. Maybe he would have heard him talk about how the judge had hoped to make him a symbol of what happens to hackers who get caught. All it took was one look around the room, with all the flashing lights and the groupie girls and the press and the glory to understand that maybe this wasn't exactly the kind of symbol the judge had intended to transform Abene into.

Would Kevin have been envious? Would he have been angry? Would he have understood that no matter how much he hacked, no matter what he stole, he would never be coddled and smooched and respected like Abene? Would he understand that he was not handsome enough, not young enough, not *simple* enough, for all of this? Abene had the glow of youth, of the handsome rebel, of a kid with an unstoppable curiosity about how things worked. He was incorrigible but unthreatening. Any fair-minded person could see that he did not belong in a federal prison shoveling snow and scrubbing toilets and staring out the bars of his window at the moon.

Kevin probably would have felt old in that pulsing crowd. He wasn't easy with strangers. Kevin had too much at stake in all this. Hacking wasn't a game for him, an intellectual quest, an exercise in personal freedom. It was a place for him to hide, where no one would ask him questions, where he could live by his own rules. He was not a criminal, his moral code was at least as solid as Abene's— *Phiber was just a kid, for chrissakes. He was still living at home with mommy and daddy.* But Abene wasn't a con artist. He didn't take pleasure in tweaking people the way Kevin did. Kevin fancied himself a one-man information economy. He collected information, and then he used it as a lever to get more.

Anyone with half a brain could see that Abene had a future in front of him. He already had a job at Echo, a hip New York City computer bulletin board. He had a sweet and attractive girlfriend who adored him. He was young and, as computer types go, handsome. It was easy to imagine him as a featured speaker at computer security conferences or, a few years down the road, as a lavishly paid security consultant.

Kevin only had a past. He had *Cyberpunk*. He had the dark memories of his stepfathers. He had a mother who didn't understand. He had a half brother dead from a drug overdose. He had an uncle who had pled guilty to manslaughter. He had friends who betrayed him. He had arrest warrants. He had paranoia. He had anger. He had fear.

6

On January 27th, a system administrator at the WELL, during a routine system maintenance check, ran a program called Disk Hog. Disk Hog looks for—you guessed it—disk hogs: it checks all the files on the computer to see which ones are taking up too much space. The program indicated that the file for the Computer, Freedom, and Privacy Conference, which was usually almost empty, was taking up an enormous amount of space: 158 megabytes.

To find out what was going on, Gail Williams, a

system administrator at the WELL, called Bruce Koball, a technical consultant in Berkeley, and one of the organizers of the annual CFP conference (the very same conference, in fact, where FBI agents had thought they'd spotted Kevin the previous March. Coincidence, or inside joke?). Koball looked over the file and realized very quickly it had nothing to do with CFP. Among other things, there were more than two megabytes of compressed e-mail, most of it to or from "tsutomu@sdsc.edu," and Koball had no idea who that was.

For the WELL, however, the implication was obvious. They had been hacked. The intruder apparently had access to the deepest recesses of their system and presumably could, if he wanted to, cause serious damage or even bring the entire system down. System administrators at the WELL called Electronic Frontier Foundation cofounder John Perry Barlow and asked "Who's the hottest hacker tracker around?"

Two names leapt to Barlow's mind: Bill Cheswick and Tsutomu Shimomura. He figured that Cheswick, a network security specialist at AT&T Bell Labs, would be unavailable, but he agreed to give Tsutomu a call. He had met Tsutomu several years earlier at what Barlow calls "a spook conference," and knew that Tsutomu was a smart and courtly fellow who might relish the chance to help.

When Barlow called, however, Tsutomu balked. He already had enough troubles of his own—at the time, he had no idea the break-in at the WELL had any connection to the Christmas Day attack on his own machine. Barlow leaned on him a little, and Tsutomu finally agreed—"basically as a favor to Barlow," Tsutomu recalls.

✣

Late that night, Koball picked up the Northern California edition of the next day's *New York Times* off his doorstep. When he sat down to read it a few minutes later, he happened to notice, on the front page of the business section, an article by John Markoff titled, "Taking Computer Crime to Heart."

It was a piece about Tsutomu, the man of the moment, and how he was grappling with the aftermath of the Christmas Day break-in to his computer. "It was as if the thieves, to prove their prowess, had burglarized the locksmith. Which is why Tsutomu Shimomura, the keeper of the keys in this case, is taking the break-in as a personal affront—and why he considers solving the crime a matter of honor," the *Times* piece read. There was no mention of Tsutomu the brilliant cell phone hacker or explorer of gray areas of the law. This time, he came off as a cartoonish superhero, a kind of cyber-batman ready to fight on the side of goodness and Mom's apple pie: ". . . more than anything else, Mr. Shimomura, who is thirty, wants to help the Government catch the crooks. And while he acknowledges that the thieves were clever, Mr. Shimomura has also uncovered signs of ineptitude that he says will be the intruders' eventual undoing . . . 'Looks like the ankle-biters have learned to read technical manuals,' Mr. Shimomura said derisively. 'Somebody should teach them some manners.' "

When Koball read this, alarm bells went off in his head. Now he knew exactly who "tsutomu@sdsc.edu" was. He called the WELL immediately, and then contacted Markoff, whom he had known for years. Markoff put him in touch with Tsutomu, and before long, it was confirmed: the files discovered at the WELL were the same ones copied from Tsutomu's machine on Christmas Day.

7

Sometime toward the end of January—Pritchett isn't very good with exact dates—Stanfill called and asked if it was okay if he drove his rental car to Hilton Head Island, a popular resort several hours north of Raleigh. He said a friend was coming into town and they wanted to take a drive, do some sightseeing, maybe a little golfing.

"The car is for local use only," Pritchett said, reminding him of the rental agreement.

"Okay, no problem," Stanfill said, then told Pritchett he'd return the car while he was away.

The call impressed Pritchett. Some people would have just taken the car to Hilton Head and never told him about it. In fact, judging from the mileage on some of the cars that are returned, a *lot* of people do that. Not Stanfill. It made Pritchett think that he had been right about him from the beginning, that he was a good guy down on his luck. You don't run across many guys like that in the bottom end of the rental car business.

Pritchett was so taken by Stanfill, in fact, that he decided to see what he could do to help him find a job. He called a couple friends in the electronics business, told them about Stanfill, and asked them if they knew of any job opening. They didn't, but they said they'd ask around.

The next day, Stanfill returned the car. Pritchett was struck by how much better he looked— shaved, his hair shorter, wearing nicer clothes. "Good news," he told Pritchett. "I think I've found an apartment." He didn't have a job yet, but said he was working on a few leads. He seemed looser and happier than the last time Pritchett had seen him, as if things were starting to go his way.

✛

The Player's Club apartment complex is Raleigh's *Melrose Place*. Everyone who lives there seems to be in their late twenties, the parking lot is full of Neons and Hondas and motorcycles and sailboats. Sixteen gray and blue townhouses are clumped around a central green. Each unit contains four or six apartments (it varies depending on whether they're studios, one bedrooms, or two-bedroom/two-bath penthouses). There are several tennis courts, a gym, a lounge area with a big screen TV, and most important, the pool. The outdoor portion of the pool is kidney shaped and surrounded by lounge chairs, which, on warm days, are inevitably populated by young, firm bodies. The indoor portion of the pool, divided by a wall that you swim under, is smaller, designed for lap swimming on winter days. There are also a Jacuzzi, a sauna, and a weight room nearby. Like a lot of places devoted to fitness and good living, it has a slightly tawdry feel to it—the water in the pool is heavily chlorinated, the lounge looks lonely when it isn't crammed with Tar Heels fans.

Kevin rented a small studio apartment, number 202, in a building on the southwest side of the complex, on the second floor. From his window, he could just see the tops of the sweet gums and red pines in William B. Ulmstead State Park, which is only a mile or so down the road. The apartment had just one room with a small bathroom and kitchen. But it was nicely appointed—nicer in every way than the depressing cave he had lived in in Seattle. It had a microwave and a sofa that folded out into a bed and silver shag carpet and matching wallpaper and a breakfast bar with two wooden stools. It was bright, clean, and friendly. It was an easy commute to Research Triangle Park. There was a McDonald's within walking distance, as well as Burger King, Domino's Pizza, Chinatown Express, Bruegel's Bagels, and Jersey Mike's Subs. There was also a Kinko's nearby, and a Circuit City. For Kevin, it had to be pretty close to paradise.

He signed the lease under the name Glenn Thomas Case. Rent was $510 a month, plus $255 for security deposit. As usual, Kevin paid in cash.

8

At about the same time Kevin was moving into the Player's Club, a posse was assembling at the WELL. Andrew Gross flew up from San Diego and met with the system administrators at the WELL to begin plotting how to proceed. Dan Farmer showed up briefly, as did several other colleagues. It was supposed to be all very hush-hush, but the computer security community is a gossipy and tight-knit group, and word had gotten around.

Tsutomu, meanwhile, had other business to take care of. On February 2nd and 3rd, he was in Palm

Springs at the posh Westin Mission Hills Inn for another security conference. He made another presentation about the break-in to his computer on Christmas Day, going over much of the same material he had gone over at CMAD a few weeks earlier. And, as before, he used this as a way to point out the larger security dangers of electronic communications. He predicted that as more material of commercial value is transmitted via the net, more attacks will be imminent. "We should predict more sophisticated attacks, as there will be more incentive," Tsutomu told the crowd.

It was an important message. By going out of his way to publicize the break-in to his machine, Tsutomu had done several things. First, he had alerted his peers to the previously overlooked vulnerability of computers on the Internet—one that posed a significant threat, even it if was, for most mortals, extraordinarily difficult to pull off.

He was also rehabilitating his own reputation. If his computer was vulnerable, it wasn't because he was less-than-attentive to the security of his own machine. It was because he had deliberately set it up that way. "Tsutomu does the software equivalent of putting a hair over the door," Larry Smarr of the National Supercomputer Applications Center says, echoing others in the computer establishment who were in no hurry to wonder why a security pro like Tsutomu had had his personal e-mail and security tools scattered all over the Internet. "He invites people in, just to see what they can do, just so they can point out the holes in his system. While they're in there, he records as much data as he can about them, so that if he wants to go out and find them, he'll have plenty of evidence."

Before the conference was over, Smarr bumped into Tsutomu in the hotel lobby. As usual, Tsutomu had a new gadget he wanted to show off—a tiny Hewlett-Packard palmtop computer with a cellular scanner—basically, a hacked cellular phone—hooked up to it. He gave Smarr a demonstration. He turned on the scanner, and a log of all the cell phone activity that was going on in the surrounding area appeared on the screen of the palmtop. Listening in on any of those calls would be, strictly speaking, against the law.

But Tsutomu, as usual, was more interested in making machines do interesting tricks than he was in violating anyone's privacy. That is one of the differences between Tsutomu and Kevin.

❖

Tsutomu spent a short time at the WELL before he and his crew determined that most of the intruder's activity was coming through Netcom. So they moved their operation down to San Jose, hoping to get a better vantage point. Netcom's headquarters are in the heart of Silicon Valley in a glass-skinned building directly across the street from the Winchester Mystery House, an enduring landmark of the Old West that was built with the fortune made from an earlier technological breakthrough: the Winchester repeating rifle.

The first night, Tsutomu and Gross set up shop in the office of Robert Hood, the network manager at Netcom. Tsutomu spent most of his time watching his screen, matching incoming logs from the WELL with outgoing logs from Netcom. By doing this they were able to determine that Kevin was gaining access to Netcom on an account named "gkremen" (not a surprising discovery, since it was the same account Kevin had apparently been using when he broke into Lile Elam's machine). When Tsutomu and Gross looked up the name in the membership directory, they discovered—as Elam had—that it was a legitimate user's account that the intruder had taken over.

Tsutomu began logging Kevin's activities. They could sit there in Hood's office and, unbeknownst to Kevin, watch everything that he was doing. Like Neill Clift, who had been monitoring Kevin over the summer, Tsutomu was using special surveillance software he had written himself. Tsutomu's gear allowed him to capture it all keystroke for keystroke in a precisely timed log, almost as if he were making a video of a burglar in action.

There was little question it was Kevin. One of the passwords they watched him use was "fucknmc"—presumably, that referred to Neill M. Clift, who had betrayed him a few months earlier. He titled a file of Tsutomu's stuff "Japboy." They would watch him skim Markoff's e-mail, looking for the letters "itni" to see if his name was mentioned. Tsutomu and Gross watched the intruder complain on IRC—a live talk feature on the Internet—that Markoff had put his picture on the front page of the *Times*, and, presumably, caused him much grief. He apparently thought Markoff was feeding information to the FBI about him, and speculated openly about what he might do for revenge.

Kevin also chatted via IRC with a friend in Israel, which brought up questions of international espionage. Was Kevin involved in something bigger than they had imagined? At that point, no one knew. It was still unfolding before their eyes.

Then there were the credit card numbers. One night Mark Seiden, another computer security consultant who was involved in the chase, was watching Kevin's activities at Internex, a small Bay Area Internet provider that Kevin was also accessing. After watching Kevin—or a person he believed to be Kevin—stash a 140-megabyte file on the WELL for safekeeping, Seiden decided to download it and have a look. It turned out to be full of goodies, including the encrypted password file for Apple's Internet gateway, various tools for breaking into Sun computers, as well as purloined cellular phone software. He also discovered the same file that Orton had discovered on "Brian Merrill's" computer several months earlier: the complete Netcom customer database, including a file named "Cards," which contained 32,000 customer records—names, addresses, phone numbers, as well as some 21,600 credit card numbers.

Anyone who has any experience with the computer underground knows that lists of credit card numbers are not rare. They are to hackers what a nice set of racks are to deerhunters—something to hang on the wall and brag about. In fact, there was reason to believe that this particular list of credit cards had been stolen from Netcom in January 1994, and had been drifting around in the computer underground as a kind of trophy for over a year. And there was no evidence that Kevin ever used any of these credit cards for personal gain. Nevertheless, purloined credit card numbers are a legal hot button—it's something everyone can relate to. And in Kevin's case, it just added weight to the argument that he was doing things he wasn't supposed to be doing.

For Tsutomu, the only real question was how to find Kevin. Because of the bust in Seattle, they knew he was probably working with a laptop computer and a cellular modem. The FBI apparently believed he was in the Denver area. But when they checked where "gkremen" was logging in from, they found that the person using the account was dialing in from all over the country via local points of presence (POPs). Like most other Internet providers, Netcom can be accessed via local dial-up numbers—POPs—so customers don't need to make a long-distance call to dial into the system. Some of the calls on the "gkremen" account were coming in from Minneapolis, others were from Denver and Atlanta. But the majority were coming in from Raleigh, North Carolina.

With the help of the FBI, they got a warrant for a "trap-and-trace" on the Raleigh dial-up number. The next time Kevin dialed in, they were able to trace the call back to its point of origin—it turned out that it was coming from the Sprint cellular phone network in Raleigh. When Tsutomu dialed that number back, however, he just got a strange "clunking" sound on the line, indicating that, in all likelihood, Kevin was playing games with the phone switch.

9

Deputy Kathleen Cunningham was oblivious to all this high-tech maneuvering. On February 9th, she and Deputy Jeff Tyler drove across the desert to Las Vegas again. They had heard about what had happened in Seattle, and figured another plea to the family couldn't hurt. If anyone was going to lead them to Kevin, they thought it was Reba and Shelly.

They decided to go to Reba's place first, since it was on their way to Shelly's. They didn't call or announce that they were coming—they just showed up on Reba's doorstep.

As Cunningham came up the walk, she glanced through the windows on either side of the front door. She could see all the way through to the kitchen, where she noticed three people sitting around a table. She recognized Reba and Shelly, but the third person was a male. Long hair, heavy-set—the thought flashed through Cunningham's mind—is it Kevin? She glanced at Tyler—he was thinking the same thing.

Tyler knocked. Shelly opened the door. She recognized Cunningham and Tyler immediately, and her face fell. But to Cunningham's surprise, Shelly was more civil this time. She invited them into the house, and they were soon joined by Reba. Tyler was checking out the guy at the table. He didn't move, he didn't try to slip off or flee. Not Kevin.

Cunningham then launched into what was becoming a well-crafted pitch: Kevin was getting himself in deeper. If he got caught in another criminal act, he could be in serious trouble. If they only had him on probation violation, that was not a big deal. She told Shelly and Reba about what had happened in Seattle, how close he had come to being caught. She argued powerfully and passionately that Kevin should turn himself in now: "I know it's not an easy thing to do, but it really is the best thing for him."

Shelly seemed to listen more closely to what she

was saying this time. "The matter is out of our hands," she said regretfully.

"What do you mean?"

"It's out of our hands," she repeated.

When Cunningham pressed for more, Shelly would only say, "He's not very happy with us right now."

Reba had dropped the Dumb and Dumber routine she had affected last time. She frankly admitted that if Kevin were hiding upstairs in the bedroom, she wouldn't tell them.

Still, it was a cordial meeting, friendly and low-key. Perhaps Kevin's mother and grandmother were coming to grips with the fact that there was nothing they could do to save Kevin. Or perhaps they were just in a good mood. Tyler used Reba's bathroom before they left; she offered them sodas for the road. Shelly gathered her things and headed off to work. On the way out, she recommended that Cunningham and Tyler check out the buffet at a casino called the Rio before they drove back to LA. "It's the best buffet in town."

Cunningham and Tyler decided to give it a try. The Rio was way off the beaten path, but Shelly was right—it was a nice spread of food.

✧

At about the same time that Cunningham and Tyler were driving back from Las Vegas, Dwayne Rathe, a fraud investigator at Sprint's corporate headquarters in Chicago, got a call from Special

Agent Levord Burns of the FBI. Burns told Rathe he needed Sprint's assistance in tracking down a computer hacker whom they believed was operating in the Raleigh area, and who might be using a cloned cellular phone on Sprint's network. Rathe agreed to help, and called the Sprint switch in Raleigh to have them check it out. But because it was a Saturday, no one was around. The call was automatically forwarded to Jim Murphy, who happened to be the technician on call.

The word "switch" harks back to the old days when telephone calls were routed by mechanical switchboards. These days, phone networks are entirely computerized, but the term lingers on. The switch is the centralized computer that sorts all the calls from a given area and routes them to their destination, whether it's local or long-distance.

It was a lucky break for Tsutomu and the FBI that Rathe's call was sent to Jim Murphy. Murphy is a big, good-humored, indefatigable thirty-four year old from Minnesota who has been around telephone networks since 1979—the prehistoric days in this rapidly changing business. He got his training in the military, where he worked on microwave radios, then moved on to U.S. West and other growing young phone companies. He came to Sprint in 1993 as a switch technician, which basically means that he oversees and maintains the complex central computers that monitor and route all the calls on Sprint's network in one region. He knows everything there is to know about how phones work, and how someone like Kevin might go about trying to beat the system.

Rathe briefed Murphy on what was up: the FBI was trying to track down a computer hacker, and they had a phone number that they believed was being dialed out of the Sprint network in Raleigh. The FBI wanted Sprint to check the number to verify that it was being used, and to see if they could determine where the caller was dialing in from.

So Murphy called Levord Burns, who was still down at FBI headquarters in Quantico, Virginia. Burns gave him the number they suspected Kevin was using and asked Murphy to see if he could find any activity on that number. So at about 5 P.M. on a Saturday afternoon, Murphy got in his car and drove in to his office at the Sprint switch in Garner, just outside of Raleigh.

The Sprint switch in Garner, one of several Sprint maintains in North Carolina, is located in a spooky and mysterious spot, cut out of a grove of red pines and poplars behind a shopping mall the size of Rhode Island. It's a cinder-block building surrounded by a chain-link fence. On top of the buildling, like an enormous horn, a tall metal tower reaches up to the sky. Several red lights pulse at the top, a warning for aircraft. Inside, there are several small offices, as well as the switch itself.

Murphy spent about four hours at the switch that night going over Sprint's calling records, but found nothing. He decided to try checking it other ways—he searched the dial digits, and found nothing. He searched Sprint's subscriber list, but found that they had no customer listed with the suspicious number. Finally, when he was just about ready to give up, he checked to see if the number had been called *from* the Sprint network, and he found it. He also discovered a very peculiar thing— it wasn't a cellular phone call at all. The call was apparently coming in on a land line, and it was going out on a land line. Very bizarre. This was, after all, supposed to be a cellular phone network. Calls handled by the Raleigh switch either came in on a cell phone, and went out on a land line, or they came in on a land line, and they went out to a cell phone.

Murphy had never seen anything like it.

It was getting late, 10:30 or so, and Murphy decided to head home. On the way, he called Burns and explained what he had found. Murphy tossed out various scenarios about how this could happen—most of them had to do with breaking into the local GTE phone switch and messing around with the routing. The level of technical detail quickly got too much for Burns, who then asked him to call back and they would have a conference call with Tsutomu.

Murphy got home, kissed his wife, wolfed down a pork chop, and then waited for Burns to call back for the conference call. Burns didn't want to talk about this anymore on Murphy's cellular line—he was apparently afraid that Kevin might somehow be listening in—so he made Murphy go down to a pay phone on the corner and call him from there. Murphy stood there in the freezing wind, waiting for Burns to get them all hooked up, but apparently the complexities of a conference call were too much, and Burns couldn't get it working. Murphy offered to drive back to his office to set up the conference call from there.

It was about midnight when all three of them finally got on the line together. They talked for a moment about the different scenarios Kevin might be using to manipulate the phone network (although Murphy didn't refer to him by name at the time—he had no idea who it was they were after). Murphy brought up the possibility that he had broken into the switch at GTE, the company that provides local phone service in the area.

"What does this guy know?" Murphy asked. "How good is he?"

"Oh, he's the best," Tsutomu replied. "He probably knows the inner workings of the switch better than the people at GTE."

"Well, if I were trying to do what this guy is doing, here's how I'd work it," Murphy said. Then he offered a scenario: maybe he had broken into the GTE switch and manipulated the call failure feature. Maybe he had set it up so that when he dialed a certain invalid number, instead of getting a fast busy signal, or an automated message that says, "Your call cannot be completed as dialed," the switch would route the call out to a local Internet access provider. It was a sophisticated trick, but it might explain why the call was both coming in and going out of the Sprint network on a regular land line.

Tsutomu agreed that that might be a possibility. It didn't help them much right now, however. They still didn't have any hard proof that Kevin was in the Raleigh area.

"What else can you do a search on?" Tsutomu asked.

"Well, if you have any other numbers that you think he might have dialed, I can check those," Murphy said.

So Tsutomu gave him a bunch of numbers, mostly Internet access points he suspected Kevin had dialed into. They were all long-distance: Denver, Seattle, a lot in Minneapolis.

Murphy said he'd check them out.

He went back to the phone detail logs, and within a half hour, he'd found the numbers. Kevin had apparently gone to great lengths to mask the local calls he was making, but he'd left himself wide open on long-distance. Once Murphy had found the calls, it was a simple matter of checking the cellular phone number where the calls had originated. It was the same process Young and Pazaski had used in Seattle—find the tower the calls are coming in on, and that will give you a general idea of where the caller is.

Murphy called Tsutomu back and said, "He's here."

⁂

A few hours later, Deputy Cunningham's home phone rang. It was 3:30 A.M. on Sunday morning, February 12th. It was Tsutomu. "We've got Kevin located at a cell site near Raleigh," he told her. He sounded rushed, almost frantic. He said he was leaving on a flight to North Carolina at 9:20 A.M. and that he wanted her to arrange for a deputy from the U.S. Marshal's office to meet him at the airport. And he wanted the deputy to be sure to bring along a "trigger fish"—a sophisticated cellular phone tracking device that could follow up to six calls at once so they could get started tracking him down immediately.

Cunningham looked at the clock again: *it was 3:30 A.M. on a Sunday morning. Was he nuts? This is not Manuel Noriega we're after. This is Kevin Mitnick, computer punk.*

"The best I can do is Monday morning," Cunningham said.

Tsutomu got upset. He didn't want to wait until Monday morning.

Cunningham agreed to see what she could do. Later that morning, she went into her office and made a few calls. She called Kathleen Carson, an FBI agent assigned to the case, and explained Shimomura's demands. "Don't worry, we've got it covered," Carson told her.

10

At about the same time Tsutomu was boarding the plane in California for his flight to Raleigh, Joe Orsak, a senior maintenance engineer for Sprint, was just coming home from church. Orsak lives in Holly Springs, a small town outside of Raleigh, very close to where he grew up. He's thirty-two years old, a big, trusting, happy-go-lucky guy with glasses and short brown hair. He looks, in fact, like the son of a career military man, which he is. When the phone rang, Orsak was outside, uncoiling the garden hose, getting ready to give his maroon 1991

Chevy Blazer a bath. Like most engineers, Orsak has a fond feeling for his mechanical possessions, and likes to take good care of them.

The call was from Orsak's boss, Gordon Fonville, the Sprint network supervisor. Orsak wasn't surprised. He often gets called in at odd and inopportune times—like when he's loading up the Blazer to go bass fishing. Unlike his pal Jim Murphy, who basically has a desk job, Orsak is always on the run. His job is to keep the physical structures of the network tuned for peak performance. When lightning hits a cell tower, Orsak is the one who drives out to the site and realigns it. The entire cellular network is surprisingly delicate. Every autumn, when the leaves fall, Orsak has to drive around North Carolina and recalibrate the towers. Then in the spring, when the leaves return, he realigns them again.

But this time, Fonville wasn't calling about a lightning strike. "We have a fraud problem in progress," Fonville said. He gave Orsak a two-minute rundown on what was going on: Tsutomu was flying into town from California, the FBI was involved. Fonville wanted him to work with Tsutomu to help track the guy down. Fonville didn't mention Kevin Mitnick by name, but he suggested to Orsak that he was a fairly notorious hacker. A hacker? Orsak didn't know much about hackers. He'd heard about them, he knew what they could do, but he'd never tried to track one down before.

He had, however, been on fox hunts. That's

what short wave radio enthusiasts call it when they bury a short wave radio receiver in the woods or in a dumpster somewhere and a bunch of ham radio guys drive around to see who can find it first. Orsak had done that plenty of times. And he was pretty good at it. More than once, he'd found the "fox" before any of his buddies.

Tracking a hacker shouldn't be much different, he thought.

❖

Orsak knew this was going to be a stealth operation. He decided to use his personal car, the Blazer, instead of his Sprint van with the big logo on the side that could be seen for miles around. He grabbed the stuff he was going to need—his briefcase, some papers, his pager, his cell phone, his Epson laptop, as well as his tracking device, a CellScope 2000. It was basically the same rig that Young had used in Seattle months earlier.

By 2 P.M. or so, Orsak was on the road. It was about a forty-five minute drive to Raleigh, first through tobacco fields and stands of pines, then gradually moving into suburbia. His first stop was the Sprint switch in Garner, where Murphy's office is located.

Orsak pulled the Blazer up to the gate, punched the security code. The gate swung open, and he drove in. He parked and headed straight for Murphy's desk. He and "Murph," as Orsak called him, are bar buddies. They're about the same age, they have the same encyclopedic knowledge of cellular phone networks. Murphy is the more settled of the two—he's married, with three kids, a desk job—but you get the sense that they were cast from the same mold.

When Orsak arrived, Murphy brought him up to speed on what was going on. He showed Orsak the call records, and they determined that the calls were coming in from sector 3 and 4 on cell tower #19 in North Raleigh. Orsak knew the spot well—he'd been out there many times.

Although tracking down criminals was all new to Orsak, Murphy had been through it before. About nine months earlier, Murphy and another Sprint engineer had been going over call records when he noticed an unusually high volume of cellular calls from Raleigh to Kuwait, Pakistan, Egypt, Sri Lanka, Nepal, Lebanon, and other countries. Sprint alerted the Secret Service, who suspected they had stumbled upon a call-sell operation. Sprint estimated that they had racked up $300,000 in fraudulent calls in just a couple of days (in contrast, it took Kevin over four months to run up about $15,000 worth of calls in Seattle).

Using tracking equipment similar to what Orsak had in his Blazer, Murphy and a couple of other Sprint technicians were able to quickly pinpoint where the calls were coming from. Late one night, Secret Service agents raided a shabby two-story house in Knightsdale, on the outskirts of Raleigh. It was a bare-bones operation—no furniture and little food in the kitchen. In one room on the first floor, agents found a thirty-seven-year-old Pakistani national talking on a cellular phone. Upstairs, they found two other Pakistanis in a room with seventeen cellular phones, a computer, and stacks of electronic and telephone equipment. They were all arrested and charged with access device fraud. Secret Service agents believed the men were part of a major call-sell operation, possibly relaying calls overseas for customers in New York. The men were convicted and received prison sentences ranging from eight to twenty-one months.

It was a dramatic arrest, but it wasn't the only high-tech crime to hit Raleigh in recent months. In September 1994, Secret Service agents arrested Ivy James Lay, a twenty-nine-year-old switch engineer at MCI's headquarters in the Raleigh suburbs. Lay was charged with installing a special piece of software into MCI's main switching computer that would allow Lay to steal calling card numbers as they flew by on the network. Over a period of several months, he pulled in some 60,000 numbers, which he then sold for three to five dollars each. Phone companies estimated the loss at $28 million; Lay's attorney put it at a more modest $7 million.

The arrest of Lay led the Secret Service to Max Louran, a twenty-two-year-old citizen of Majorca, Spain, who had purchased thousands of numbers from Lay, and who they believed to be running an international ring of criminal phone hackers who had cost phone companies upwards of $140 million.

In a sophisticated sting operation, FBI and Secret Service agents lured Louran to Dulles Airport near Washington, D.C., where he was seized. He eventually pleaded guilty to wire fraud and conspiracy to traffic in unauthorized calling cards and was ordered to pay $1 million in restitution.

All in all, it was one of the biggest high-tech busts in history, with millions of dollars at stake, international intrigue, a dramatic arrest, and clear criminal intent. What it didn't have was media coverage. The story got five hundred words in *The Washington Post*, one paragraph on the second page of the business section in *The New York Times*, and two sentences in *Newsweek*.

11

Although they had never met, Murphy didn't
have much trouble finding Tsutomu at the Raleigh
airport that night. He was at the phone bank in the
American Airlines terminal, just as he had said he
would be. And he was, of course, as usual, *as always*,
on the phone. Tsutomu had given Murphy a description of himself earlier—"I'll be wearing a purple jacket," Tsutomu had said—but that detail
wasn't exactly necessary. Here it was the middle of
winter, and Tsutomu was standing there in shorts,
sandals, and a purple fleece jacket, his long black

hair flowing over his shoulders, his big laptop slung over one shoulder. Not your average tourist in the land of Jesse Helms.

Orsak was waiting in Murphy's Sprint van at the curb. Murphy and Tsutomu hopped in, and immediately Tsutomu started filling them in on what was going on. For the first time, he told them that the guy they were going after was named Kevin Mitnick, that he was a hacker who had been on the run for several years, that he suspected him of breaking into his computer and the computers of friends of his, and that, come hell or high water, they were going to catch him now. Orsak and Murphy felt as if they had stumbled into a movie of the week. They drove around the parking lot in circles for a few minutes, listening to Tsutomu's rapid-fire delivery.

They finally ended up at the Budget Rent a Car office. Tsutomu hopped out and rented a clean little Geo Prizm.

Tsutomu followed Orsak and Murphy back to the switch, which would be command central for the operation. It was Sunday night, the streets were empty. As they approached the shopping mall near the switch, the parking lot looked like a vast asphalt prairie. Sodium streetlights gave everything a yellowish cast. They wound along the access road behind the mall, making a right turn into the woods. The lights from the mall were gone now, blocked out by a thicket of pines. They drove several hundred yards to the entrance to the switch, where they found Special Agent Lathell Thomas of the FBI waiting for them. He had parked his white Crown Victoria just outside the gate. It was a cold night, perfectly silent. High above them, the red lights of the tower pulsed slowly.

Murphy got out and punched the code; the gate swung open. Orsak pulled the van in, and Tsutomu and Agent Thomas pulled their cars in behind them. The four of them shook hands and chatted a little as they walked into the cinder-block building. Agent Thomas, a local FBI man who worked out of an office in Raleigh, was no expert in computer or cellular phone hacking. That was clear to Orsak right away. Thomas had a file with him—pictures of Kevin, a physical description, copies of his arrest record, etc. In his slow, bluesy North Carolina drawl, Thomas went over basic surveillance tactics: don't drive around in circles because it looks suspicious, don't use your cellular phone because someone might be monitoring it, keep a low profile. Although it would be a nice dramatic touch to paint this scene as full of prehunt tension, it really wasn't. At least not to Orsak. They all knew there was nothing dangerous about what they were going to do—Mitnick had no history of violence, it wasn't as if he were going to come after them brandishing a gun. The worst that could happen is that Kevin might get wind of what they were doing and disappear again.

Once the procedural matters were out of the way, Tsutomu, Murphy, and Orsak decided that the best thing to do would be to visit the cell tower where most of Kevin's calls had been coming in. It was about twelve miles away, on the north side of Raleigh. Murphy decided he would stay behind so that he could watch what was going on at the switch.

So Orsak and Tsutomu hopped into Orsak's Blazer and headed across town. They were followed by Agent Thomas in his Crown Victoria, who wanted to stick around for a while just to make sure everything went smoothly. On the way, Tsutomu and Orsak talked about where they'd gone to school—Orsak was a graduate of North Carolina State, where he had majored in electrical engineering, and where he now tutored select groups of graduate students in the design and maintenance of cellular phone systems. Tsutomu talked a little about Caltech, but mostly he seemed anxious to get going. He was nervous, fidgety, talking a mile a minute.

Orsak stopped at a BP station across from the Crabtree Valley mall. It was about 11 P.M.. He filled the Blazer with gas and stocked up on munchies: peanuts, crackers, Doritos, Cokes. And for Tsutomu, lots of Mountain Dew.

❖

Like most cell towers, this one is on a hill. It's maybe two miles from the Player's Club apartments, just down the road from Circuit City. Orsak drove down Glenwood Avenue, the main pipeline out of downtown Raleigh, then made a right turn onto Hilben Street. The road was dark (no streetlights), woodsy, and lonely. He drove past several warehouses and a new Post Office that was still under construction, up a long steady grade, then turned into a driveway beside a large warehouse. He followed the driveway along the side of the building until he came to the loading dock area in the rear, where he parked beside a chain-link fence. Agent Thomas pulled his Crown Victoria up nearby. Straight above them, rising a hundred and twenty feet into the sky, was Sprint's cell tower #19.

Orsak got out, unlocked the fence around the base of the tower. Inside was a small, cinder-block building about the size of a two-car garage. While Tsutomu talked with Agent Thomas, Orsak went inside and set up his laptop computer, which he plugged right into the cell, and which allowed him to scan the channels that fed into that cell tower. Then all they could do was wait. And listen. As the scanner bounced along the channels, it picked up snatches of a conversation. Usually it was somebody coming home from a bar, half drunk, kissing up to or making up with his wife or girl-friend.

Tsutomu is not good at waiting. He bounced around in the little shack, nervous, edgy. He wanted to get this over with. He pushed Agent Thomas to get more agents on the scene so that when they tracked Kevin down, they could bust him. According to Orsak, Tsutomu was afraid Kevin was going to slip through their fingers. The moment they found him, Tsutomu wanted a team of agents to bust down his door and make the arrest. He was worried that if Kevin got wind of what was going on, he might go out in a blaze of glory. There was always the fear that he might delete files and destroy information at the WELL or Netcom or other systems he had access to. Kevin had no record of such destruction before, but if he felt cornered, if he knew he was about to go to jail, well, who knew what he might do?

Orsak didn't know what to make of this speculation, whether it was rooted in reality or paranoia. To him, Tsutomu just seemed unfamiliar with the way the law worked. The need for a search warrant, for example, seemed to be a detail that was beyond him.

Agent Thomas handled Tsutomu's protestations gracefully enough. "Well, the experts are coming down from Quantico tomorrow," he told Tsutomu. "I think it's best if we put off any decision until then."

Tsutomu fumed. To keep busy, he and Orsak went for a drive in the Blazer to test the equipment. When they returned about a half hour later, Agent Thomas was gone. Orsak wasn't surprised— he had not seemed too enthusiastic about being out on a Sunday night, and had spent a good deal of time earlier on the phone, trying to line up someone to come out and replace him. Apparently, he hadn't been able to find anyone.

✣

At the cell site, Tsutomu and Orsak could use a regular telephone, where they could speak without worrying about being overheard by any cellular phone scanner Kevin might have (as it turned out, he didn't). Orsak called Murphy at the switch, and Tsutomu called his people in California—mostly Kent Walker, apparently. Walker was a U.S. Attorney who had been working with Tsutomu on the case in California, and who was friendly with Markoff. From what Orsak could hear of the conversations, Tsutomu was pressuring him to push the FBI into issuing the warrants.

It was sometime after midnight when Tsutomu got a page—it was Markoff, calling from the airport. Tsutomu called him back and told him what they were up to, then Orsak took the phone and gave him directions to the cell tower. Tsutomu and Orsak were waiting for Markoff and listening to the scanner, hoping to pick up modem tones or other evidence of Kevin's activities, when a voice crackled over the airwaves.

"I think we got something," Orsak said hopefully.

It was a conversation between two men—one with a slight Long Island accent. There was no urgency to the conversation—they talked about the weather, mostly. It was difficult to hear much through the static and fuzz, but after a few moments, the name "Fiber Optic" leapt out.

"It's him!" Tsutomu exclaimed. "It's Kevin!"

They jumped in the Blazer and headed down the hill. On the way, they noticed headlights approaching—it was Markoff. Orsak flashed his high beams, and Markoff pulled off to the side of the road in his Geo Prizm (a car that, coincidentally, was almost identical to the one that Tsutomu had rented). Markoff parked and jumped into the Blazer while Kevin's voice was still crackling out of the speakers. According to Orsak, Tsutomu and Markoff quickly determined that the other voice— the one with the Long Island accent—belonged to Eric Corley, a.k.a. Emmanuel Goldstein, the publisher of *2600: The Hacker Quarterly.*

The next half hour was extremely tense. Orsak and Tsutomu could track the signal only as long as Kevin stayed on the line . . . and he might hang up at any second. Orsak drove down the hill, back out to Glenwood Avenue, while Tsutomu watched the signal-strength meter on the tracking gear. They turned right, heading away from downtown Raleigh, but they didn't have to go very far before they could see that the signal was fading. So Orsak flipped a U-turn and started heading back the other way, past Circuit City, past McDonalds. . . . The signal strength increased.

They came to the intersection of Duraleigh Road. They turned right, passed the furniture store on the corner, and started heading down a small two-lane road. The signal strength was getting stronger. . . . When was the call going to end? They couldn't believe they were this lucky. Tsutomu was extremely nervous, afraid they were going to be seen. They drove a quarter of a mile or so down Duraleigh, past a strip mall and a bunch of apartments, heading into the woods . . . the signal faded again. Orsak turned around . . . the call was still holding . . . drove more slowly, the signal got stronger as they got closer to some apartment complexes on the left side. They turned into the parking area of the first one . . . the signal strength dropped. This wasn't it. They drove back out onto Duraleigh, made a left, and approached the Player's Club apartment complex, with its cheery sign illustrated with stick figures of swimmers and tennis players.

Tsutomu was practically vibrating with anxiety. What if Kevin was looking out the window? What if he spotted them at the last moment and fled? Orsak turned left onto the access road, and the signal strength maxed out. This was it, this was the place.

The problem was, the signal was coming in from the apartment complex, which was going to make it doubly difficult to track down. There were thirty or so separate buildings in the complex—a cellular phone signal can bounce all around in a place like that, making it very difficult to get a precise fix on it.

But they were sure as hell gonna try. To keep

from being spotted during their surveillence, they drove out of the apartment complex area and into the strip mall across the street, where they cut the lights, pulled up in an alley behind the shops, and waited for Kevin's calls—which had stopped—to resume. It was an eerie, lonely spot. A jumble of discarded appliances—stoves and refrigerators and dishwashers—were piled up against the cinder-block wall. A few feet away, behind a car repair shop, was a drooping banner that read: "Sludge-master—the Ultimate Engine Care. Now Available."

Orsak was amused by Tsutomu: he was so nervous and hyper, then all of a sudden, bang, he'd be zonked out, snoring. They tried to keep it in rotation—one of them slept, while the other kept an ear on the scanner. They downed their Cokes and Mountain Dew (neither one of them drank coffee). They talked about Kevin's exploits. Tsutomu, with some bitterness, mentioned the file that had been found on the WELL called "japboy."

During these and other conversations, Markoff never mentioned that he was a journalist who was covering the story. Tsutomu said nothing about it either. It wasn't a big deal—Orsak just assumed he was another member of Tsutomu's team. According to Orsak, "He asked a million questions," and seemed surprisingly knowledgeable about the details of cellular technology. At one point, he overheard them talking about whether or not Markoff should attend a dinner that had been arranged the next night with Levord Burns, who had traveled up from FBI headquarters in Quantico, Virginia. Markoff was apparently worried that the FBI might not take kindly to his presence. Tsutomu suggested it would be no problem, just keep quiet, don't ask too many questions.

Technically, cellular phone tracking isn't much of a challenge. In fact, there was really no reason for Tsutomu to be along—other than, of course, to get the satisfaction of being there to see Kevin's capture. He was clearly caught up in the drama of the chase—besides his monstrous SPARC portable, he'd brought along his little Hewlett-Packard palmtop, which he had hooked up to his OKI portable phone (it was the same setup he'd demonstrated to Larry Smarr a few weeks earlier). While Orsak was scanning the channels with his equipment, Tsutomu scanned the same channels with his laptop. It's wasn't necessary—Orsak was perfectly capable of tracking the guy down on his own. But Orsak didn't mind. In fact, he liked Tsutomu—he thought he was an odd but extremely intelligent creature, and he was glad for the company.

✦

The three of them went out on several expeditions to try to pin down Kevin's location more precisely. Tsutomu was still worried about being seen, so on a couple of occasions they made their expeditions in Markoff's Geo. If Kevin was looking out the window, at least he wouldn't get suspicious of the same Chevy Blazer driving by all the time.

The calls would stop and start, sometimes too brief for them to get a good read on. They spent a lot of time just sitting in the darkness, waiting.

Kevin's calls continued, off and on, until about 5 A.M. By that time, Orsak and Tsutomu had narrowed Kevin's location down to one building on the southeastern edge of the Player's Club complex. There were four units in the building—it was impossible to tell exactly which apartment the signals were coming from. For that, they would need more precise equipment that only the FBI could supply.

It was about 6 A.M.—just before daybreak, Orsak says—when they finally called it quits. Orsak hung around until about 9 A.M., shooting the shit, still high from all the excitement of the night. Then he noticed people were starting to show up for work, and figured it was time to go home and get some sleep. He drove home through the tobacco fields and pine woods, then collapsed into bed for about eight hours.

12

The following night everyone met for a powwow at Ragazzi's, an Italian-theme restaurant about a half mile from the Sprint switch in Garner. It was the kind of place that has door handles the shape of chianti jugs, an open fire brick oven, and bags of garlic and dried red peppers hanging from the walls for decoration. Tsutomu and Markoff were there, as were Tsutomu's friend Julia Menapace (she had arrived earlier that day), Orsak, Jim Murphy, and a third Sprint technician, as well as Agent

Burns, who had driven up from Quantico that afternoon.

It was part celebration, part strategy session. After two years, the search for Kevin was finally nearing an end. There was a lot of talk around the table about Kevin's history, what he had done in the past, what had motivated him, how smart he was.

Orsak, who was sitting between Murphy and Burns, noticed what a nice Italian suit Burns was wearing. A classy guy, Orsak thought. While he was clearly interested in arresting Kevin, he didn't act as if he were about to bust Al Capone. In fact, Burns commented to Orsak that, as far as hackers go, Kevin was known more for his annoyance than anything else. Orsak got the sense that they were here to do a job, and that was it.

At the other end of the table, in contrast to his millions of questions the night before, Markoff was subdued. Tsutomu had introduced him simply by name, and then didn't mention that he was a reporter with the *Times*. Markoff volunteered nothing. Both Orsak and Murphy were still under the impression that he was working for Tsutomu.

The secretiveness was an understandable maneuver on Markoff's part. Journalists (including myself) do similar things all the time. This was a story he had been following for years, and here he was on the final turn, with a great seat on the rail. Who would have given that up? Still, it was a gutsy move. Burns wasn't an Atlantic City mobster. He wasn't corrupt. He was the FBI. They do not, as a rule, warm to the notion of journalists sitting in on what they believe to be private conversations.

There was some subtle irony here, too. One of the sins Kevin apparently committed was to eavesdrop on Markoff's personal e-mail. A violation of privacy, to be sure. But one that bears some interesting comparison to what Markoff was doing by sitting in on this private dinner with an FBI agent.

The dinner lasted over an hour, and Markoff made it through alive. Then it was time to go find Kevin.

✥

A short time later, everyone met back at the switch. They were joined by two cellular phone experts from the FBI, who arrived with a station wagon full of fancy equipment, including a trigger fish. Tsutomu immediately went to work with Murphy trying to correlate the latest call records, while Orsak, being the hardware junkie that he is, checked out the FBI's cellular tracking gear.

Instead of using Orsak's Blazer, which they feared might look too familiar to Kevin if he happened to be peering out the window, another Sprint technician, a bearded, colorful character named Fred (he prefers that his last name not be used), volunteered to drive them around in his Dodge Caravan. It was the perfect cover vehicle— roomy on the inside, inconspicuous on the outside. They spent a half hour or so setting up the trigger fish in the rear of the van, then attaching several directional finder antennas on the roof.

When they were done, Tsutomu was worried. The antennas on the roof were a dead giveaway. They were like a big neon sign that said "We're on to you, Kevin." But what could they do? Without the antennas, the trigger fish was useless. Then somebody came up with the bright idea of disguising them. Murphy ran inside and grabbed a Phillips lightbulb box, and amidst wisecracks about this "urban assault vehicle," used some tape and string to attach it onto the roof in away that covered the antennas. Now it just looked like a cardboard box on the roof of the van. Bizarre, but not necessarily alarming to someone like Kevin. And with a scruffy guy like Fred at the wheel, it would just look like some Deadhead was taking off on a camping trip.

✛

They left the switch around 11 P.M. Burns and Orsak took Tsutomu's Geo, while the two FBI technicians rode in the Dodge Caravan with Fred. Tsutomu and Markoff stayed behind with Murphy to keep an eye on Kevin's electronic adventures from the switch.

During the forty-minute drive over to the Player's Club, Fred was apparently chatting with the two technicians in his van and happened to mention that Tsutomu's friend John Markoff was a reporter for the *Times*, and had coauthored a book about Kevin called *Cyberpunk*. He knew this because, not long after the dinner at Ragazzi's, Markoff had given him his card, and Fred recognized the name.

Oh really?

A short time later, one of the FBI agents called Tsutomu at the switch and, in no uncertain terms, asked who the hell Markoff was and why he was around. Tsutomu won't talk about the call, but Murphy, who was sitting nearby, says Tsutomu was straight up with him about it. He told the agent that he'd gotten an okay from Kent Walker to bring Markoff along.

That didn't seem to carry much weight with the FBI—especially with Levord Burns. According to Murphy and Orsak, it wasn't just that Markoff had failed to disclose his profession and, in some quiet way, played games with the trust of an FBI agent. What Burns was really afraid of, apparently, was that Markoff was going to tip off Kevin and send him on the run at the last minute so that it would make a better final chapter for the book that everyone knew he would end up writing about this. A wild idea, to be sure. But Burns was the point man in the closing moments of a high-profile arrest—he had a right to be jittery.

Markoff didn't fight it. "I think I'll go back to the hotel," he said after Tsutomu hung up. Then he gathered up his notes and went back to the Sheraton, where he and Tsutomu were staying. He kept in touch by phone, but stayed out of sight until Kevin was arrested.

✛

Fred pulled the Caravan into the parking lot of the strip mall across the street from the Player's Club. The only thing left to do was figure out exactly which apartment Kevin was in, get a search warrant, and go in.

Unlike Tsutomu, Burns seemed to be in no hurry. He wanted to take things one step at a time, make sure he did things right. He needed to devise a strategy for making the arrest, get it approved by his bosses, then execute it. If he was worried that Kevin would get wind of things and take off, Orsak didn't notice it.

While they were getting organized in the parking lot, Murphy was sending Orsak messages on his pager about which channel Kevin was using on his cloned phone. By this time, Kevin had quit using Sprint and was now using CellularOne for access. So back at the switch, Murphy was talking to the CellularOne people, who were tracking Kevin's calls, then relaying the information to Orsak, who passed it on to Burns. Unbeknownst to Kevin, who believed that by switching cellular phone providers and using new access numbers he was keeping one step ahead of the law, his every move was being watched.

Fred and the two FBI technicians made several passes by the Player's Club in the van. Essentially, that told them the same thing that Tsutomu and

Orsak had learned the night before—that Kevin was somewhere in the apartment complex. They needed a different strategy. Fred drove back to the parking lot across the street, where they would be out of sight in case Kevin looked out the window. One of technicians jumped out of the van with a small black bag. Inside was a small handheld version of a radio directional finder. It was designed to be used in close circumstances like this, where the larger trigger fish is impractical and too imprecise. Essentially, this instrument allows an FBI agent to walk down a hallway and zero in on exactly where the calls were coming from. That was the theory, anyway.

The technician walked across the street to the Player's Club. He just looked like a guy out for a midnight stroll with a camera bag over his shoulder. He quietly walked up along the sidewalk to the apartment where they suspected Kevin might be living. By watching the dial in the directional finder, he hoped to pin down Kevin's location once and for all—a difficult task, even for technicians with their expertise.

It was about 2 A.M. when Fred and the two technicians met up with Orsak and Burns again. They had apparently narrowed the search for Kevin's apartment down to building 4640, which was on the opposite side of the complex from where Tsutomu and Orsak had determined he was the night before. Kevin was in apartment 107 or 108, the FBI still wasn't sure. But it was too risky for them to keep walking around in the open at this time of night.

Burns decided to call it quits and return the next day.

13

"Investigation conducted via electronic tracking measures has narrowed the citus of the target's cellular phone operations into the computer networks to Apartment No. 107 and Apartment No. 108, located in Player's Apartment Complex on 4640 Tournament Road, Raleigh, North Carolina," Agent Burns wrote in his affidavit on Tuesday, February 14. "Investigation of the leases on these apartments reveal that Apartment No. 107 was leased on February 4, 1995, by a new lessee. This is the precise date on which the target began operating out of the Raleigh, North Carolina, area. The other apartment is leased by the girlfriend of the apartment complex's manager, who is not a suspect.''

The only problem was, despite all the effort and high-tech equipment, they still weren't sure which apartment Kevin was in. In fact, they were not even close. Building 4640, which Burns identified in the affidavit, was on the other side of the Player's Club complex from the building 4550, where Kevin actually lived. Burns had apparently made an educated guess in the affidavit—but what if it were wrong? What if they got a search warrant for the wrong apartment, made a big fuss about going in, and then scared Kevin off? But if they waited any longer, they ran the risk that Kevin might get spooked and disappear—they all knew it wouldn't take much. A strange car. A voice on the cell phone. A ripple in cyberspace.

Confusion ensued. John Bowler, the U.S. Attorney in Raleigh who was handling the case, contacted Judge Wallace W. Dixon, who lived in North Raleigh about ten minutes from the Player's Club, and asked him to make himself available that evening—they might need him to sign search and arrest warrants at the last minute.

Meanwhile, Tsutomu and Menapace were hanging out in the mall across the street from the entrance to the Player's Club. Murphy was keeping an eye on his activity at the switch, and the guys from CellularOne were doing the same. Out in California, at the WELL, system administrators were nervously monitoring their system, watching for any sign of trouble. At Colorado SuperNet, they were doing the same, and at Netcom. They need not have worried. Up until the last minute, Kevin was merrily hacking away, still poking around in Markoff's e-mail, oblivious to the net closing around him.

The big question on everyone's mind was, what would Kevin do when the moment came and the FBI knocked on his door and Kevin realized he was going to jail? Tsutomu had been thinking all along that he might do something crazy. No one knew exactly what. He had root access at the WELL, at Netcom, at Colorado SuperNet, among other places. If he wanted to, he could cause a tremendous amount of damage. All it would take would be a few keystrokes, and he could destroy accounting files, directories, virtually the entire system. All the Internet providers who were involved in the hunt had taken precautions: they had backed up their files and were ready to shut things down if it looked as if Kevin were going to do anything nasty. They couldn't shut him out all together, however, because if they did, they were afraid it might tip him off. So they just waited, most of them monitoring their system on a twenty-four–hour basis, waiting for word that Kevin had been arrested.

There were other worries. What if Kevin retaliated with a more sophisticated attack on the Internet itself? What if he launched a lethal virus into thousands of computers at once? A farfetched notion, but who could say for sure? If he was a terrorist, if he had havoc in mind, it was quite possible that he had rigged up some kind of doomsday program, something he could launch at the last minute and which would be impossible to stop, something that would swing like a wrecking ball through the electronic universe. It would be his farewell gift, his good-bye bomb.

Not everyone's worries were technological. Kevin's fear of going back to jail was well-known. He had talked about it many times. He believed that he would never get a fair shake, that if he went in again, he would never come out. He had told people he had been assaulted in jail before. He knew he would be assaulted again. It was very possible that he would decide that he would not go back to jail. That anything was better than sharing cell space with other men, men who might reek, in some indefinable way, of the darkest moments of his childhood. It might feel like going back to hell, and he might just decide not to do it. He might just off himself instead.

✛

At about 9 P.M., Bowler and several FBI agents met at Judge Dixon's house. They told Judge Dixon that they were still not sure which apartment Kevin was in, but that they were sure he was in the Player's Club complex somewhere. Agent Burns gave him his ten-page affidavit, but the judge noticed that they had forgotten to propose a search warrant. Bowler made arrangements to have some delivered from his office, and then Burns and the other agents went back to the Player's Club to see if they could pin down Kevin's whereabouts. They told the judge they'd call if they got any new information.

A few minutes later, a secretary from Bowler's office arrived with preprinted search warrant forms. Where the name and address of the property to be searched was supposed to be filled in, it said only "Kevin Mitnick" and "Raleigh, North Carolina." Nevertheless, the judge signed the forms, which were delivered to Bowler at the Player's Club.

Meanwhile, things were getting tense at the Player's Club. About five officers from the Violent Crimes Task Force for the Eastern District of North Carolina, including Deputy U.S. Marshal Mark Chapman, had been summoned to the scene earlier in the day, and were eager to make an arrest and get this over with. But Murphy and the rest of the electronic monitoring team had detected no activity on Kevin's phone in the last couple of hours. Had he gotten wind of the investigation and split? By now everyone knew all about the near-miss in Seattle. Had they gone through all this . . . only to have Kevin slip away in the final minutes? It certainly seemed possible.

Then sometime after midnight Kevin returned. He would later tell his attorney that he had gone out to get some dinner. How he had gotten in and out of his apartment while a half-dozen cops were supposedly watching the complex remains a mystery. Perhaps it was just dumb luck. In any event, not long after midnight Kevin's hacking activity resumed, and the FBI's cellular phone technicians again tried to use their handheld receiver to determine which apartment he was in. Chapman happened to be downstairs in building 4550 with one of the technicians when he heard a door open above. What happened next is a matter of some dispute. Chapman says he looked up through the spaces between the stairs and saw a person matching Kevin's description step out of his apartment and look around, as if he were checking out a suspicious sound. Kevin, through his attorney, claims he did no such thing.

However it happened, the cops no longer had any doubts about which apartment Kevin was in. Agent Burns, along with FBI Agent Lathell Thomas, Deputy Chapman, and two other members of the Violent Crimes Task Force, gathered at Kevin's door.

Burns knocked.

A voice from inside: "Who is it?"

"FBI."

A bolt of terror must have shot through Kevin's heart. Nevertheless, he remained fairly calm. He spoke with Burns through the door for several minutes. He insisted they had the wrong apartment, he wasn't Kevin Mitnick, he had no idea what they were talking about. At one point Kevin opened the door slightly and spoke through the crack—Chapman noticed that he had a cellular phone to his ear, and was apparently talking to someone. When Burns asked if they could come in, Kevin demanded a search warrant. What happened next is, again, a matter of dispute. Kevin says he tried to close the door and Agent Burns blocked it with his foot. Then five agents forced themselves into his apartment. Chapman says Kevin allowed them in.

Once they were inside, they saw his computer in plain view. They checked the apartment for weapons, then looked Kevin over. He was wearing a black sweatsuit and running shoes, as if he had just come back from the gym. Burns asked him to identify himself. "My name is Thomas Case," he said. He showed the agents a North Carolina driver's license, credit card, and checkbook all under the name Thomas Case. While Kevin was rifling through his wallet, agents saw that it contained several other IDs. When he set it down on the counter, one of them grabbed it and looked inside. Kevin claims they began searching his apartment despite the fact that he told them that unless they could show him a search warrant, they had to leave. Kevin was allowed to call his attorney, John Yzurdiaga, in Los Angeles. Yzurdiaga told Burns to produce a search warrant or get out. So Burns left.

Chapman and the other agents stayed behind to keep an eye on Kevin. "He seemed extremely nervous," Chapman says. "He reverted to an almost childlike state." He asked to call his mother, but the agents, wary of Kevin's telephone skills, refused. "You can call her when you get to jail," they told him. He asked for his medicine—his lifelong stomach problems were acting up again. Chapman got him his pills.

Burns returned a few minutes later with an arrest warrant, but no search warrant. "You still don't have a search warrant," Kevin told him. Despite much evidence to the contrary—like the name on his bottle of pills—he maintained that he was Thomas Case and he was being unjustly harassed by the FBI.

Burns left again and called Judge Dixon. The judge gave him verbal authorization to conduct the search. Burns returned to Kevin's apartment and showed him the warrant. The correct address and apartment number were handwritten in the top corner.

Not long after that, Kevin was handcuffed. They read him his Miranda rights and placed him under arrest. Then he was led outside—it had started to rain now, a light drizzle—to a waiting police vehicle.

✣

It took FBI agents an hour or so to search Kevin's apartment. They seized about eighty items, including a Toshiba laptop, cell phones, and various cell phone paraphernalia. Nothing surprising there. There were a few items, however, that suggested that Kevin was truthful when he told Charlie Pritchett that he had come to Raleigh to get a job. There were two books, *The 100 Best Companies to Work for in America*, and *Knock 'Em Dead*, a well-known guide to job-hunting tactics, as well as a pile of forty-four job application letters. To Chapman, the oddest thing about Kevin's apartment was that there was absolutely no food anywhere—there was nothing in the refrigerator but a box of baking soda.

The FBI also confiscated a copy of a two-day-old *Raleigh News & Observer* that Kevin had lying around, dated February 12, 1995. Kevin's horoscope in the paper that day was weirdly prescient:

> **Leo (July 23-Aug 22):** Someone you are trying to impress will state, "You undoubtedly are psychotic." Backstage maneuver featured, you'll have advance information relating to secret files. Discretion necessary.

❖

It was after 3 A.M. by the time Kevin was finally transported to the Wade County Public Safety Center in downtown Raleigh. On the way there, he made repeated requests to talk to his mother. But he refused to tell the agents what his mother's name was or whom they should say was calling. He was still insisting that they had the wrong guy, he was Thomas Case, he had no idea why they were taking him downtown.

Finally, after hours of denials, it dawned on him

that he was not going to be able to hack his way out of this. "Okay, you got me," he finally confessed. "I'm Kevin David Mitnick. I want you to know I am not a spy. I am very loyal to the United States." He then sent his apologies to Agents Ken McGuire and Kathleen Carson, whom he had harassed with phone tricks and anonymous messages. He said, "Tell them it was nothing personal."

V

SNOW JOB

1

Two weeks after Kevin's arrest, I found myself in LA, working on the story for *Rolling Stone*. Like the rest of the world, I had first heard about Kevin's capture when I read Markoff's dramatic account in the *Times*. I had never met Tsutomu (or Markoff or Kevin, for that matter), but I dutifully put in a half-dozen calls to the San Diego Supercomputer Center, hoping to talk with him. No luck. I also left several messages for Ann Redelfs, the friendly media relations person at the Supercomputer Center.

When Redelfs called me back a few days later,

she sounded overwhelmed. "Excuse me for not calling sooner," she explained. "There have been about two hundred requests for interviews with Tsutomu in the last week. Calls from Japan, New Zealand, Europe, you name it. I've been a little crazy."

"So I'm out of luck?"

"No, I don't think so. I discussed your request with Tsutomu, and he's agreed to talk to you."

Good news. "Shall I fly down to San Diego tonight?"

"No, he's not here."

"Where is he?"

"I don't know. Maybe up north. He doesn't tell me these things. He just sends me e-mail."

"Is there a number where I can call him?"

"No. He doesn't give out his number. I don't even have his number. What's your deadline?"

I told her.

"Okay, I'll relay that to him. You'll probably be hearing from him in the next couple of days."

"Are you sure this is going to happen? If not, I'll fly back to New York—"

"Yes, it will happen," she assured me. "Tsutomu is a man of his word. If he says he'll talk to you, he'll talk to you."

✛

I hung out in LA for a few more days, waiting for Tsutomu. As my deadline approached, I e-mailed him several notes saying that if we were going to talk, it was now or never. Just before midnight on March 9th, I received a reply: "i'll be in truckee ca at the tahoe donner cross-country ski center tomorrow (friday), if you want to find me there i'll have some time to chat," he wrote. "mostly i'd like to talk about related issues such as ethics and privacy. i'd also be curious to hear what other viewpoints you've heard . . . will be in ram mobile range for a few more hours tonite, then will be radio-less . . ."

Well, great. The only problem was, I was in LA, he was in the Sierras, and there was a whale of a storm between us. On the evening news that night, there were pictures of houses floating down rivers, swamped cars, landlocked cats. In the Sierras, there were reports of three feet of new snow. Driving to Tahoe—a six- or seven-hour journey if the roads were clear—was out of the question. I called the airport—too late to catch a flight. The first flights in the morning would probably be delayed.

I e-mailed Shimomura back, telling him I wasn't sure I would be able to make it tomorrow. Could we do it the following day? By the time I went to bed at 2 A.M., he hadn't replied.

I understood Tsutomu's reluctance. All this badgering by the media, myself included, must have been hard to take. Until that moment, he'd lived a life of science, working on complex computational problems far from the public eye. No longer. Just days after the story appeared in the *Times*, Markoff's agent, John Brockman, negotiated a reported $700,000 deal for a book coauthored by the *Times* reporter and Tsutomu. Movie and CD-ROM rights went for another hefty chunk, as did foreign rights. Almost overnight, Markoff and Shimomura were millionaires. Who needed publicity?

✢

When I got up the next morning, I still hadn't heard from Tsutomu. Nevertheless, I booked a 9 A.M. flight to Reno. When I arrived at LAX, however, I discovered the flight was canceled due to bad weather. So was the 10 A.M. flight. And the noon flight. I finally boarded the 1 P.M. flight, which was supposed to arrive at 2:30 P.M.. It was, of course, delayed.

The plane ended up bouncing onto the tarmac in Reno just after 3 P.M. It was pouring rain. An hour later, I was on my way up Interstate 80 toward Lake Tahoe in an Alamo rental car. The rain turned to hail, the hail into snow, the snow into a blizzard, the blizzard into a whiteout.

It was nearly dark by the time I arrived at Tahoe Donner ski area. Tsutomu was long gone. The parking lot was empty except for a few snowed-in cars and an idle snowplow.

I called Ann Redelfs again and explained my predicament. I assumed she really did have Tsutomu's number, and that when things became dire enough, she'd give it to me. I was wrong. "I'm telling you the truth," she said. "I have no way to reach him. He does not give out his phone number to *anyone*—not even me. The only thing I can do is e-mail him and tell him what hotel you're at and hope that he gives you a call. "

I got a cheap hotel and flopped in front of the TV and waited. I sent him several e-mail messages, but got no response. I presumed he either hadn't made it to Tahoe, or that he was already gone.

At 2 A.M., just after I had fallen asleep, the phone rang. "Hi. It's Tsutomu."

I explained what had happened. "Can we meet tomorrow?"

"I don't know."

"I've come a long way for this, Tsutomu. . . ."

"I might ski at a different place tomorrow. I'm not sure yet, I have to check with the ski patrol. I'll call you by eight o'clock tomorrow morning and let you know, okay?"

At 8 A.M., the phone did not ring. I waited until 9:30. Still no call. At 10, I called Ann again. What was going on? "It's nothing personal," she assured me. "He does this with everyone. It's just the way he is."

Enough. I'd write the story without him. I packed my bags and headed back to Reno.

When I hit the highway, however, I had a change of heart. I turned off and drove up the long, windy, icy road to the Tahoe Donner ski area. It was a long shot, but what the hell. I parked in the snowy lot and walked into the ski lodge—a small, simple modern building not much bigger than a gas station. Because of the bad weather, the place was almost empty—there were a few people renting skis, and a woman sitting in the window blowing on a cup of hot chocolate. Then I noticed someone in purple Lycra ski pants standing by the cashier with his right foot perched up on the counter, stretching his leg like a gymnast. A black ponytail swung between his shoulder blades. Even from a distance, he gave off wired, high-energy vibes. It was Tsutomu.

When I introduced myself, he looked shocked, like *how the hell did you find me here?*

✛

The game was over, I thought. I figured we'd just sit in the lodge and talk. "We can wrap this up in an hour," I told Tsutomu. Then I'd be out of his hair and on my way.

Again, I was wrong. Tsutomu said something about having to go look at his skis, and then disappeared upstairs. He returned about ten minutes later in the company of his cabin mate, Emily Sklar, a grad student at San Jose State. Tsutomu looked ready to go—a purple parka, Oakley sunglasses, neon green and pink Salomon ski boots, skis, and poles.

"My friend is giving a ski lesson," he said, pointing to Sklar. "I have to go with her."

"When will you be back?"

"Sometime later this afternoon."

"But I have a plane to catch—"

"I came up here to ski," he said. By that he

meant, he had not come up here to be interviewed. "You're welcome to come along if you want," he said generously.

He could see I was dressed for LA. I had no ski gear, no hat, no gloves, no tight purple Lycra ski pants. "Maybe I'll just wait here in the lodge," I said. "What time do you think you'll be back?"

"Sometime this afternoon."

"Can we talk then?"

"Oh, sure."

Then he turned around and headed out toward the mountain. I watched him and Sklar put on their skis—she was a ski instructor, I learned, and he was following along to learn how to become an instructor himself. Tsutomu and Sklar were joined by a middle-aged man and woman—their students. They shook hands and chatted for a few moments, then the four of them kicked and glided off into the woods. As I watched Shimomura's purple pants disappear among the sugar pines, I had the strange feeling that I wasn't going to see him again for the rest of the day. There were miles and miles of trails, as well as several lodges on distant mountains. He could easily be gone until sunset.

So I did the only sensible thing. I went to the ski shop, plunked down my plastic, and bought a hat, gloves, and pullover. Then I rented skis and continued the chase.

✛

By noon, I was Tsutomu's student. If he wanted to learn to teach people to ski, he could teach me. Actually, the lesson was with Sklar, and Tsutomu was her teaching assistant. It is one of his goals in life to become a ski instructor, and he was as intense about skiing as he was about everything else—at one point, when I was having trouble with my poles, he offered a long and complex theory about why elliptical-shaped baskets at the end of ski poles are more desirable than regular round baskets.

By two o'clock, we were back in the lodge for lunch. Tsutomu ate almondine couscous and a banana. Sklar joked about the motley crew of reporters who had been trying to track Tsutomu down. A week earlier, a crew from CNN had ambushed him in the ski lodge. Tsutomu avoided them until one of the producers volunteered to be hauled around the slopes in a metal sled because he'd heard that Tsutomu, who was also training to be on ski patrol, wanted to practice dragging injured skiers out of the woods. After that gesture of goodwill, Tsutomu gave them a five-minute interview.

I wondered about Tsutomu's love/hate relationship with the media: if he didn't want me up there, why did he invite me along? And if he invited me along, why was he so reluctant to talk? Clearly, Tsutomu is too complex of a creature to fit easily into the world of sound bites and spin. One part of him seemed to think that he was above it all, that he shouldn't have to be bothered. But there was also the understandable desire to bask in the glory of the moment—*yes, he had taken Kevin down.*

Perhaps he was just shell-shocked by all the attention. At the WELL, the arrest was the subject of immediate and intense fascination. Although some wagged their fingers when U.S. Attorney Kent Walker called Kevin "an electronic terrorist," very few rushed to support him. Maybe it was a sign that the computer culture was growing older, that it was losing its patience with young adventurers. Some worried about the long-term impact the case would have on cyberspace. "Great changes are afoot in the technical and legal underpinning of the net," Bruce Koball wrote in a post on the WELL. "To the extent that Mitnick and his ilk get demonized, and the Net and cyberspace get painted as a sinister, anarchic, lawless wilderness requiring legal intervention, we all lose."

Others saw it as a call to action: "The 'Evil Empire's' Sputnik was the spark that lit the U.S. roman candle of science and math education renovation in the late '50s and '60s, as well as fueling the costly rockets of the competitive U.S. space race," read the announcement to one computer conference. "Perhaps the Evil Kevin Mitnick—the FBI's favorite Devilish Computer Cracker—will end up fueling a similar wake-up call across the nation, among citizens, businesses and industry leaders."

The *Times* came under scrutiny, too. When Markoff's dramatic story of Kevin's arrest ran two days after he was captured, the paper of record did not bother to disclose the fact that Markoff had himself been deeply enmeshed in the hunt for Kevin. Nor did they disclose Markoff's relationship with Tsutomu or his grudge against Kevin (although three days later, in a brief follow-up piece, Markoff did admit that he suspected Kevin had read his e-mail). Then there was the question of that million-dollar book deal. As Jon Katz, the media critic for *Wired*, put it: "You have reporters for the first time having a chance to become millionaires. How does that affect reporting?"

Many hackers, as usual, smelled a conspiracy. Markoff and Tsutomu had had it all worked out from the beginning: they would catch Kevin and get rich at the same time. Chris Goggins, a.k.a. Eric Bloodaxe, the editor of *Phrack*, an electronic magazine popular with the underground, imagined this exchange between Markoff and Tsutomu: "Hey Tsutomu, you know, if you went after this joker, I could write a book about your exploits! We stand to make a pretty penny. It would be bigger than *The Cuckoo's Egg*!"

"You know John, that's a damn good idea. Let me see what I can find. Call your agent now, and let's get the ball rolling."

2

While Tsutomu slurped couscous almondine, he talked about his motives for chasing Kevin. "I didn't want to fuck with his mind," he said. "I just wanted to find the warm body and then get back to skiing." To Tsutomu, Kevin was a bug in the system. Nothing more, nothing less. "I decided to go after him, basically, because he was a pain in the ass. At some point, it's easier to deal with the problem once and get it over with."

"How did you know it was Kevin that broke into your machine?"

"I didn't. The things he was interested in on my computer were the kinds of things Kevin would go after, but the attack was very sophisticated. IP spoofing is a complex attack, and I don't think he had the talent. He had no coding ability, so far as I could tell. His technical skills are very limited. He mostly used tools that other people built. And even then, he has trouble. If someone hasn't given him instructions, he doesn't know how to use it."

After a few minutes of talk, Tsutomu abruptly left. He was expecting a Fed Ex package at his cabin, and he wanted to make sure it arrived. I was sure he was gone for the rest of the day.

But again, I was wrong. He returned about ten minutes later with the package from Japan. He opened it with a great deal of anticipation; inside was a small piece of computer hardware. "It's a new eight-hundred–meg hard drive," Tsutomu explained. Most hard drives are about the size of a portable CD player. This was the size of a cigarette pack. Despite his obvious glee, Tsutomu balks if he's accused of techno lust: "I am not a computer person. I am a user, that is all. To me, computers are simply tools for doing other work." He sometimes calls computers doorstops, or big, expensive room heaters.

Maybe so, but he sure surrounds himself with a lot of gadgets. He had his OKI phone with him, a pedometer, a multi-function wristwatch. His mountain cabin was better wired than many small companies. At one point during lunch, he and Sklar plotted a 50-mile trans-Sierra cross-country ski trip. They discussed wax types and weather conditions. But Tsutomu's biggest concern was his cell phone—should he bring it along? It meant extra weight and bulk, but clearly the idea of leaving it behind made him uneasy.

The cell phone is his constant companion. To Tsutomu, there is no meaningful distinction between cell-phone chat and face-to-face chat. In the middle of a conversation, he will pick up the phone, dial it, and start talking. At one point during a discussion of Kevin's hacking skills, he abruptly dialed Mark Lottor and tried to get him to drive up to Tahoe for the weekend. "It's only one hundred eighty miles from San Francisco," he told Lottor, sounding a little lonely and bored. "Yeah, I'm sure. I drive it all the time." Pause. "I don't know about the road conditions. The storm is supposed to pass." Pause. "Then fly, if you don't want to drive. Okay. Okay. See you."

Then it was back to Kevin. After hyping Kevin as a dangerous outlaw in order to get law enforcement to go after him, he now wanted to downplay Kevin's talents. "If he had shown cleverness, if he had at least done something interesting with his skills, I would have had more respect for him. Instead, he was doing something else. He was just making a nuisance of himself."

"Have you ever cracked a computer system?"

"What do you mean?"

"I mean, have you ever tried to gain unauthorized access into someone else's computer?"

"That's difficult to say—"

"You know what I mean."

"I did hack some systems while I was working at Los Alamos," he said. He hesitated for a moment, then added, "but we always had blanket approvals for what we were doing."

"Blanket approvals by whom?"

"I don't want to talk about that."

He also did not want to talk about the details of the chase. He was saving that for his book, he said. Okay. He did not want to talk about his relationship with John Markoff, either, except to say that yes, they had been cross-country skiing together, and no, he didn't think Markoff had done anything wrong.

At that point, Tsutomu got down on the floor and started doing some stretching exercises. He was thinking about one more trek around the mountain before darkness fell.

"How do you feel about the idea that Kevin might spend ten years in prison?"

Tsutomu hesitated, as if there had been a momentary power loss in his circuitry. "He took a lot of proprietary software, which a lot of companies have a lot of money invested in. He had the Motorola cell phone source code—what was he going to do with that? How did we know he wasn't going to sell it overseas? That is an incredibly valuable software.

"I don't know what else to do with someone like him," Tsutomu continued, beginning to look vaguely troubled. "I think it was important to send a signal that this was not acceptable behavior. He was not polite. I agree that prison is not a great way to stop him, but it is an effective way."

Later he said: "I think there are lessons to be learned here. One of them is, we have to ask ourselves—what are we going to tolerate on the net? The system is not secure, but we like to trust them as such. I think we have to look at this three levels: first, what the net already does. Second, what it claims to do. And third, what we want it to do. People treat the net as if it were secure, and it really isn't. Just because we want to use the net for something—say, commercial transactions—doesn't mean we should do that. We need to be more realistic. We need to learn what the net can provide, and use it accordingly."

What did he plan to do himself, now that this episode in his life was over? He mentioned getting involved more in shaping laws and public policy that affect the Internet. He also wanted to get back to physics. "Life is short," he said. "There are lots of interesting problems to work on."

Meanwhile, Kevin sat alone in his jail cell in North Carolina, indicted on twenty-three counts of computer and communications fraud. He complained about skin blotches to the prison doctors. He ate his meals off a metal tray and tried to keep in shape by running up and down a short flight of stairs on the prison grounds. The only people he was allowed to speak to in the outside world were his lawyers, his mother, and his grandmother. On the net, a few hackers tried to take up his cause, but got nowhere.

There was not much profit or honor in defending Kevin. He was a troubled, lonely, self-mythologizing outlaw adrift in an electronic world that had outgrown its countercultural roots. He had a kind of hubris that far overshadowed his actual hacking abilities, and in the end his singular achievement was to piss off and offend virtually everyone he encountered. Some might argue that the hunt for Kevin showed the community spirit of cyberspace in action, that it was the electronic equivalent of the Guardian Angels collaring a well-known thug in Times Square because the cops are too lazy to do the job. Others might say it was high-tech vigilantism.

My own feeling is that ten years from now the idea of Kevin Mitnick as a national menace will seem quaint, even amusing. Our culture is rapidly becoming more technologically sophisticated—in the future it will be much harder for the media to inflate the Kevin Mitnicks of the world into digital parade floats for computer crime. By then the real cybercriminals will have blossomed, and Kevin will look like a two-bit shoplifter. He will be remembered as a creation of a particular moment in the civilizing of the electronic frontier, a time when our ignorance and fear about how technology is changing the world was on the rise, and when law enforcement needed a symbol to show that they were cracking down on the wild, uncharted lawlessness of the Internet. The media was only too happy to provide that symbol. It happened to come in the shape of a screwed-up Jewish kid from Panorama City. Kevin's pursuers became millionaires; he ended up sitting behind bars in orange coveralls.

It wasn't all bleak for Kevin. In July 1995, in exchange for pleading guilty to one count of access device fraud in North Carolina, the twenty-two other counts were dropped. He was sentenced to eight months in prison. He was then bussed out to the Metropolitan Detention Center in Los Angeles to serve his term and to face more charges, including probation violation. David Schindler, the U.S. attorney who was handling the case, promised to throw the book at him.

✢

At the end of the day, Tsutomu decided not to take another run. It was still snowing hard. We walked out into the parking lot and brushed the snow off our cars and loaded our skis. We made plans to meet at a cafe in Truckee later that night (it didn't work out—I fell asleep). He planned to bring his laptop with him, so he could log onto the net while he was there and hang out with his friends, both virtual and real. I had the strong sense that he was not easy with what had happened to Kevin. The ending of the story did not fit with his physicist's demand for an elegant solution to every problem. This was human. This was too complex, even for Tsutomu.

"I think Kevin is a broken person," he said at one point, apropos of nothing.

"Broken?"

"Yes. Broken."

Then he got into his car and headed down the icy mountain road.